MATEY

Patricia W Grey

The Chinese say that once you've saved a person's life you are responsible for it forever.

John Scottie Fergusen

This novel is entirely a work of fiction. Names, characters, businesses, organisations, places and events are either a product of the author´s imagination or are used fictitiously. Any resemblance to actual persons, living or dead, or to events or locales are entirely coincidental.

This cover was devised and designed by Mark Lodge.

With thanks to
Gordon Fairman
and
Clare Allcard
for their unfailing help.

Author **Patricia W Grey** has lived in Europe for the past twenty plus years. Previously she and her husband owned and ran a cultured pearl farm in Broome, Western Australia. There they introduced new methods of cultivating pearls in their underwater farm. She is a keen skier, hiker, Bridge player and member of the Andorran Writers´ Group.

Also by the author:
Death has a Thousand Doors
Taboo

Short stories:
Kissed by a Stranger
Thirteen Families

And with the Andorran Writers´ Group:
The Five Senses

MATEY

Chapter 1

He marched down the street, nappy loose and with mismatched shoes, the Velcro latched tight. His focus was intent and he ignored the cars and trucks rocketing past on one of Perth's busiest thoroughfares. The pavement was uneven and once or twice he lurched close to the road, but managed to steady himself and continue on his way. A black Labrador joined him when he was five minutes into his quest. It walked a foot behind him, focus equally committed. The dog looked at the boy, and the boy looked ahead at the pink-hued horizon.

Tracy saw them from the overpass, where she'd stopped on her morning run to stretch a tight calf muscle. She searched the street to find the irresponsible adult who'd let a toddler forge ahead at 6 a.m. and barely light. What could they be thinking? Although the car headlights bounced off the little boy's white singlet and dingy nappy, none of the early Sunday morning drivers appeared sufficiently worried about the potential for tragedy to stop or slow down. The child paused for a moment, turned his body as if searching for something and then headed for a crossing manned by stoplights fifty metres ahead.

Tracy began to run, taking the steps down to road-level two-at-a-time.

"Stop! Stop!" she screamed over the thunder of a passing semi-trailer. The dog crept closer to the child and cautiously head butted him away from his trajectory. The toddler paused to examine this new sensory attraction. He seemed surprised at the intervention but gave the dog a casual caress that was more like a smack. He looked around again as if woken from a dream, and carefully examined the row of identical red brick houses and scrubby front lawns illuminated by the early morning street lights. His shoulders squared and he took off again at a trot. The dog sprang after him and Tracy started mouthing, "Oh God, Oh God, Oh God," as she sprinted towards them.

Just as the boy came abreast of the crossing, the dog flanked him and knocked him to the ground. The child rolled over, and legs scrabbling, tried to regain his feet, but the dog would have none of it. Softly whining, it knocked him back towards the weeds and empty soda cans that bordered the pavement. There the child sat until Tracy reached them.

"Good dog! Good dog!" she panted, and the dog looked up at her with grateful eyes. She crouched down and said, "Hello, my name's Tracy. What's yours?"

"Dog," said the boy, emphatically, blue eyes on hers. Someone had pierced his ear. There was a small gold sleeper in it. His soft downy hair had one long piece at the back like a silky ribbon, a look that was somewhat out of date. His lips were rimmed with red. A wet finger and swipe diagnosed tomato sauce. He'd wiped his fingers on his T-shirt. She took out a tissue and spat on it and dabbed at his mouth. The sauce had dried hard and after a bit of scrubbing with little result, she gave up. The boy puckered his lips and blew her a kiss with an extravagant opening of his fist, throwing his arm up in the air. He was left-handed.

"Where's Mommy?" she asked.

"Dog!" he said. And turning, he pounded the dog on the head.

"Gently!" Tracy shook her head, afraid the dog might retaliate and snap at him. But the dog just inched away a little. The boy gave him a feather duster pat and looked at Tracy for approval.

"Good boy," she said – not sure if she was addressing the dog or the boy. The dog thumped his tail and the boy wriggled his noisome nappy-encased butt. Yellow excrement was beginning to escape down one leg. For a horrible moment she thought the dog might be inclined to lick it off, so she grabbed hold of its collar and checked the worn metal disk hanging from it. It was engraved with 9245 and then it looked like either a 1 or a 7 plus 345. A Scarborough Beach phone number like her own. The boy hadn't strayed far. The parents were probably blissfully asleep and unaware the boy was missing. Maybe he was a sleep-walker but there'd been an unnatural sense of purpose about his determination to reach the crossing. Unusual in what she surmised was a two or three-year-old. An only child, she hadn't had much to do with babies plus, until she turned sixteen, her mother thought her too young to earn money baby-sitting. Sixteen seemed to be the magic number. She could do any number of things when she turned sixteen.

"I'm calling your Mommy OK?" she said, holding out her pink-cloaked cell phone.

The boy put two hands together under his cheek in the universal sign of sleeping. "Dog," he whispered.

"Yes, I'm sure she's sleeping. She'll be surprised, won't she?"

But this went over the boy's head. He lay back against the dog to wait. The dog sighed. Whether in pleasure or impatience, Tracy couldn't tell. She didn't know much about dogs either. She and her mother had a cat.

Detective Inspector Bailey looked at the bedside clock. 6.15 a.m. He grabbed the phone and cupped the receiver under his chin before it woke Sara. Her head was under the covers but her waist-long hair had escaped – a black wave on the cotton bedspread. The mobile number on the LCD screen was unknown. Another drunken misdial he presumed, unhappy at the quantity of wrong numbers he received for the local taxi service.

"Bailey," he said—waiting for the inevitable, slurred, *send a taxi to…*

“I’ve got your little boy,” a high, clear voice said.

“What?” Bailey shook his head to clear it.

“Your little boy!” said the girlish voice. “He’s been walking on his own down a busy road. He could have been killed. You should lock your doors if you’re going to sleep in.”

“I think you have the wrong number!”

“Do you have a black Lab?”

“Have you been drinking, young lady?”

“Do. You. Have. A. Black. Labrador?” The voice was now brook-no-nonsense terse.

“I do. Why?”

“He’s here with me and the little boy. That’s how I got your number. From the dog’s collar.”

Bailey sighed and sat up. “Where are you?”

“Near the school overpass.”

“I’ll be there in five.”

“Bring a nappy!” the voice said, ringing off.

Bailey padded quietly into the bathroom and pulled on his jeans, hopping from one leg to the other. Zipped his fly and threw on a t-shirt. Trainers. No socks. Wallet and police ID. Gun? he wondered. Then smiled. No matter the provocation, he wasn’t going to shoot his dog. He whistled, just to make sure this wasn’t some kind of prank, but when Shooter didn’t appear he had to assume the phone call was ridgy didge. *Back soon* he wrote on the kitchen whiteboard, underneath *Jasmine tea, rice, and Wasabi paste* in Sara’s neat hand.

The Camaro let out a throaty roar when he backed out of the driveway, but he was careful to keep the squeal of tyres to a minimum. Sundays the neighbours liked to sleep in. He did himself.

It wasn't far to the overpass, nor was it hard to see the huddle on the pavement. A toddler seemed to be sitting on his dog. Beside them crouched a teenager in short shorts that showed off a good amount of sleek tanned leg. Her red hair was scraped back into a ponytail and as Bailey drew up beside them a ferocious frown marched across her forehead. It quickly morphed into bemusement when he put the blue flashing light on the roof of the car.

"Now what's all this about?" he said, hoping that Shooter hadn't bitten anyone. Normally the dog was good with children but any dog might bite if provoked. "Who's the kid?"

"Thought he was yours! Who're you anyway?"

"Police. Detective Inspector Bailey," Bailey produced his badge and the girl had a good long look at it. Shooter gave him a doggy grin and thumped his tail. Bailey reached out to pet him, but changed his mind and tousled the little boy's hair instead.

"Tracy Keller." The girl had the posh diction of a private school student. "I found him wandering down the street on his own."

"Dog!" affirmed the little boy.

"That's all he says."

"How did my dog get involved?"

"Beats me! But he deserves a medal. He

knocked the little boy over to stop him crossing the road. Otherwise he could have been killed. I wouldn't have got there in time."

Bailey looked at Shooter, who thumped his tail again. He'd never shown signs of being a wonder dog. In fact, Bailey had always thought him particularly untrainable. "Outstanding," he said. "Well, we'd better head to the local police station and clock in," he looked at his watch. "The parents will be beside themselves by now."

"Where's the nappy?"

"The kid's not mine, remember?"

She shrugged. "Well, it's your car."

Bailey got her point. The upholstery might never recover. Lacking a rubbish bin nearby, he stood up and walked around to the boot and pulled out an evidence bag to dispose of the noisome nappy. "Come on, matey," he said, reaching down to the child and hoisting him to his feet. "What's this?" he said, indicating the row of small red fingerprints on the child's singlet.

"Tomato sauce," she grinned.

Bailey undid the nappy and bagged it, then used a bottle of water and his chamois to clean the child off, tossed the chamois into the evidence bag as well. The boot of the Camaro hadn't produced anything that could be fashioned into a nappy so he stripped off his T-shirt and, with a bit of ingenuity, used that. Seemed a small sacrifice. A T-shirt versus the car's interior. Sara might not think so. It was

Versace. She'd bought it for him on sale.

The girl was checking him out. "You moonlight as a Chippendale?" she asked.

Smart mouth, thought Bailey, full of confidence. "Call your parents, Tracy. Let them know where you'll be."

"No need. Mum won't be up before ten. Lucky it's a Sunday."

Bailey almost shuddered at the thought of the child staggering out into Monday morning traffic. Mayhem.

Shooter bounced to his feet and pranced around, giving Tracy a gratuitous lick or two.
"I've never been a dog person," she mused.

"In the back, Shooter," said Bailey. The dog scrambled into the car and over the front seat, tail wagging on overtime. The Camaro was normally out of bounds. "You too Tracy. You can hold the kid on your knee."

"Why can't I sit in the front?"

"If the front airbag deployed it could kill him."

"I didn't know that," she said, and climbed happily into the back. "D'you think there'll be anything to eat at the police station? I haven't had breakfast."

"Sure to be," said Bailey passing the boy back to her.

"Dog!" said the boy, enthusiastically smacking his lips. His little legs drummed on the back seat and Bailey noticed each shoe was a different colour and the soles had the imprints of a different animal.

The Police Station was only a few blocks down Scarborough Beach Road, but a large sign posted out the front said *Closed for Major Renovations. For general enquiries contact Mirrabooka Police station at 50 Chesterfield Road.*

"That's miles away!" Tracy met Bailey's eyes in the rear vision mirror.

He sighed. "We'll go to my place, it's close and I'll call DCP when we get there…Department of Child Protection," he added, to clarify.

"Mum wouldn't like me going to a strange man's house. Even if you are a policeman."

"My girlfriend will be there. Call your Mum to come over and pick you up."

"What's your address?" she asked, jiggling the boy up and down on her knee as far as the seatbelt would allow. He was humming a tune and Shooter was joining in the chorus with the soprano whines and whimpers that Bailey normally heard during a thunderstorm. Tracy put her head down and listened intently, "It's Spongebob Square-pants," she said, humming a few bars to encourage him, "The theme song. He's got it down."

"He looks like a square-pants." Bailey laughed, thinking of his inexpert effort at fashioning the nappy.

While Tracy used her mobile to call home, Bailey drove to a Vietnamese-run 24-hour store to buy staples for breakfast plus a packet of disposable nappies. He cast his mind back twenty odd years and tried to remember what a toddler ate for breakfast. His only clue as to the boy's preferences was the tomato sauce around the child's mouth. Milk obviously; yoghurt and banana mashed together always seemed to go down well; and maybe toasted vegemite soldiers made with white bread. Buy a sippy cup? Or did toddlers drink from a mug? Children seemed to bring themselves up these days. Parents complained they didn't have the time. They didn′t seem to have the inclination either. Social media said children were turning up for their first day at school without being potty trained. The mind boggled. Maybe buy a baby bottle? Bailey reviewed a mental snapshot of Sara's list on the whiteboard. He'd buy the tea and some dumplings stuffed with bean paste too. They were her favourite.

Tracy was giving her mother an abbreviated version of her morning, followed by Bailey's address and the telephone number from Shooter's collar. "Can we come in the shop too?" she asked when he pulled up in front of the store.

"I don't see why not?"

A battle ensued to get them all out of the car at the same time. Shooter leapt over Tracy's legs to be first out of the passenger side door. He left a bloody scratch in his wake, spoiling the tanned perfection of her legs. Bailey got out and handed her a handkerchief. "Sorry," he said.

She dabbed at the scratch and said "Bloody

dog," without putting any venom into it.

They trooped into the shop, earning a hard look from Mrs Trang. "Where your shirt, JB?" she asked. "No respect."

Bailey pointed to the boy's t-shirt clad bottom, "I need a packet of disposable diapers, Mrs Trang." He gave her what he hoped was a winning smile. She and her husband rarely smiled back. They were refugees who worked hard to glean barely a living at the corner shop. Boat people. He wondered, as he always did without voicing the thought, if the trip from Vietnam and the stay in the refugee camp was worth it. Perhaps for the next generation?

"Boy, has she got your number," said Tracy, browsing around the store. Most things were kept behind the counter, safe from light-fingered shoppers, but she picked up a couple of snicker bars and added them to the goods Mrs Trang was piling up in front of Bailey. She shrugged, "Matey pointed at them. The only thing we know about him is that he likes tomato sauce; and now snicker bars. And he watches TV and hums along. Might as well keep him happy." She had him on her hip, and gave a little dip and twirl that made him crow with laughter.

Bailey picked up the snicker bars and put them back. "I'm not being mean," he said to Tracy's frown. "Some kids have nut allergies. I do myself. I'd like to keep him healthy until I hand him over!"

"Maybe you should reconsider the DCP. It might cause a problem for his parents." They could just be sleeping in. Why not give ‘em a break? Child Protection might take him away and put him in a foster home.”

“How old are you? Sixteen going on sixty?”

“Fifteen. And I′ve had some experience with the DCP. Long story. Irrelevant now.” When her parents split up, she’d first lived with her dad. It was a happy time. Then her mother, the lying bitch, had reported him for inappropriate behaviour. The DCP had put her in a foster home while the court sorted things out. Now she lived with a mother who stumbled through life in an alcoholic haze and who’d probably still be over .05 when she drove over to the detective’s house. Maybe if her mother was convicted of DUI Tracy could go back to her dad’s house. How great would that be? But he hadn′t contested the custody arrangements. “Too much trouble,” he′d said wearily and now he had a steady girlfriend so she probably wouldn’t be welcome.

“I’ll call headquarters first,” Bailey conceded. “See if he’s been reported missing.”

Chapter 2

The following week was abnormally quiet on Perth streets. Friday saw Bailey in Langford's glass-walled office reviewing the week's crime statistics. No murders. No hotel glassings. No domestic violence. None reported, anyway. With the weather turning cold, more people were staying at home to watch television instead of hitting the bars. DUIs were way down as well. Darkness was falling early.

"Not a bad month in all. The Police Commissioner will be pleased." Langford said, gazing absentmindedly into the large room housing the elite homicide squad. The boss liked to say his glass wall made him accessible for any problem a subordinate might want to discuss with him, but Bailey suspected the transparency was more about Langford taking the team's measure. Checking who was doing his or her job. "Nothing yet about the kid?" Langford asked as a parting query to Bailey's back.

Bailey had been stealing towards the door. He turned, and leaned on the door frame. "A two-year-old goes missing and no-one notices? Or reports it? Makes no sense. Nothing from the public, although the media is saturated with his photo. It's all over Facebook. About 250,000 shares to date." Bailey sighed with exasperation. "Not a whisper. Poor kid."

Langford waited for more.

"Tracy, the girl who found him, bugs me about him every day. Wants to visit the kid in the foster home. Keeps asking why we don't do more to find the parents. When she says 'we' she means me in particular, even though I keep telling her Missing Persons are on the job. She comes over to my house. Swims in the pool and takes the dog for a walk. And I find her sitting on my porch, waiting for me after work."

"Her mother OK with that?" Langford asked—scepticism evident.

"Mother's a drunk."

"Drunks still worry."

"This one doesn't."

"Be careful, JB. Fifteen-year-old girls spell trouble."

"Tell me about it."

"How does Sara feel about a nubile young girl stalking you?"

"She´s studying for exams right now." Bailey and Sara's relationship had settled into a routine. She stayed with him most weekends, but weekdays were for classes and she spent nights at her university digs.

Langford smirked. A smirk that said *You dog, you! Dating a woman half your age and now a fifteen-year-old is lining you up.*

Bailey took that as a sign he could get back to work. All the same, Langford had set his mind travelling on a well-worn track. Where were the child's parents? When he'd visited the foster parents, who had taken to calling the boy Mark—Markey being close to Matey—

the toddler had pointed to Bailey in delight. "Da Da Da..." he'd yelled with joyful bonhomie, and although he went on to say, "Da Da Da Dog!" the couple gave Bailey a pretty hard look.

Initially the Child Protection Department was disinclined to tell him anything at all about where the kid had been placed. In their experience a witness was so often a perpetrator. Cops had no more rights than Joe Public. But Langford had pulled a few strings to get Bailey the information. It wasn't every day one of his officers found a toddler wandering around the streets unsupervised. In the media he and his dog were overnight heroes, whereas Tracy, at her mother′s insistence, was only mentioned as 'the resourceful young teenager who first found the toddler'. Tracy was not OK with that.

At that moment, Tracy was looking at her mother, sprawled in front of a daytime soapie, fast asleep—or more likely unconscious. Why did alcohol have such a hold on her? Tracy's grandparents had shrugged weary shrugs when she'd asked. There was nothing in the past to suggest her mother would take to the bottle with such relentless enthusiasm. She'd been a good child, they avowed. Obedient. Quiet. It had taken her a while to perfect her English when they immigrated to Australia from the Netherlands, so she'd been slow to make friends at first, but by high-school her blonde good looks had ensured she was part of the in-crowd.

A ruined marriage had done nothing to make

Tracy's mother reassess the way she was leading her life. It seemed to Tracy that although her mother could have had it all, she was just pissing it away. She was still good looking, despite a face starting to turn puffy with excess. Well, OK, she was now a bottle blonde, but she kept it looking real with weekly visits to the hairdresser. Short, curly hair without dark roots. Maybe she'd had it too easy after marrying a well-to-do husband who hadn't wanted her to work.

Tracy would make sure she had a profession when she left school. Currently she was leaning towards working for the police department. It's true her crush on Bailey might be influencing her a bit, but she was well on her way to getting over that, since he refused to give her any information about Matey. Or Markey, as JB usually referred to him now. All the same, being a policewoman would allow her to help people in a way she hadn't been able to help her mother.

"Mum, I've made you a cup of tea," she said, placing the tray with the tea and some cheese sandwiches on the coffee table. "Wake up. It's past ten o'clock."

Her mother opened one eye and mumbled, "—not hungry. Had something earlier."

"I can see that!" There were no dishes in the sink.

"Don't be a nag." Her mother rolled to face the back of the sofa.

"Get a life, Mum. Get up and do something!"

But it was no use. The tea would go cold. Tracy would end up eating the sandwiches, toasted, when she came home. Her mother would have showered and changed and be out with one of her boyfriends. An empty house was the rule, not the exception. Getting custody rights back from Tracy's dad was all about spite. There was no motherly care involved. It was about winning, not to mention getting more maintenance. Tracy was counting the weeks until she turned sixteen. Then her life would start and she could make her own decisions.

She slipped her feet into running shoes and decided to jog down to JB's and get Shooter. It was great to have a dog to run with instead of exercising on her own. JB said he didn't mind. And Shooter seemed to like it. Tracy hurried into the kitchen and called, "Misty!"

The Siamese cat came running at the sound of the electric can opener. It twined around her ankles and gave her socks a thorough sniffing, rubbing its chin against her shin. *I smell Dog!* it miaowed—a singsong falsetto that drove her mother mad. Tracy smiled, again thinking of toddler Matey and his dog fetish. She was slowly being converted into a dog person. But before she left the house, she'd better change the cat litter. The kitchen smelt. Mould could grow in the corners and her mother wouldn't notice. As long as the freezer was plugged in, keeping the vodka on ice.

The call came in at noon, just as Bailey was about to slip down to the canteen for lunch. A woman's body had been found at a tourist apartment in North Beach. Despatch had sent an ambulance and one of the local coppers to secure the site. Bailey copied the address to his phone and looked around for his partner, Palfrey.

"Thought it was too good to be true," said Palfrey, referring to the major crime hiatus which had left them catching up on overdue paperwork. "Grab a sandwich to eat in the car?"

"Might be better if we eat later," said Bailey. Despite years of experience, dead bodies could still make the attending detectives feel queasy.

"Why is it that we always get called out at lunchtime?" Palfrey groused, shutting down his laptop. "Or when we're just about to clock off. There goes the fucking weekend."

Paid overtime was in short supply after the latest budget cuts. And it was no good telling Langford you were heading home early to make up for missing lunch. Detectives worked long, unpaid hours to put the bad guys away. No wonder the force was losing five officers a week to private security positions in the lucrative mining industry. They got double the pay and didn't end up in a hospital emergency room with a knife stuck in their guts. Not that the voting public was aware of the problem. According to internal gossip, the officers who resigned were recorded as being ′on unpaid leave′ in the hope that, once out in the private sector, they would change their mind. Kept the loss looking manageable.

So far Bailey hadn't lost anyone from his team, but it was only a matter of time. Ninety police officers had resigned in the first four months of the year, and ten had retired. What had started as a slow bleed a few years before had turned into a serious haemorrhage. Not enough funds. Not enough support from the politicians or the public. And as a result, when Bailey and the team's success rate plummeted, so too did their job satisfaction. With fewer feet on the ground, and fewer experienced detectives, investigations suffered from competing demands on their time and the force's budget.

"Ever think about chucking it in?" asked Palfrey.

"Reading my mind," said Bailey as they stepped into his Camaro.

"Got all the gear we need in the back?"

"Teaching me how to suck eggs?"

"You look like you've got a bad taste in your mouth, that's for sure."

Bailey just shook his head and accelerated up the ramp and out of the department's car park. He'd be losing Palfrey to retirement the following year, and then he'd have to decide who to pair up with. It would be difficult to impossible to find a partner with the same rapport, but at least Palfrey would last the distance. He wasn't looking forward to what his family had in store for him when he retired.

Grandfather duties. Repairs and maintenance. Not only of his own home, but those of his children—all of whom seemed to have inherited the *useless when called upon to do anything practical* gene. Fortunately, one of them lived in the Eastern states.

"Not far from your place," Palfrey commented, looking at the address Bailey had punched into the dash-mounted GPS.

"Yeah," Bailey said. "Forensics on their way?"

Palfrey nodded. "Should arrive just after us."

Exiting the Mitchell Freeway towards Scarborough Beach Road, the traffic thickened and slowed. They turned into the West Coast Highway and pulled into the parking lot of a cream stuccoed complex called Blue Seas Apartments. A wooden sign with an arrow pointing the way to reception also advertised short and long-term holiday lets. They followed a mossy path set between thickly planted palm trees. Out of control purple bougainvillea bushes attempted to detain them as they scraped past their prickly branches.

Palfrey plucked at the branch caught on his sleeve "Could do with some pruning."

"The whole place could do with some TLC," said Bailey. The stucco was shadowed with grey exhaust fumes and the corners of the building sprouted patches of unsightly mould. "Using too much water for a start."

Using too much water in a state with very little rainfall was as politically incorrect as smoking. Not that Palfrey paid any attention to restrictions on either. "I like a green lawn," he said. He'd scoffed at Bailey for putting in pavers and low maintenance plants. "Flowers. A bit of colour. That's what I like. Otherwise, what's the point?"

"You'll be out there ten hours a day maintaining it when you retire."

"Could be worse."

Bailey slid open the glass door into the reception area. The bottom left-hand corner was starred from connection with someone's foot. A piece of glass had fallen out and been stuck back on with masking tape.

"You the manager?" Bailey asked a short-set man with dark curly hair.

"Malcolm Birch," The man nodded and held out his hand. "This is my assistant, Beverley. She found the body." He indicated a young woman with a greenish complexion, seated unobtrusively behind a filing cabinet.

"I've been sick twice," she announced. "I don't have to go back there, do I?"

Palfrey shook his head. "Have a cuppa tea with lots of sugar, love. We'll come back and talk to you when you've settled down. Don't go anywhere."

"The registration details?" asked Bailey, economically. Birch pushed over a piece of paper with round loopy handwriting. *Hannah De Graaf. Amsterdam. The Netherlands,* it said. *12th May to 29th May.*

"We'll need her payment details."

"She booked ahead through booking.com. Used a Visa card. Beverley will get you the number." He lifted his chin at Beverley who tottered to her feet and moved to the Formica reception desk. "We clean the apartments once a week, or when the tenant vacates if it's a short-term rental."

"Did you take a copy of her passport, or check any identification?"

Birch shook his head. "We don't do that with a pre-booking, as long as the credit card is verified."

"Get many overseas guests?"

"It varies. Mostly in summer. They like to stay by the beach."

Down at heel the complex might be, but its location perched across the road from the beach, with views up and down the coast, was indisputably prime. "Want to show us the way?" Bailey asked the manager.

He took a large set of keys and they set off back the way they'd come until they reached a stairway to the second floor. Doors to the holiday apartments were set along a balcony come corridor.

"Looks like there's eight apartments to each floor on each wing. What's the occupancy rate at the moment?" asked Palfrey, calculating the number of inhabitants they'd have to interview.

"Yes, eight to each floor, thirty-two apartments overall. We're about forty percent full right now. Going into winter isn't a busy time."

"Twelve, maybe thirteen apartments to interview," said Palfrey.

Number 22 was two from the end. A uniformed policeman stood at the door, his back to them, texting. Palfrey coughed to get his attention then Bailey showed his ID.

They looked down at the traces of blood evident on the young policeman's boots and sighed. When would the first responders learn not to contaminate the crime scene? "You'll have to hand over your boots to forensics when they get here, for elimination purposes."

"Couldn't avoid it, sir. You'll see."

"Don't let anyone by without writing down their details." Bailey was terse. Excuses. Excuses.

The door opened into a room containing a small kitchenette, a square table with three upholstered chairs and two sofas set at right angles to a flat screen TV. The air conditioner was noisy and blasting away. Before moving into the room, the two detectives suited up and put on gloves and covers for their shoes. "She's in the bedroom," said Birch who was hovering by the door. He indicated an open door leading off the main room, and sounded nervous for the first time. "You don't want me to show you, do you?"

"No, Mr Birch. You can wait with Beverley."

The room was dark. The blinds pulled down and the curtains drawn. Bailey flicked on the light switch by the entrance, and noticed the fourth upholstered chair pushed at an angle close to the wall beside him. Then he saw the bloody footprints. They led from the bedroom and around in circles and figures of eight, like Piglet and Winnie the Pooh's snowy footprints in the story he used to read to Kate at bedtime. *Pooh, Piglet and a Woozle.* He could nearly recite it from memory he'd read it so many times.

There were several sets of these footprints overlaid, one on top of the other. The young policeman's size 12 prints only encroached into a 15cm area near the bedroom door.

"Fuck," said Bailey. "Fuck, fuck, fuck." The initial footprints were small. Tiny. Made with bare feet. Then one set with shoes. The right shoe had a different sole pattern to the left. Dolphins on one and zebras on the other. On top of these again, faint prints. Shoes with that distinctive toe pattern that meant the person had run through the bloody prints after they'd dried.

"Beverley," said Palfrey.

"Matey," said Bailey.

The first clue to the toddler′s identity had surfaced at a blood-soaked crime scene. The two policemen exchanged grim expressions.

"Moving on," said Bailey.

Chapter 3

Arcs of blood had spattered the walls and floor. "Who would have thought the old man had so much blood in him," Bailey said, recognising a tragedy from close and frequent acquaintance.

"What are you blathering on about?" asked Palfrey.

"Macbeth. Sara and I watched the old Sean Connery movie a week ago."

Palfrey raised his bushy eyebrows towards the ceiling. "Typical woman. She found you, liked you, but now wants to change everything about you. What happened to action movies? At least you can understand the dialogue."

It was one of Palfrey's traits to portray himself as an inveterate ignoramus. As part of his modus operandi when he was interviewing suspects, it led to unwary admissions. "I like Sara's different point of view," was all Bailey had to say in reply.

Palfrey nodded. Detectives were always canvassing different points of view to ensure their investigation didn't get stuck on the one track that could lead them astray.

The body was near the bedroom door. The ambulance man who had first attended the scene had left it as he found it, after confirming death. A yellow chenille bedspread lay on top of the body. Bailey took several photos with his mobile phone then folded it back. Features swollen and marbled in death, Bailey could discern a snub nose, a scattering of freckles and blonde hair with matching eyelashes topping the bloated corpse beneath. The stink immediately invaded the four corners of the room. They stared down in shocked silence.

"Eviscerated," said Palfrey after a long moment, a touch of horror in his voice. "You don't see that often." The woman's stomach was disembowelled, with slashed fragments of her paisley patterned shirt seemingly caught up in her intestines.

"And I never want to see it again." Bailey was having trouble holding down his breakfast. Acid rose to his throat from his morning orange juice. "Hope the bedspread wasn't Beverley's idea. Looks like it doesn´t get cleaned between guests. Imagine the amount of DNA."

"Shouldn't think Beverley spent more than a second in here."

Bailey nodded agreement. "Maybe the perp covered the body because of the kid." They'd found Matey's cot hidden behind the sofa, pushed against the wall. It hadn't been visible from the entrance.

Palfrey continued the thought, finishing Bailey's sentence as he often did. "—he came in and did what he did without realising Matey was in the apartment, probably sleeping, then threw the cover over her so Matey wouldn't see her like that."

Bailey nodded. "A kid-friendly murderer. I guess they come in all shapes and sizes. I'll get Hunter onto that. See if he'll work up a profile. That'll give us a different approach to combine with forensics."

The team's scepticism about profiling had taken a hit after psychologist Hunter's inspired notion about a certain POI in a recent case. He was now the go to guy for 'persons-of-interest' when they were fresh out of ideas.

The forensic team arrived not long after Bailey and Palfrey. First taking numerous photos of the scene, they were hard at work in the kitchen and entryway under the direction of the Forensic Forward Co-ordinator. Well known by both Bailey and Palfrey, the sergeant groaned and commented that rental accommodation crime scenes were a nightmare to process, there were so many trace elements to collect.

"Do tell!" Palfrey moved towards the jumble of clothes upended from a small Travelpro suitcase set by the bed. He stirred the clothes with one gloved finger and then checked the case's various zipped compartments. "No wallet or handbag that I can see. So maybe it was just a robbery gone wrong."

"She's still wearing a watch. Looks expensive." Bailey stepped over to the wardrobe and checked the interior. A grim man dressed in a clown's costume sprang out at him. His reflection in the full-length mirror. He was starting to look his age. The internal battering he'd experienced from images of murder victims over the years showed in the set of his mouth and the deepening lines of his face. No doubt this case would lead to further erosion. He projected a hard man with no sign of the hidden self—the one who wanted a more balanced life.

Hanging from the cupboard's rail, a grey quilted jacket was paired with a pair of fashionably torn jeans. Nothing in the pockets. Opening a drawer, Bailey found two passports hiding under a plastic laundry bag. The first photo showed a pretty, translucent face far different to the purple hue of the woman on the floor. The freckles and the snub nose were the same. The second passport showed a baby, fifteen months old, a younger Matey. His name was Bram.

"Who was Hannah de Graaf? Why did she travel to Perth?" Murders were rarely random despite all the crime novels filled with sociopaths and serial murderers. "Long day ahead, Palfrey."

The homicide squad would soon arrive to begin interviewing people in the neighbouring units. Back at headquarters Evan would process the details of the holiday apartment customers that Malcolm Birch had emailed from the guest register to see if there were any outstanding warrants or guests with form. Bailey and Palfrey continued to search the bedroom, but apart from the passport and a paper bag containing an empty takeaway box from KFC kicked under the bed, there was little to see. Bailey took the carton out of the bag and discovered empty tomato sauce sachets. A cash receipt revealed a purchase of chicken nuggets, coleslaw and two serves of chips, a coke and an apple juice, and two snicker bars. Looks like Matey didn't have a peanut allergy.

He waved the receipt at Palfrey. "At least we can pinpoint the murder date. She picked up the takeaway at 5pm— the night before we found Matey."

"How did she get there from here?"

"Walked. KFC is on the Esplanade. I wonder why they didn't eat there?"

"Maybe she left Matey behind to finish his afternoon sleep."

Bailey looked at Palfrey. He wondered if young parents today kept their children to a routine of afternoon sleeps. Palfrey, as a grandparent, would know better than he did. "Anyway, it's a break to have a timeline. I'll call Evan and have him start looking at CCTV." He looked down at the receipt, frowning, "Sometime after they eat dinner, the killer comes in… no wait, how does the killer come in? No sign of forced entry." Bailey rubbed his nose with the back of his gloved hand. "According to her passport, this is her first visit to Australia. She′s hardly arrived. Maybe she meets someone on her walk?"

"Or maybe he knocks at the door. *Hi miss, have you seen my cat?*" Palfrey tried to add some texture. "She's from Holland. Expects Australia to be a safe, friendly country. Wants to help. He overpowers and kills her. Then Matey, who's been put to bed after his supper, wakes up. Cries. Whatever. Asks after the perp's dog, since that's the only word in English he seems to have taken to. Surprises the killer, who throws the bedspread over the body and skedaddles."

"Does he want sex or money for drugs? Evisceration is a weird route to choose." "Telling me!" Palfrey belched, hand over mouth. "Let's step outside for a moment. Smell's killing me."

It was six days since Tracy had discovered Matey trotting unattended down Scarborough Beach Road. Even with the air-conditioner on its coolest setting, putrefaction was well underway. Not to mention blood had its own distinctive smell.

They backed out of the bedroom and tiptoed around the periphery of the lounge to avoid stepping on the bloody footprints. The crime scene was already contaminated by the ambulance man, and the local policeman. Bailey wondered if they had taken photos with their mobiles. It was becoming more and more common for the first responders to take images on their phones, which could be useful—or problematical— depending on why they took them, and if they were shared on social media.

Outside, on the long second floor corridor, a welcome sea breeze flooded their lungs. Bailey looked towards the Indian Ocean, where rank andf ile whitecaps marched towards the shore. A platoon of surfers dressed head to toe in black neoprene wetsuits sat on their surfboards waiting for the next big wave. The apartment complex had a great view; that was for sure.

"OK. Say the vic knows him. They have a prearranged date. She's already fed Matey something—probably the take-away, since his mouth was ringed with tomato sauce when Tracy found him—and put him to bed." Bailey tried to imagine what happened next.

"The perp could be her drug dealer."

"It's possible— although she'd been in the country barely a week."

"Addicts always find a dealer."

"No tracks on her arms. She looked well nourished. Have to wait and see if the coroner finds any trace of drugs in her bloodwork. There′s no purse, which points to a robbery. But on the other hand, she′s still wearing a Cartier watch."

"Young people today." Palfrey looked sad. "They all take drugs. They call it recreation, not addiction. We used to call tennis or golf recreation."

Bailey wondered who in Palfrey's close family circle was responsible for the more than usually hangdog expression. But before he could ask, a police car drove into view, Pamela Page at the wheel. Tony Caravelli was in the passenger seat talking on his mobile. Hunter lounged in the back. Dark sunglasses on an inscrutable dark face.

"Good. They're here. Let's hope interviewing the remaining guests give us something to work with."

Tracy tooled down the road on her bike, cycling home from a fruitless visit to her father's apartment. Today he'd gone in to the office instead of telecommuting.

She should have called ahead. It was hot for an autumn day, but she turned and peddled back up the hill past the Blue Seas Holiday Apartments to have a second look. Yes, that was JB's distinctive silver Camaro parked at the front, together with a lot of unusual activity; police cars, an ambulance, and men in weirdly coloured jump suits on the second floor balcony. A policeman appeared to be guarding the door to one of the apartments.

What was going on? Beyond the alcohol-fuelled fights and hoons leaving rubber behind in public car parks after doing donuts, not much happened in Scarborough. She cycled up to reception, took off her helmet and padlocked it to the handlebars. Looking around for a non-existent bike rack, she leaned her bike against the stuccoed wall. Hopefully the bike would still be there when she came out again.

"Hi," she said, carefully shutting the sliding door behind her, "I'm looking for a friend of mine. Detective Bailey. Is he here?"

The young woman behind the desk was collating sheets of paper from the printer. Her short spiky hair and a nose piercing indicated the lack of a dress code at work. Her jeans were purchased for a thinner woman and the flip flops on her feet displayed chipped dark blue toenail polish. She looked Tracy up and down, her lip curling at Tracy's sleek figure-hugging biking gear. "The detective won't want you bothering him today, Sweetie."

The 'sweetie' was definitely extraneous. Meant

to annoy.

"Why? What's happening?" Tracy found a quick straightforward question was the route to an honest answer. People usually responded without unduly filtering information.

The woman hesitated. Tracy could almost see the lies backing up behind her mouth before the effort became too much and the damn burst. "There's a dead body in one of the units. It was me who found her."

"You poor thing," Tracy said, putting a lot of sympathy into her voice. "That must have been a terrible shock."

"Too right. I was sick twice." The woman walked to the counter. "There was blood everywhere. I stepped in it. Had to give the police my shoes." Her eyes opened wide, like an old-fashioned doll. Tracy half expected her to bleat *Mama* as she leaned forward to speak in a conspiratorial whisper. "Someone murdered a young Dutch tourist. She booked in a week ago with her little boy, but he seems to be missing."

"No way!"

It didn't take a genius to figure it out. Tracy thought of Matey in his droopy nappy, trotting beside Shooter. The red stains on his T-shirt could have been his mother's blood. She felt slightly sick. What would happen to him now?

"Beverley!" Behind her, a thickset man with an abundance of ebony hair was giving the receptionist the evil eye. "The police haven't appointed you as their public relations officer. I'm sure they don't want you gossiping with any Tom, Dick or Harriette who happens by. In fact, I think they'll be pretty pissed off with you."

"Oh, don't worry," Tracy interrupted breezily. "I'm a good friend of Detective Bailey. He's mentoring me. I'm planning to enter the force myself, shortly."

The man frowned at her, giving him a faintly menacing appearance. The widow's peak over his white face and slit eyes was perfect for a horror movie. "How old are you?"

Tracy laughed a shrill yap that even to her sounded false. "I always get that. Especially down the pub. Can't go out without my ID. No one ever thinks I'm old enough to drink. JB says the bad guys would never take me for an undercover cop so it will give me an edge."

"Jesus," said the man. "You look about twelve years old."

"Paedophiles watch out!" said Tracy, congratulating herself on her dissembling skills.

"—telling me!"

"Although I'd rather be in the canine division. I love dogs." A few weeks before Tracy could never have imagined she'd say that. Shooter had converted her.

"I could never be a policewoman," Beverley chipped in. "I don't have the stomach for it. Hope I never have to see anything like *that* again."

Beverley had rather a pronounced stomach and a shirt that was far too short to hide the belly-button piercing. Not a good look. Too much sitting behind a desk. "Oh well," said Tracy, backing up towards the door, "You're right. It's not the best time to catch him. I'll see him later, when he gets home."

"Jailbait if I ever saw it," she heard the man say as she closed the sliding door. She pushed her bike to the Camaro, took off her backpack and scrabbled inside for the yellow post-it stickers she used to communicate with her dad. Normally she left one on his keyboard and signed off with a little smiley face. Not for the first time she wondered why her father wouldn't communicate with her with WhatsApp or Twitter. She was scratching her ear with her biro and thinking about how to sign the message to Bailey when she heard her name.

"Tracy. What the hell are you doing here?"

She looked up at the activity on the balcony and saw Bailey standing with his hands on his hips, behind him two men carrying a stretcher. Matey's mum. Off to the morgue. Or so she supposed. She suppressed a shiver.

"Just stopped by to say hi to Beverley in reception. What are you doing here?"

"Don't move from that spot, young lady. I want a word with you."

"What? I can't hear you." A tiding of magpies warbled in a nearby gumtree adding credibility. She cupped her ear. "Say again."

But before Bailey could repeat his instruction to stay put, Tracy jumped on her bike and coasted down the hill, making for Liam's house. Not only was it downhill, but Bailey didn't know the address. In fact, aside from her mother, no-one knew she'd been seeing Liam. Why she couldn't have a gainfully-employed boyfriend of twenty just because he was older was a bit of a conundrum. What made a schoolboy more acceptable? Wasn't maturity supposed to be an asset? Teens were always being told to 'grow up'. Liam had a car. A car was a useful tool for a would-be policewoman.

Bailey stopped by the Camaro and pulled the yellow post-it from the windscreen. "Need glasses?" Palfrey asked as Bailey squinted at the tiny writing. "What is it about teenagers and green ink?"

"*Hond is* dog in Dutch," Bailey read out loud, "and mother is *moeder.* Mum is *ma ma.* You could call my mother, JB. She speaks Dutch. Maybe she could talk to Matey."

Bailey thought about the petite blonde who'd come to collect Tracy on the day they'd found Matey. Joanna Keller. By then it had been mid-morning, she was sweating booze.

Palfrey patted his pockets and pulled out a packet of drab, dark brown, plain wrap cigarettes. In another country, the colour would be called olive green, but the Australian Olive Association had objected to being linked to a package that said "contents toxic." He lit up and took a deep breath, holding the smoke in his lungs. When he breathed out, he said, "Two-year-olds do have a limited vocabulary. Probably around one hundred words. Similar to an average dog, although there's a Border Collie that has learnt 1,022 words. Verbs and nouns."

"You're not starting to google trivia are you, Palfrey?"

"Have to keep up with the grandkids. Anyway, I'm looking forward to meeting this young woman." said Palfrey

"Who? Tracy?"

"No. Princess Katherine. Who d'you think?"

"She's all yours, Palfrey. I'm out of practice with teenage girls—plus I could do with some peace when I get home after work instead of finding her there waiting to interrogate me."

Palfrey blew a cloud of smoke in his direction. "An interpreter is not a bad idea."

Bailey coughed, waving the smoke away. He looked at his watch. "It's 3pm. She's bound to be asleep on the sofa after drinking a bottle of vodka for lunch."

"Cruel."

"What me? Or the way she's bringing up her daughter?"

"Alcoholism is a disease, JB."

"Since when did you become so politically correct?"

Palfrey sighed. “Since one of my grandkids started drinking and driving. And God knows what else she’s imbibing, and doing, although the tattoos might give me a clue if I looked closely enough. I wonder if tattoos can prove intent in court.”

“I thought your grandkids were toddlers.”

“My eldest boy married twice and has two families. The first lot have just come back to haunt me. They’ve been overseas with their mother for the past few years.”

“Oh yeah? How’s that working out?”

“Not well. The mother’s taking my son to court for years of unpaid child support.”

“Remind me what your son does again?”

“As little as possible. At the moment, he drives a taxi. The owner pays him in cash so the ex-wife can’t get her hands on it.”

Bailey gave him a considered glance. No doubt he’d hear more about it as the week progressed. He drew his mobile from his breast pocket and called Evan back at HQ. “Get onto Child Protection Services and see if they have a Dutch interpreter. It seems Matey might speak Dutch and could tell us something about the scene here. If not, see if we can set up a time to visit the boy with our own interpreter.”

“We have an interpreter?” asked Evan. But Bailey had already rung off.

The sun was starting to sink due west over the sea. Bailey raised his hand to shade his eyes and stared out at the silhouettes of the surfers, black against the gold hued sky. Not for the first time, he wondered why he'd become a policeman. It was a dark profession.

Palfrey threw the half-smoked cigarette to the pavement and stamped it out. "What now? Help the team with the interviews?"

Bailey patted the victim's passport in his pocket. "Let's get onto the Consulate for the Netherlands first. See if we can fast-track information on the woman and her family. Get things rolling. No doubt a member of the family will want to fly out to take care of Matey."

"Might give us a clue as to why she's in Perth."

"That's the general idea."

"Life´s a bugger," said Palfrey about things in general.

"That it is."

Bailey called the number listed on the consulate web page. He had little hope of anything but a recorded message since the hours listed were 10:00-13:00 four days a week. It was an honorary consulate, whatever that was. Perhaps the people who manned the desk weren't paid. They just loved the kudos of being bureaucrats. As if.

"—if the matter is urgent please call 948x3##2." The recorded voice was garbled and Bailey had to listen to the message three times to decode the number. He punched it into his cell phone. The number rang eight times and Bailey was just about to give up when a breathless voice said, "Yes? Hello?"

"Detective Senior Sergeant Bailey here. I'd like to speak to the honorary consul."

"That would be me. Greta Meer. What can I do for you Detective Bailey?" The voice was of a woman who'd smoked a packet of cigarettes a day for life. Husky. Sexy. Bailey pictured her as petite, around late forties, with a mouth striated from smoking.

"I'm afraid we have the death of one of your nationals to report. We'd like to get some information about the deceased family, so we can contact them."

"Give me half an hour, and I'll meet you at the office. Hay Street…"

"We'll be there," Bailey cut her off. The address was staring back at him from his iPhone. As was a picture of the office from the web cam. It showed a four-story building with a large "For Lease" sign on the ground floor. He looked at his watch. Half an hour. They should make it easily.

The woman who unlocked the glass door after closely examining their credentials was tall and willowy. A blonde. No wedding ring. 34D cup, Palfrey mentioned with authority later. The husky voice was the same.

"A death you said?" She ushered them into a spartan office sporting a steel desk, three chairs, and a dusty rubber plant in the corner. Probably fake. No filing cabinets. Technology and iCloud made physical files redundant. Bailey and Palfrey sat at the brown ergonomic chairs behind the woman's desk, Palfrey a little awkwardly, shoulders hunched, foot tapping. His body automatically recoiled at any attempt to reform his unhealthy ways.

Bailey pushed the passport across the desk. "I'm sorry to say the death of this young woman was a very brutal one. There is a child involved—still alive," he added as the woman flinched. "Two and a half years old. He's in the charge, the safekeeping, of the CPFC,"

"Department for Child Protection," Palfrey clarified in case Ms Meer hadn't dealt with them before. She nodded, paused for a moment to look at the passport photo, and then without comment typed Hannah de Graaf's details into the battered computer on the desk between them. It whirred and creaked as if tectonic plates were shifting. Her eyes met Baileys' and she smiled.

"It's old, but reliable. Like my car."

Bailey was tempted to ask what kind of car, but Palfrey asked, "Is it normal for the child not to be included in the mother's passport."

"In the Netherlands all children, even babies, need their own passport or identity card in order to travel. That way, if the parents aren't married, or are separated, either parent could travel with the child, according to custody arrangements."

"Anything in there about the father?" asked Bailey, indicating the computer.

Fingers flying on the keyboard, she said, "I'm still waiting. I'm trying to access the BRP. The *Basisregistratie personan,* or Municipal Personal Records database." Looking up again, she said, "It contains date of birth, details of parents and children, home addresses and so on for every resident of the Netherlands."

Bailey shook his head. Big Brother was apparently Dutch.

"Residents have to inform the database when certain changes occur in their lives. If they have a baby or marry abroad, for example."

"Isn't that an infringement of their civil liberties? Or data collection laws?" asked Palfrey, who normally didn't bother with such issues.

"We like to have an ordered society. Services are delivered faster this way. Not to mention there is less abuse of the public services."

A win-win situation. People got their social services more rapidly while the authorities monitored those who received them. Something for everyone. To his surprise Bailey wouldn't be against a similar database in Western Australia. He was beginning to think like Palfrey. That's what happens when you spend a lot of time with an older partner. You started to clone. Soon, without being able to help himself, he'd vote for the Liberal party like his dad, even though he knew he'd be just as unhappy with them as with the other lot.

It was another few minutes before the printer spat out the details. Ms Meer handed them two copies, and looked at the one she'd printed for herself. "It may be better for our own police force to contact the parents to advise them of Ms de Graaf's death, and…" she looked again at the paper in front of her, "—since the father is Australian, and resides here, we'll leave contacting the father of the child to you."

Bailey and Palfrey exchanged a glance. Progress of a sort. "Perhaps the Dutch officers would like to talk to us first. We′ll run them through things."

"Of course. Give me your details and I'll ask them to contact you."

Bailey handed her his card. She stood up. In her patent leather high heeled shoes, she had no need to look up to meet the gaze of the two tall detectives. Bailey caught the wisp of scent that surrounded her like gossamer. It whispered nature. Did tulips have a scent? He had to stop himself sniffing the air like a bloodhound.

"Please keep me informed," she said.

"Of course," they chorused. That wouldn't be a hardship.

Chapter 4

The morning dawned grey with a light drizzle. Bailey woke, patting Sara's side of the bed, searching in vain for her warm peachy bottom. For a moment he'd forgotten the emergency that had called her to Singapore after her grandmother had just been diagnosed with a glioblastoma brain tumour. Sara's return airline ticket was open-ended and he had no idea when she'd be back. Family first. Fair enough. Back to bachelor ways.

Shooter got up a touch arthritically, walked stiffly towards the bed and wagged his tail. Pat me, his eyes beseeched. Bailey ruffled his black head, noticing the threads of silver on his muzzle for the first time. The dog put one front paw on the futon and levered himself up to get closer.

"You're my boy," Bailey whispered. Shooter licked his face. "Wanna pee?" He walked through the house with the dog close at his heels and let him out into the rain, then backtracked to the bathroom to run the shower. Sara didn't like Shooter sleeping in the bedroom, so lately the dog had been banned. But what she didn't know wouldn't hurt her. With that in mind, his thoughts turned to the honorary Dutch Consul, Greta Meer. Bailey had googled her when he finally got home the night before. He wasn't thinking about her economics degree or the fact she was twice divorced, he was thinking about Palfrey's comment that she was a 34D cup. That comment had snagged in his brain and he was having a hard time getting past it. He′d hoped to see her again. It was a shame she wasn't available to act as an interpreter.

The front door slammed Was Shooter letting himself in now? He quickly pulled his jeans over his wet naked body. "Hello?" he called out.

"You there, JB?" Tracy's familiar voice rang out. "I found Shooter halfway up the street. You shouldn't let him out on his own like that!"

Bailey poked his head out of the bathroom. "Then he wouldn't be wonder-dog of the year, saving little boys from the traffic, would he?" Tracy was in her running gear looking like the front cover of Sports Illustrated, or possibly the winner of a wet t-shirt contest.

"You got any Cheerios? I didn't have breakfast."

"You going to haunt me night *and* day now?"

Tracy laughed. "I gave you the clue about Mum speaking Dutch. And I'm staying home from school today to keep her sober until her appointment with you and Matey. The least you can do is give me breakfast."

"Help yourself. And put some coffee and toast on for me at the same time. I'll be out in a minute, just have to shave."

"What did your last slave die of?"

Nevertheless, when Bailey emerged from the bathroom, Tracy—her hair still dripping— had coffee, toast and jam waiting for him. She'd even plucked some Jasmine from the bush in the garden, and stuck it in an empty jar. The powerful scent invaded the entire house. It was a million times better than the spray he used to sanitise the bathroom but it did clash unpleasantly with the aroma of newly toasted bread. He tossed her a dry towel and said, "Thanks. That looks great."

"I thought I′d come with you to see Matey," said Tracy.

Bailey was on the point of saying absolutely not, when he realised the little boy already had a connection with Tracy. Perhaps her presence would make the interview go more smoothly. He wasn't convinced it would yield a result, but it was worth a try.

"OK. Since you made me breakfast." He winced. That was no way to discourage the girl from visiting him. With Sara away, the neighbours would talk. And he'd seen how talk about inappropriate relationships could derail a man's life. "All the same, Tracy. You shouldn't visit me like this without Sara here to act as chaperone. I know that sounds old fashioned, but it's a fact of life that people wouldn't understand a friendship with such a large age difference."

Tracy smiled at him, and looked pleased.

"What?" said Bailey.

"It's nice that you consider me a friend."

As discouragement went, he'd failed miserably.

When she saw him frown, Tracy said "I have a boyfriend you know. And anyway, you're a policeman. Aren't they supposed to be..." she searched for the phrase, "above reproach?"

"Only in an ideal world. No chance of that." He attended to his toast. "Make me another slice, there's a good girl."

Matey was in the temporary custody of a couple in the northern beach suburb of Kingsley. Bill Peach worked for the Australian Taxation Office and specialised in mining company audits; his wife, Norma, was a masseuse who worked from home. This had caused the Department of Child Protection a moment's pause before agreeing to add the couple to their register of suitable guardians. They had inspected the studio where Norma worked her magic on tired muscles, and ensured the massage oils were kept in a locked cupboard. They had checked for pornographic magazines, found them lacking, and then they had interviewed the neighbours.

"No worries," had been the uniform response. "She only works on Sheilas. Gives the wife a discount. Helps calm her down at that time of the month."

With a husband at the tax office, the DCP was also sure Norma declared her cash income, unlike many who worked in her industry. Not to mention before applying to be a foster mother, she had undertaken a first aid certificate and a parenting course. The psychological profile indicated a woman with both feet planted firmly on the ground. The husband's profile was less straightforward. But that was often the case with professional men. They equivocated from habit, being used to second guessing the wishes of upper management and living life on the fence—ready to jump on either side to preserve their jobs and promotion prospects.

Bailey pulled the silver Camaro to a stop in front of a generic three bed, two-and-a-half bath brick and tile home. The distinguishing feature was a studio built onto the attached double car port. A small sign read "Sports Massage" with a phone number. He let out Tracy and Joanne Keller and the trio hustled past frangipanis and oleander bushes to the tiled porch. The front doorbell chimed *I get by with a little help from my friends*. Perhaps a clue that the couple were fans of the 60s.

Norma answered the door with Matey on her hip.

"Naked!" He screamed at Bailey, throwing his arms up and falling upside down, chubby legs clinging around Norma's waist.

Bailey grabbed him before he could fall. "You've learnt a new word," he laughed. "You're not naked, silly. I'm not either."

"He comes into the studio with me when I'm working," apologised Norma. "He sees a lot of naked women and seems to thoroughly approve of them. They all love him."

Be that as it may, nudes hadn't overtaken his original obsession.

"Dog?" The little boy asked, looking back towards the car.

"Sorry matey. The dog's at home today." Bailey cursed himself. He should have taken up Tracy's offer to meet him at the house and brought Shooter along. But he didn't trust her mother to drive, even when sober. "Tracy's here though." He pointed her out, and Tracy now reached for the little boy, provoking a clumsy exchange. They were still in the front hall and so far Matey had been handed around like a prized parcel. Tracy's mother was left standing uncertainly by the entrance, looking like the world had changed in unexpected ways since she'd last left the comfort of her sofa.

Bailey made the introductions. "Norma, this is Joanne Keller and her daughter Tracy. Tracy is the teenager who found Matey. Her mother speaks Dutch and we're hoping Matey's vocabulary is sufficiently developed that he can tell us a few things."

Norma knew this of course, the DCP had explained. "Come into the lounge." They followed her down the passage to a dark room decorated in various shades of beige. She'd set up a child's table and chairs in front of the L-shaped couch. Joanne Keller sat on the sofa and Bailey brought in two dining room chairs so he and Tracy could sit opposite. Norma hovered, uncertain where she should sit.

"Out of his line of sight would be best," said Bailey. "Where's the woman from DCP?"

"Held up with another case. She could be another half an hour."

"Since this is a murder case, I think we′ll start."

Norma's startled eyes flashed to Matey. "He's a very bright child, detective. Be careful what you say. Although he doesn′t say much, he understands more than you'd think."

Bailey nodded, then waved his hand at Joanne, gesturing for her to begin.

Dutch was quite a guttural language, somewhat like German he thought, as the words washed over them. He'd already discussed how to proceed with Joanne Keller, and she took it slowly, smiling, telling Matey her name, and making eye contact with the little boy. She started with a compliment.

"That's a pretty shirt," Bailey knew she'd said. "Blue, like your eyes."

Matey pointed to his eyes, and Tracy exhaled audibly by Bailey's side.

"Pink," the boy said in English pointing to her dress. He looked around for more colours to identify but seemed stumped by the monochrome room. His gaze travelled down Bailey's Khaki shirt, brown belt and khaki pants until it fixed on Bailey's shoes.

"Black," he said, then he looked up, eyes narrowed. "Black dog," he said in English.

Bailey felt like applauding, but didn't want to distract Joanne's gentle interrogation.

"We've been working on colours," said Norma, quietly.

Joanne's voice continued, with short sentences and long pauses. Bailey wondered how much of the Dutch Tracy understood. She was staring intently at her mother, focussed on her pale face and crimson lipstick. Joanne must have asked something about Norma, because the boy turned and pointed at her, and said "Norma mama," which gave Joanne the entrée to ask about Hannah.

She said *Hannah* and added something ending in *Mama.* The little boy repeated the gesture he'd first shown Bailey. Two hands under his cheek showing that Mama was asleep. Then he put his finger to his lips.

Joanne took him back a bit, obviously asking about the plane ride, because Matey said "vroom, vroom" and, turning his arms into wings, jumped up from the chair and zoomed around the room, showing impressive enthusiasm. It took Norma's intervention to get him to sit down again.

Despite his lack of Dutch, Bailey was monitoring the thread he'd coached Joanne to follow, helped by the pantomiming. Joanne made her hands into waves, and asked about the sea. Matey shivered, and said "*Koud,*" which was pretty close to cold.

Matey smacked his lips, and looked hopefully towards Norma and said, "Hungry now."

"I'll bring you some milk and cookies in a minute," said Norma.

The little boy moved his legs restlessly and looked away from Joanne. Body language conveying succinctly, that enough was enough. She asked him, quite sharply now, "*Wist mummie kennismaken met een man*?"

Matey shook his head. Mummy didn't meet a man.

"*Wist je vader komen?*"

Matey's eyes filled with tears. He shook his head. His father didn't come. He began to sob in an ever increasing crescendo, "*Mama, Mama,*" and Norma rushed to pick him up and cuddle him to her.

"That's enough!" she said, a red mark like a slap on her cheeks. "He doesn't know anything." She bent and kissed his fair hair. "Come with Norma for a chockie bickie." She immediately corrected herself, "chocolate biscuit."

Matey brightened. Chocolate was top of his pops.

Bailey looked at the little boy's feet, swinging to and fro. He was still wearing his mismatched shoes. Norma looked down to see what had caught his attention. "He won't wear any other shoes. I guess they remind him of …her."

"I'm surprised forensics didn't take them?"

"He screamed so much when they tried; they just took scrapings off the soles."

Of course. The nappy he was wearing on the day Tracy and Bailey found him was long gone, his stained T-shirt went to forensics, so the shoes were the boy's only link to his *sleeping* mother. And over time, would he remember anything of his mother? The way she smelt. How she laughed. Her kiss. Her voice. Perhaps not remembering was for the best. Best that he wasn't a witness to his mother's murder. Best for Matey—but not for the investigation.

"Thank you," he said to Norma. "It was worth a try. I'll bring the dog one day if that's OK? And I'll keep you informed about the family." She nodded.

"We'll let ourselves out."

Tracy stepped forward, and stroked Matey's cheek. "I babysit," she said to Norma, "You know—if you and your husband want to go out any time. He'd be safe with me. I've never had a complaint. My mum's in the book."

She took her mother's hand as they walked back to the car. "You were great, Mum. I was proud of you. Maybe you could do something like this for a living—something with children, or maybe translating."

"No complaints about your babysitting? That was a whopper. You've never babysat in your life." Her mother pulled her hand away and said crossly, "You've broken one of my nails!" Her nails were scarlet talons. With her slightly beaky nose and tufted blonde hair she reminded Bailey of a bird of prey. Unforgiving.

"No reason I can't start," said Tracy, voice even. She turned and waved at the house before getting into the car. Bailey saw Matey's chocolate smeared face pressed to the window. He was mouthing something. Probably "dog", or possibly "black, naked dog!" Bailey grinned and waved too. The kid was making him soft.

"There's not a large call for Dutch translators in Perth." Joanne snapped, once she got into the front passenger seat.

Bailey could see sobriety was taking its toll. It was all very well to value and encourage your mother, but respect needed to travel both ways. Maybe Tracy should try giving as good as she got. Jolt her mother out of her narcissist rut. Although with alcoholics—what could you do? No point in reasoning with them.

Joanne put her hand on Bailey's arm, a flirtatious gesture he tried to ignore. "It's amazing how your birth language comes back though. I haven't used it for years."

"You did well in there. Were you born in the Netherlands?" Bailey shrugged off her hand as he put the car in reverse.

"Yes. We immigrated to Australia when I was eleven."

"That must have been difficult, adapting to a new culture and language."

"Yes. It wasn't quite the land of milk and honey that we′d been led to believe."

"How so?"

"My father's professional qualifications were never recognised here. He ended up stocking shelves in a supermarket. He and my mother were very bitter about that."

"Couldn't he have sat some type of exam?"

She sighed and shook her head. "It's a long story…"

"—Why did you want to know if Matey's father had visited?" Tracy interrupted. "I understood that bit of Dutch."

Bailey saw no harm in answering. "Turns out he's Australian."

The suburbs flashed by and they all sat quietly, ruminating on the missing father and why he wasn't in the picture. "You don't think the father did it, do you?" Joanne asked, her voice an octave higher, appalled. "Murdered his wife in front of his child?"

"They weren't married—but I don't think anything right now. We′re just gathering facts."

That wasn't true of course. Bailey thought a lot of things. Mainly about soaring domestic violence statistics and the odds that murders were usually committed by a member of the family or someone with a close relationship to the victim. The most common cause of death for women aged 15 to 44 wasn't cancer, heart attack or road trauma, but 'intimate partner violence' according to all the latest reports. He certainly considered the father a person of interest, and wanted to trace where he'd been in the days since Hannah and her son had arrived in Perth. Perhaps the victim's parents could shed some light. Hopefully, by the time he got back to the office, Palfrey would have managed to talk to the Dutch authorities who would, in turn, have contacted the woman's family.

So far forensics had only revealed a plethora of fingerprints from a badly cleaned rental apartment. Hundreds. Well, that was an exaggeration. More than thirty anyway. Mainly taken from inside the fridge and the cupboard doors. The door handles had been wiped so that only manager, Malcolm Birch and his receptionist, Beverley's fingerprints were evident. The perp had obviously thought about what he'd touched, which would indicate he had a criminal record. Maybe he'd have missed something under stress. The law of averages said at least some of the fingerprints would be a match in the computerised national crime register. But whether their man's fingerprints were to be found only time would tell.

"Drop you off at school, Tracy?"

"In this dress—short, pink and frilly? Are you insane? I'd never live it down."

"Tracy!" Joanne warned her.

"It'd be asking for trouble. Girls can be such bitches," she explained. "Anyway, Mum's taking me out to lunch."

"If you're good!"
"Somewhere fancy. You can drop us at home."
"You must be proud of Tracy, Mrs Keller."
"She has her moments."
As an accolade, it wasn't much.

Chapter 5

When Bailey made it back to headquarters Palfrey was on the phone. He glanced up and pointed to the chair in front of his desk then pressed the button for speaker phone. Bailey sat.

"—The mother is booked KLM flight 835 to Singapore and from there she'll be on Jetstar flight 131 to Perth, arriving at 11.10pm." The voice sounded vaguely British.

Palfrey leaned forward, his considerable bulk making the chair creak ominously, "Would you like us to arrange accommodation?"

"The honorary consul, Greta Meer, offered to pick her up and take her to the hotel. I'll email you Mrs de Graaf's personal details."

Bailey was struck by the perfect English and lack of accent of his Dutch counterpart. He wished he was fluent in a second language. But what language would be as useful internationally as English? He dragged his thoughts back to the conversation.

"Hannah's father isn't coming?"

"He has a medical condition, which makes such a long flight inadvisable."

"Does Mrs de Graaf," Palfrey looked at the printout on his desk, "Ines," he amended, "speak English?"

"She does, but Ms Meer will translate for you if necessary."

"OK," said Palfrey. "You have my number; we'll be in touch."

He hung up the phone and took out a packet of cigarettes. The debriefing would obviously take place outside. Bailey pushed back his chair and without comment they strode towards the elevator. "Matey was a bust," he told his partner as the doors closed. "He understands Dutch, but had nothing to say."

"Figured as much. He is only two, three in September."

"What about the father? Tom Watts, isn't it?"

"Evan tracked him down. Believe it or not the guy lives in Broome, so since Hunter comes from there, he got onto his contacts and discovered Watts is a deckhand working in the pearling industry. It's neap tide, whatever that is, and since he was out on the boat when the murder occurred, he has the perfect alibi."

"Is he coming down to see the boy?"

"He's out on the boat again, but they're putting him ashore at the Eighty Mile Beach caravan park near Wallal Downs. From there he'll be driven to Pt. Hedland for the flight to Perth.

Palfrey yawned. "Late night," he said and continued, "Hunter doesn't know him. Watts hasn't come to the attention of the local police. No warrants or arrests in his past."

"I don't much trust perfect alibis," said Bailey. "Get Evan onto the airlines to see if he flew down at any period from the day Hannah de Graaf arrived."

"On it already."

They stepped out of the lift and Palfrey lit up as they walked through the automatic doors into the grey autumn day.

"Fair go, Palfrey. You're not supposed to smoke within four metres of the entrance."

"Get stuffed. Who's gonna stop me?"

Good point. Palfrey was well liked, even by the receptionists who were the butt of his sexist jokes. How he got away with it, Bailey would never know.

Palfrey inhaled and held the smoke in his lungs for longer than Bailey thought wise, and then expelled it, turning away in consideration. Nevertheless, the wind blew the smoke straight back into Bailey's face.

"For fuck sake Palfrey, when are you going to give it up?"

"Never gonna happen."

"What else did the Dutch authorities say?"

"Hannah met Tom Watts in a bar when he was on holiday in Amsterdam. They connected, she got pregnant. He hung around for a few months, but took off before the birth. He's never seen his son, or expressed any interest in him as far as the parents know. Nor sent any financial support."

"Nice guy," said Bailey, before remembering that Palfrey's son had essentially done the same thing.

"Not really. Anyway, Hannah thought she'd bring Matey over so they could get acquainted. The parents were against it, but they paid for the trip anyway."

“How come Watts didn’t come down to Perth?”

“She was planning to go up to Broome.”

“We didn’t find any airline tickets.”

Palfrey raised his eyebrows. “She had eTickets, probably on her mobile phone.”

“We didn’t find a mobile phone.”

“Exactly.”

“You get her cell number?”

“Of course. Evan’s getting Telstra to triangulate it, assuming it’s on. See where she′s been.”

A bus went by close to the curb, surfing through the puddle left by the previous night’s rain. The two detectives hastily stepped back. “Bugger,” said Palfrey, looking down at the spots on his trousers.

“Hannah have any form?”

“Pot’s legal in the Netherlands. So is prostitution.”

“They tell you that? Without you asking?”

Palfrey nodded. “Without me asking, but they also said she was a normal girl who worked in the family business.”

“What sort of family business?”

“Diamonds. They’re diamond merchants who cut and polish diamonds.”

Detective Bob Hunter, the indigenous member of the Perth Major Crime Squad, was glaring at the screen of his desktop computer when Bailey and Palfrey returned. He was a recent addition to the tightly knit squad who were still coming to terms with him. The fact he didn′t turn up at the celebratory beer fests when the team cracked a case wasn't helping. Bailey had a sneaking admiration for his intellect, but was having a hard time actually liking him. Hunter held them all off. Aside from his psychology degree from a prestigious Melbourne university, they knew little about his personal life, and it seemed that he preferred it that way.

"What's up, Bob?"

"Trying to see what I can come up with for the boyfriend. Looking at his Instagram page right now."

"Oh yeah?" Bailey peered over his shoulder. "Anything weird in there?"

"Surfing. Diving. Boozing. The usual. He′s a nice enough looking guy. There are photos of the boat he works on. The crew. Cleaning pearl shell. Girls in bikinis. Typical."

"Anything about Hannah or Matey?"

"I'm still on recent posts, haven't got into the prior years yet. Hadn't we better get used to calling Matey by his real name."

Bailey had to think for a moment to remember what it was. "I don't see him as a Bram. Reminds me of Bram Stoker and Dracula. Who'd name their boy after a horror story."

Hunter gave him a considered glance. "Bram was the author. Not the character. Short for Abraham. He was Irish."

"Whatever," said Bailey, shorthand for get stuffed. Sometimes a conversation with Hunter was like talking to Wikipedia. Hunter, like Palfrey, was prone to getting the last word in. Last words actually, since he usually spoke in paragraphs. Bailey was bookended by the two of them. He felt like he was in a verbal straightjacket.

"Interesting combination," said Hunter. "Pearls and diamonds."

Ding dong, thought Bailey. Now this was an angle he and Palfrey hadn't thought of. "Go on," he said. "Got a theory?"

"It could be something. It could be nothing. One thing a lot of people don't know about Broome—aside from it being," he made quotation marks above his head, "*the pearling capital of the world*, quite a few of the residents work for Argyle Diamonds in Kununurra and commute. Although the mine is slated to close next year, Rio Tinto will be rehabilitating the site until 2025. Living in Broome by the beach is more congenial than living inland. Although the mine is 1,000 kilometres away or more by road, it's only an hour and a half by plane. The work schedule leads itself to living away from the work site. Two weeks on, two weeks off – which puts far less strain on a relationship than the six weeks on, six weeks off in the offshore oil industry."

Bailey wondered why Hunter hadn't gone into education or the private sector, rather than entering law enforcement. He'd make a good professor. He had thought of pairing him with Pamela, the only female detective in his team, but she'd said that since she knew everything and Hunter thought he knew everything, it would never work. She also complained that she always got paired with the odd one out. First Tony when he came out as gay—and now Bailey was trying to fob Hunter off on her. Fair comment.

"Hannah has no convictions in her past, but I wonder if her parents have had any brushes with the law? Dealing in blood diamonds and so on," mused Bailey. "I'd better get onto Palfrey and see if the Dutch authorities indicated anything like that."

"If Palfrey didn't ask, they probably wouldn't volunteer negative information on a victim's family. It would be disrespectful to the victim. Europeans are more mindful of the courtesies than we are. Even cop to cop."

Bailey nodded, "Been to Europe, have you?"

"After I graduated, I spent some time in Vienna. Carl Rogers said *This is where the trouble all started."*

"Who's Carl Rogers?"

Hunter reared back from his computer. "The famous American psychologist! *Client-centred therapy!* I thought you took an interest?"

Bailey's introduction to psychology was through his relationship with Sara and her choice of study. If she'd been studying French or maths, he'd have bought a different book instead of 'Elementary Psychology.' He hadn't got around to Carl Rogers.

Mind you, rogering, yes, plenty of that. Bailey had been making up for his past dating failures. A good-looking university student half his age dating him? That needed analysing in itself.

"Vienna. Freud's birthplace," he tried for a quick recovery. "How did you like it?"

Hunter had lost interest. "When I've finished working up a profile on Watts, I'll see what I can turn up regarding the De Graafs. Practically everyone turns up on Google in some shape or form."

"Would it show if they had any form?"

"You never know."

The guy was useful, that's for sure. With good instincts.

Palfrey came shambling over. "Where to now?"

A good question.

"Lunch," said Bailey, and as an afterthought, "want to come, Bob?"

"Sure," said Hunter, surprising them both.

They headed to Joe's Oriental Diner at the Hyatt Hotel. It was on the street level of Adelaide Terrace and the detectives only had to stroll across the road from police headquarters. Bailey greeted the hostess by name and she ushered them to his favourite table by the window.

"First time I've been here," said Hunter looking around at the unpretentious wooden table and chairs and open kitchen where chefs were busily chopping and sautéing ingredients. "I thought a restaurant at the Hyatt would be fancier." They plopped down and perused the menu. The degree of heat in the spicy dishes was graded by the number of chillies beside its description. "I like it hot," said Hunter.

Palfrey and Bailey exchanged a look. They liked it mild. Normally they shared two or three dishes in perfect harmony. "Fine," said Bailey. He beckoned the waitress over. She was young with spiky hair, a pierced nose and a happy face. "I'll have the crispy duck with plum sauce and noodles."

"Nasi Goreng," said Palfrey, playing it safe.

"I'll have today's special. Mongolian beef, extra spicy with steamed rice, and garlic spinach on the side."

The waitress moved closer, checking Hunter out. "Don't I know you?"

"Bob Hunter," he said.

"Oh yeah. Claire Foy."

"How long've you been down, Claire."

"Oh—a few years now. Ever since culinary school. I'm usually the sous chef here, but one of the waitresses didn't turn up this morning. Anything to drink?"

"Water."

They all nodded. Water was fine. "A Broome connection," said Hunter in explanation to his colleagues.

"Cousins," chirped the waitress. "Two or three times removed."

They smiled at each other, and Bailey saw how attractive Hunter could be when he relaxed. He hoped the Broome connection would bear fruit in the current investigation.

The food came quickly and as they used their chopsticks to dexterously pick their way through it, Bailey asked Palfrey if he'd got any impression that Hannah's parents were already known to the Dutch police.

"No—although when I asked if the vic's father was coming over, there was a longer than usual pause. I didn't think anything of it at the time."

"I don't know. Maybe it's my overactive imagination, but diamonds and pearls have me wondering if this is something more than a murder of opportunity."

"Especially with no evidence of rape or sexual activity," said Palfrey.

"Plenty of rage though," said Hunter.

"Don't mention intestines right now," said Palfrey, looking at Bailey's noodles.

"—so Bob," cut in Bailey, "what do you know about the Argyle Diamond Mine?"

Hunter scratched his head. "It's a sacred women's site. The Gija call the land where the mine is situated, Barramundi Gap, after the dreamtime story where a barramundi swims into a cave and the old women try to catch it with their net woven from spinifex. The barramundi jumps over the net, and scrapes itself on the side of the cave, leaving some of its scales behind. The scales are the multi coloured diamonds found at the mining site."

Palfrey took out a handkerchief and blew his nose long and hard. "I don't see how that helps us, really," he said at last.

Impressed by his partner's restraint, Bailey wondered if Hunter was having a go at them. Had the story come from anyone other than Hunter, he was sure Palfrey would have given a lot of grief. Wasn't tiptoeing around an indigenous member of the force discrimination in itself? Why not say the giant mining conglomerate, Rio Tinto, who operated the mine, had used block cave mining techniques to extend the diamond pipe's life to 2020? Bailey had shares in the company and he read the annual reports but he let Hunter have his moment. "O.K. Speculation over. Let's follow the facts."

They finished the rest of the meal in silence, only broken by Claire's return to slip Hunter her telephone number. Hunter tucked it into his pants pocket without comment. It made Bailey realise how little he knew about the squad's latest recruit. Did Hunter live with anyone? Have a long-term relationship? Children? Married, single, divorced? Bailey was ashamed to realise he'd never asked. When the time was right, he'd try to get to know him better. The way he knew the rest of the team.

Chapter 6

The morning brought heavy rain. Bailey's Camaro surfed down the highway creating a wake that engulfed cars on either side. It needed new tyres but who had the time? Aquaplaning at speed wasn't a good idea. He slowed and reviewed the previous afternoon's work to stop him thinking about Sara's phone call. Her grandmother had taken a turn for the worse and Sara couldn't see herself returning to Perth any time soon. In fact, she was thinking about transferring the final year of her studies to Singapore. Graduating with an international degree would help her future employment prospects. She hoped Bailey would understand and they could still be friends.

There went his love life.

"You're quiet," said Pamela.

Bailey had brought Pamela with him in lieu of Palfrey, who was in court that day giving evidence about a neighbourhood brawl. Palfrey had gone next door when a pool party rampaged out of control, and the inebriated neighbour had punched him in the nose, breaking it and thereby risking a 3 to 6 month term in jail. Palfrey, mindful of the effect this would have on the family's young children, was speaking in his defence.

"Just thinking about the interviews at the holiday apartment. Someone surely must have heard or seen something. Wondering what we might have missed."

"You mean wondering what Hunter, Tony and I missed!" said Pamela, who was touchy about implied criticism.

"I didn't mean that at all, Pamela. Get over yourself."

Pamela looked down at her phone and started texting. Insubordinate bitch. Wait—cancel that thought. It was OK to call Hunter an insubordinate bastard, but apparently there was no equivalent for women. No way to insult them even in thought without being a rampant misogynist. Mind you he was feeling just a tad anti-woman today. He flashed his lights at a car in front, which moved over to the side. Unusual to find a driver with manners in the morning commute, looked like a woman driver too. OK, enough with the overreacting.

"Heard from Sara?" asked Pamela, looking up from her phone. Sometimes he didn't appreciate how intuitive she was. Call him grumpy.

"Grandmother's getting worse."

"Are you on the *ran tan* again then?"

"Did you know that the B side of *Babooshka* is *The Ran Tan Waltz …She saw me coming for miles…*" he sang in an off key staccato.

"Don't be so put-upon, JB, life is what it is, not what you want it to be."

"Right," said Bailey. He swerved into a park outside the Dutch Consulate's building. "I'll try to remember that."

"Don't confuse a bit of skirt for the love of your life. You should know better."

Bailey thought about mentioning her going nowhere affair with the boss, or asking why she didn't switch careers and write an agony column, but quickly discarded the idea. "Don't hold back, Pamela," he said instead.

"Stop moping and get on with the job then."

They got out of the car without further discussion and put on their professional faces. Inscrutable. All seeing. Forgetting temporary team dynamics. They saw so much of each other they sometimes overstepped boundaries but the job always came first. To have a common goal was a great panacea for hurt feelings.

Hannah's mother, Ines de Graaf, was a plump woman with a robust bosom. When she stood up from consul Greta Meer's comfortable chair to shake their hands, this and the ultra-high stacked soles of her shoes made her look like she was in danger of tipping over and severely compromising her top shelf.

Pamela was looking unfavourably at the large diamonds flashing on the woman's ears and ring finger. "My mother always told us diamonds were only for evening-wear," she told Bailey later, when the interview was over.

"Our condolences for your loss, Mrs de Graaf," Bailey said.

The woman pursed her lips as though sucking something distasteful through a straw, then brought a lace square to her eyes. "We thought Australia was a safe place," she said, dabbing at invisible tears, "and the police here… they have done nussing!" Her accent was thick and added unpleasantly to the ungracious response. Still, Bailey was used to being blamed for society's ills. The police were everybody's whipping boy these days.

Pamela rocked forward on her toes and growled something that sounded like "harrumph," followed by a spirited, "Detective Bailey personally rescued your grandson from falling under the wheels of a truck! I'd think that warranted some gratitude."

"Well," said Bailey, "my dog did that. I got there later."

"Not much later!" said Pamela.

Greta stepped in front of her fellow countrywoman in what looked like a blocking move and said; "The police are doing all they can."

Mrs de Graaf was unimpressed. "My husband showed me the statistics. Crime is double here than what it is at home. We should never have allowed Hannah to visit." She put her hand out and leant on the top of the upholstered chair. As an indication of her age, state of mind or the shoes, Bailey was not sure.

"My grandson. When will you bring him to me?"

"It's not quite that straightforward, Mrs de Graaf. You can have a supervised visit in his current foster home this afternoon. Child Protection Services will interview both you and the child's father to ascertain suitability for custody."

"The father!" She almost spat the word. "He's unfit to be a parent."

"That will be for the judge to decide. Obviously there'll be a court hearing." Pamela's response in a contrived monotone was pitiless.

"Obviously? Obviously? I see nussing obvious in this, except that I have flown all this way to bring the poor little boy home with me, together with my daughter's ashes! Our flight home is booked for one week's time."

"Bram," said Bailey.

"Excuse me?"

"Your grandson's name is Bram. Isn't that right?"

"What is it to you, his name?"

This wasn't getting them anywhere. "Please sit down, Mrs de Graaf," he said. "Interviewing you here at the Dutch consel's office has been a courtesy, but we have some questions we'd like answered. As you so rightly indicated, we have a murderer to apprehend."

She couldn't tell them much. Hannah worked in her parents' diamond-cutting and polishing business; She'd met Tom Watts while conducting a tour of the facility; He asked her out to a discotheque that night and she fell pregnant not long after; Once her bump became more pronounced he left, not hanging around for the birth.

At the beginning of the relationship Mr and Mrs de Graaf had invited him into their home. He'd seemed like a nicely behaved young man, so they'd expected he would do the right thing and marry Hannah. They'd even offered to find him work in Amsterdam. It had been very disappointing to discover his true colours. Hannah had moped around for a period, but once Bram was born, she took to being a mother and it wasn't until recently she'd started to obsess about visiting Australia to introduce the child to his father. Mrs de Graaf had been against it, but she and her husband were eventually worn down by Hannah's arguments and they paid for the tickets.

"I blame myself for letting her come to such an uncivilised country," she said, introducing the square of lace to her eyes once more and clearly not blaming herself at all.

"I believe the Netherlands has a permissive attitude to drugs, Mrs de Graaf. Was Hannah a drug user?" Pamela's voice was studiously neutral.

Greta interrupted. "The Netherlands tolerates soft drugs, and sells marijuana in coffee shops—mainly to residents with a specific "weed card" they've had to apply for—but growing and distributing hard drugs is strictly prohibited."

"And yet most of the cocaine and amphetamines sold in Europe enters through Dutch ports like Antwerp," said Pamela.

"Antwerp is in Belgium," said Mrs de Graaf.

Score one. Pamela scowled.

Bailey stepped in. "Getting back to Hannah," he said, "did she…partake?"

Mrs de Graaf waved a delicate hand at them. Flash, flash, flash went the marquise diamond on her finger. Bailey estimated two to three carats at least, thinking of his long-ago foray into buying a miniscule engagement ring for his now ex-wife.

"Psh. She may have gone to a coffee shop to smoke once or twice—everyone is curious to try it. But as a mother, of course her focus was on her child. And she couldn't do the precise work she's required to do with diamonds if she was taking drugs."

"So Hannah also cut and polished the diamonds? She didn't just run the tours?"

"Diamonds are our life, Detective. Hannah was brought up to do everything from a very early age. We will bring her child up the same way."

"Do you test for drugs in the workplace, Mrs de Graaf?"

"There is no legislation to require this." Greta again answered out of turn. "It is possible only if there are health and safety concerns to a third party, or national security issues."

"You think my daughter's death is drug related, Detective Bailey?" The sour mouth turned down even more. “You imply the victim of this terrible murder has brought it on herself with her lifestyle. Or the lifestyle you imagine she has.”

“We have to canvass all possibilities.”

Pamela added, “I noticed your business premises back onto the famous red-light district in Amsterdam where many of the marijuana cafes are located. With violent deaths such as this, a connection to drugs is always a possibility.”

Mrs de Graaf shook her head emphatically and jabbed an index finger in their direction. “Hannah would never invite this sort of problem while she was with her son. She was a mother first. Above and beyond all else.”

Bailey thought about Matey. What a calm little boy he was. A reflection of his mother and her love for him? Probably. Much as he failed to appreciate her attitude, Mrs de Graaf was probably right. Looked like Hannah was clean.

Chapter 7

Tracy stepped out of her boyfriend's Countryman Mini, and waved him goodbye. At Norma's request, she'd come to spend some time with Bram, that is—Matey. It was hard to think of him as anyone else.

Norma had a special client with aches to soothe. Not only of the physical kind, although the damage the client had suffered at her husband's hands was bad enough. No, there were psychic wounds that needed lancing like a boil. Norma believed in letting things out with primal screams and felt this might be a little too much for Bram to bear. With good timing, she'd told Tracy on the phone, the session would be over by the time his grandmother, Mrs de Graaf, and the woman from the Child Protection Agency arrived.

Tracy had come prepared with jelly beans of different colours and flavours, and a colouring book full of animals. They could colour the cow that says *moo* and the dog that says *woof woof.* She'd considered kidnapping Shooter for the afternoon, and taking both Matey and the dog to the park, but on second thoughts Detective Bailey might get a bit cross. She hadn't seen that side of him but she had a feeling it was there. She'd caught the look that passed over his face when her mother had tried to paw him in the car. When he'd shook her off not so gently. The well-muscled arms and torso she'd seen when he'd sacrificed his t-shirt for Matey weren't there just for show. Some of the characters who came across his path would need roughing up for sure.

She found the memory of his naked chest rather enticing and thought about it far too much when she was in bed at night. She′d added a couple of extra weights to her upper-body machines in the gym. When she became a policewoman, she'd obviously have to subdue or handcuff a bad guy or two. Sometimes in her dreams she found herself wrestling with the detective instead. Something she didn't mention to her boyfriend, Liam.

Norma looked flustered when she let Tracy in. "My client′s already arrived. She's waiting in the treatment room and she's not in good shape. Bram's watching a SpongeBob SquarePants DVD. But he's a little tearful. The lady was crying and it distressed him."

"OK. I hope jellybeans can fix that."

And they did. Before long Tracy and Bram lay sprawled on the tiled floor lining up a rainbow of the coloured sweets. Norma looked like the sort of woman who was houseproud, so Tracy didn't worry about germs. In fact, they were having a competition, seeing who could hoover the most jelly beans into their mouth without using their hands when the doorbell rang.

The woman at the door had a miniature superman outfit hanging from a hanger. Tracy thought the outfit and the diamonds on the woman's fingers were completely over the top. Would Bram have even heard of Superman?

"You must be Mrs de Graaf. We weren't expecting you until much later."

A yellow taxi did a squealing U turn in the cul-de-sac, and the woman brushed past Tracy, her large leather bag catching Tracy a hard smack on the arm.

"Come in!" said Tracy—redundantly—rubbing the sore spot.

Bram pattered quickly down the passage. "Ooma!" he blurted, "Mama?" He pushed past them, legs churning, and ran outside. "Mama? Mama?" The little boy was beating the bushes. "Mama come."

When Tracy reached him and bent to pick him up, he let out a piercing shriek, his legs kicking, his body writhing. It was hard to hold him. He slid down her chest back onto the path and crawled under the flowering bushes where he sat wailing, petals raining down on his head.

Tracy squatted down. "Sh-sh-sh," she hushed. "Mama's not here, sweetheart."

She turned a furious look at the woman, who was hovering by the front door. "Now look what you've done. That's why you were supposed to come here under supervision so you wouldn't upset him." Leaning forward, she attempted to pull him back onto the path but through some expert wriggling on his part he simply left his empty T-shirt in her hands. "Gotcha, you little escape artist!" This time she caught the back of his nappy, as he crouched on hands and knees, ready to make another escape bid, this time towards the road.

The woman shrugged. "Was I supposed to sit in ze hotel doing nussing, when my whole purpose was to come here and take my grandson home?"

"You were supposed to do what the CPS asked you to do."

Norma had left her studio at the noise and stood, hands on hips, a worried frown directed at them. "What on earth is going on?"

"What was the harm?" Mrs de Graaf walked towards Norma with hand outstretched. "My dear woman. So kind of you to look after my grandson." She picked up Norma's unresponsive hand and pumped it. "Let us have tea. I have presents for you all." She turned and glared at Tracy. "Not you."

"I wouldn't accept one if you did," said Tracy.

"I'm in the middle of a very delicate appointment right now. The timing is most inconvenient," interjected Norma. "Tracy, would you make Bram's grandmother a cup of tea. I´m afraid I can´t join you until the appointed time."

Tracy had scooped a now unresisting Bram up from the path. "What's that in your mouth? Spit! Spit!" Instead of spitting the little boy swallowed. Tracy dug around and pulled a pink petal from his mouth. "Bloody hell. Norma, Oleander plants are poisonous."

"I thought that was an old wives' tale."

Tracy shook her head. “The whole plant is poisonous. Flowers, leaves, roots, sap—with a toxin similar to digitalis. We learned about it in Nature Study at school. He’s got sap on him too from beating the branches. His skin’s already coming up in welts.”

An alabaster-pale woman with rivulets of mascara under her eyes appeared behind Norma. She was wrapped in a towel, dark bruises evident above and below the flimsy covering. “Just a minute, pet.” Norma patted the woman’s arm. “I’ll call the poison centre while you...” She put a hand to her mouth. “Tracy?”

“Don’t worry,” said Tracy. “I’m on it.”

The ambulance arrived in less than 15 minutes, but it was the longest 15 minutes of Tracy’s life. She’d stepped fully clothed into the shower with the little boy and washed him down with soap, than wrapped him in a fluffy beige towel. Even in her distressed state, she noticed the home’s bland interior had continued into the bathroom. Beige on beige. She supposed she was disassociating. She’d read about that.

Norma and her pallid client, who was now dressed in jeans and boots, waited out the front for the medical crew. Mrs de Graaf bounced between the two groups. When the ambulance attendants finally rushed down the passageway, Bram vomited multi-coloured jelly beans over Tracy and started to convulse.

"Jesus. Jesus. Jesus," Tracy said, half in protest, half in prayer.

"Give him to us, love," said the taller of the two ambulance men. "Quick as you can."

She passed him over and followed them back to the ambulance.

"Only one of you can come with us," the smaller attendant said.

Tracy, Norma and Mrs de Graaf all stepped forward.

"The mother!"

"I am the grandmother," said Mrs de Graaf with authority. She stepped up into the ambulance, elbows out, as if blocking shoppers in a bargain basement sale.

They quickly pulled away with just enough time for Norma to shout, "which hospital?"

"Osborne Park."

Norma looked at Tracy and seemed to realise the teenager was wet through and covered in puke. "I'll lend you some clothes. We'll follow on behind."

"—'kay." Tracy's teeth were chattering with both cold and delayed shock. It had all happened so quickly.

The client hugged them both, not concerned with Tracy's wet, vomit-stained clothes.
"Puts things in perspective," she said quietly. "A sick child's worse than anything. Don't worry about me, Norma. I'll call you later to see how the child is."

The hospital waiting room was cheery, with prints by famous Australian artists on the walls. Tracy identified an Albert Namatjira, Sidney Nolan and a Brett Whitely. Talk about eclectic, catering to all tastes. There was also a child's finger painting in vivid reds and blues. She moved closer to read the plaque. *With thanks to the hospital staff for their exceptional care of our son, Peter Fitzsimmons, during his last days. In memory.* Gah. Not good. Whoever hung that on the wall had obviously not spent any time there waiting for good news of a loved child.

The overbearing Dutch grandmother, Mrs de Graaf, was deep in conversation with Norma, giving her the details of her daughter's life. Tracy supposed she should feel some sympathy, but she couldn't help noticing the egoism. It was all about the woman's loss.

Norma caught her eye. "You all right, love?"

"The waiting's hard."

"I'm sure he'll be OK. You caught him right away."

Tracy nodded glumly. Her first babysitting job and the kid ended up in emergency. Perhaps she wasn't cut out to be a babysitter after all.

Norma must have been thinking along similar lines as she said, "I don't know what Child Protection Services will think of me as a foster mother now. I'll probably never get another opportunity."

"Course you will. If certain people had stuck to their schedule, it would never have happened." Tracy gave the oblivious Mrs de Graaf a hard stare. The woman was busy filing her nails as if she hadn't a care in the world.

"Now, Tracy. It was just a convergence of events we couldn't anticipate. We can't live our lives trying to control the whole world. It isn't sensible."

Was that true? Tracy tried to ensure her small part of the world made sense. She turned her head as a blue gowned man stepped into the room.

"Mrs de Graaf?" he asked, looking around. The older woman put her hand on Norma's shoulder and levered herself to her feet. "You can go in. He's a little drowsy, but you should be able to take him home in an hour or two."

"He's in my custody," said Norma, asserting her rights in a quiet voice.

The doctor nodded, obviously used to the complicated family circumstances that came through the emergency room door. "I'll make a note of that for the duty nurse when she completes the discharge formalities."

"Pfff. Such nonsense," said Mrs de Graaf. "So much bureaucracy for a little boy!"

They tiptoed through the ward to the alcove at the end. Three cots with rails up to stop the children falling out were set up side by side. The first cot was empty. The second held a toddler swaddled in lint.

Norma stopped abruptly. "I read about this child in the paper. Her father doused her in lighter fluid and set her on fire. He'd had words with his wife and wanted to make her pay."

"Psycho. Hope he kills himself with the shame of it." mumbled the obviously angry male nurse who had followed in their footsteps. "He was high on methamphetamine. People should be blood tested every week and be forced to go to parenting classes and take an exam before they're allowed to have children."

Tracy shuddered. "What will happen to her?"

"Untold skin grafts, pain and foster care."

"Perhaps I could visit her. Read her stories. Sing nursery rhymes."

"You have a kind heart, sweetie."

Matey was in the final cot, dreamily sucking his thumb. "He's such a darling," said Norma. "I wish he were mine."

"Vair are his clothes?" demanded Mrs de Graaf. He was in a tiny surgical outfit. Blue. The same shade as the doctor's.

"In the console beside the bed," said the nurse.

Tracy and Norma hung over the cot, while the grandmother rummaged through the plastic bag containing his shoes and a spare nappy that Norma had brought with her.

Tracy couldn't imagine anyone stealing something from a child this age—but then she couldn't imagine a father setting fire to his child either.

Matey opened his eyes. Blue sparks flew towards them. "Dog," he said.

"Thank goodness. No damage then," said Tracy. She and Norma laughed and hugged each other, happy with relief.

"I'll take a taxi back to my hotel," said Mrs de Graaf. "I don't want to get in the way."

That would be a first, thought Tracy.

"We'll be in touch after I've spoken with the CPS," said Norma, holding out her hand.

Mrs de Graaf shook it. A limp up and down. "I hope there is no more inconvenience."

"Inconvenience!" Tracy shouted at Bailey as she recounted the day's events later in the day. "Poor Matey was almost poisoned, and she thought it inconvenienced her."

"Settle down."

Bailey had arrived home to find a ballistic Tracy waiting for him. Shooter was cowering under the kitchen table. The dog could sense dissention and didn't want any part of it. His tail between his legs, he whined his apologies. Not sure what he'd done to bring down the wrath of his goddess.

"It's OK, fella." Bailey patted his legs to encourage the dog to emerge, but he simply backed further away, eyes on Tracy. "You're scaring my dog, Tracy," he said. "And another thing. Will there be a day any time soon, when I don't find you waiting for me after I finish work? I could do with a rest."

"What?" Tracy blinked at him. "I thought you cared about Matey."

"I do. But he's in good hands right now with Norma. Right? Not our responsibility."

"Of course he's our responsibility," said Tracy—irritation ploughed across her forehead. "We found him! We have to make sure he's safe." Mouth turned down, about to cry. "You have to find his mother's murderer."

Bailey nearly said that if you found a dog, you took it to the pound and they looked after it, but understanding it would add fuel to the fire, he said, rather weakly, "There are procedures we need to follow. Family rights under the law."

"Isn't there some way we can ban Mrs de Graaf from taking him? You'll never guess what else she did!"

Bailey sighed, and popped the top off a can of light beer. "Go on then. Tell me."

"She tried to take his shoes. The ones he loves so much."

"Why would she do that?"

"Because she's a fucking witch."

"Language!"

"Friggin' witch," amended Tracy.

"Not much improvement!"

"Anway, I wrestled them off her." She plumped down on the kitchen chair. "Can I have something to drink?"

Bailey waved at the fridge. "Help yourself. To a Coke." He watched her bottom in her short shorts as she stomped away. Two perfect globes perched on long, long tanned legs. "On second thoughts, take a can and best be off."

She turned a wounded face towards him.

"Enough Tracy. I have a date and I need to get ready for it."

He didn't. But what the hell. He couldn't have this fifteen-year-old making herself so entirely at home. It would lead to trouble. His boss's warning rang in his ears. Langford was right. Time to back away.

Chapter 8

With busy mornings, tasked to go in opposite directions, the Homicide squad met for an early breakfast. Their regular café in Northbridge was open 24/7. It was old, with 1970s orange and brown décor, but the food was cheap and the service welcoming. Night Patrol first discovered it; then by word of mouth, the police force started to filter through its doors. The Greek owners liked their presence. Northbridge was the centre of the drug and prostitution culture. Fights broke out regularly in the wee hours. Windows were broken. Doors kicked in. Tills burgled. But after the cops turned it into their personal bolthole, this run-down café with its flashing neon sign was left alone.

"The usual?" the waitress asked Pamela.

The usual was oatmeal with a sliced banana and blueberries covered in natural yoghurt and a beaker of black coffee. The rest of the squad tended towards full English with an extra plate of chips, but today both Palfrey and Bailey opted for the Pamela option.

"With skinny yoghurt," said Palfrey, mournfully ogling the fried food. "Cholesterol."

Bailey didn't comment. He was still in denial about his racing heart. One day soon, he'd go to his GP. Get an opinion. One that wouldn't make it onto his annual police medical if it was bad news. By the baleful look on his face the squad knew better than to comment.

Hunter, as usual, was the odd one out, ordering a meat pie with a diet coke to chase it down. No one took it up with him either. They expected him to be different.

"So," said Bailey, "anything to report?"

They liked meeting here where it was ex-official with no Langford breathing down their necks for word of a breakthrough. Cases took time to crack and were solved with painstaking work. The top brass didn't always appreciate that.

Tony shook his head. Bailey was still getting used to the earring. "Nothing from the street." Each member of the squad dobbed in a tenner a week for snitch petty cash. Tony was responsible for doling it out. Cash for information. If it came to light in court, it could be a problem but usually it didn't. And the money was responsible for solving many a case.

"Tom Watts," said Bailey—"Matey's father. Been onto your mates in Broome to see what's happening there, Hunter?"

They were still waiting on Watts. His non-appearance at the airport had something to do with the tides not being right and a stiff easterly breeze. It sounded like a poor excuse.

"Neap tides end tomorrow and then he promises to be on the next plane."

"Did you talk to him personally?"

"No—to the skipper of his boat on the ship-to-shore. It sounded reasonable to me. Pearling is dictated by the tides and Watts can't come ashore without a great deal of inconvenience and expense to the rest of the crew and to the company. They're fishing off the eighty-mile beach, an eight-hour steam from Broome. Using the dinghy to drop him on a beach to catch the plane from Port Hedland just wasn't realistic."

"Anything from the CCTV footage in Scarborough?"

Evan leaned forward. The youngest in the team, he often got what the others considered the shit jobs, sifting through hours of mindless CCTV footage from the cameras variously located throughout Perth, this time near the Scarborough apartment complex where the murder had taken place. "Nothing that stands out. People walking their dogs. Going out for a burger. Surfers coming back from a day on the waves. The usual. I don't want to sound defeatist, but I doubt we'll get a break there."

They all nodded and tucked into their breakfast. Silence, if not defeat, reigned.

"Think I'll go by Mrs de Graaf's hotel on my way into headquarters. See what she's got to say for herself after yesterday's brouhaha with Matey," said Bailey.

"The woman's a weirdo, that's for sure. Doubt I've ever met anyone less grandmotherly. Want me to come with you?" Pamela looked eager to lock horns with Ines de Graaf once more. Which is why Bailey said no. He wanted compliance from an interview not World-War-Three. Suddenly anxious to go, Bailey stood and slapped a $10 note on the table and headed for the car.

The receptionist at the Sheraton Hotel gave him a polished smile. Red lipstick and white teeth. The nametag said *Sheila.* Being called Sheila in Australia must be a bitch.

"I believe you have a guest here, a Mrs de Graaf. What room would she be in?" Bailey asked.

The woman checked the computer in front of her. "Whom shall I say is calling?"

"No need for that. I'll pop up to see her."

The smile slipped a little. "I'm not sure that…"

"Something I want to sort out with your guest." He could see she was thinking about explaining company policy. The policy that said no information was to be given out about guests. He slid his badge across the counter. "I′d like to be as discreet as possible."

She nodded, curls bouncing. "She has a junior suite. 501. Fifth floor."

There was no real reason not to notify Mrs de Graaf he was on his way up. But Tracy's complaint about the woman's behaviour stuck in his gullet. Why would she try to take the boy's shoes? He'd thought about it during the night, and here he was before 9.00 a.m. making an unannounced call despite not wanting to court a complaint to the police commissioner, or to be labelled as insensitive and intrusive. Langford had given the squad a bollocking about the escalating number of complaints from the general public. Joe Public had Legal Aid on speed dial. They wanted safe streets without being personally responsible for them. Any questions about what they saw or heard and you can bet their rights were being disregarded.

The woman didn't ring true. Yes, she was the victim's mother. Her passport and the Dutch consulate had confirmed that. But her general demeanour was off. Bailey had learned not to dismiss his gut instincts.

He rapped on the door, and answered "Detective Bailey," to the muffled response.

The door opened a crack. "Yes?"

"I was on my way to headquarters and thought I would go over a few things with you, if that's convenient."

"It′s not. You should have called," she said, but she opened the door wide and ushered him in. "This would not happen in my country."

Today she was minus her diamonds and looked more grandmotherly, to use Pamela's term. Her hair was imperfectly coiffed and she wearing the hotel slippers. Her choice of dark purple skirt and lilac top indicated subdued colours suitable for mourning. Not every bereft mother wore black. Bailey was used to seeing the whole spectrum, from relatives who didn't wash and who wore the same stained clothes for days, too devastated to contemplate the smallest tasks; and those who clung to routine as a way of coping with their grief. They dressed to keep up appearances.

Mrs de Graaf checked her watch, an unadorned Seiko. "Will this take long?"

Bailey looked around for a place to sit. The sofa was thick with shopping bags, paper not plastic, with multiple logos. He pulled a chair from the walnut desk and asked, "May I?"

Mrs de Graaf merely waved a hand.

"Been shopping?"

"For my grandson. New shoes. New clothes to wear on the plane and for a different climate back in Holland."

"Didn't Hannah have clothes for him?"

"I feel the clothes from the apartment where she was found have been…" She paused and looked at the ceiling for a moment, a tear hovered on her eyelashes, "—contaminated. I don't want him to wear them or have any memory of them. How much does a child remember? It´s best not to dredge up something that may upset him."

"Good idea," Bailey nodded. "I heard about what happened yesterday. That he associated your appearance with his mother and had a meltdown."

"Yes. He was extremely upset. I don't want to see that again. We have to start a new chapter." She walked over to the sofa, picked up a bag seemingly at random and tipped the contents onto the coffee table. Tiny shoes tumbled out. Shoes with soles that depicted animals. Giraffes. Dolphins. Kangaroos. Bailey didn't know the name of the brand, but he knew they weren't cheap. Five pairs seemed a bit excessive. The next bag she tipped out was full of T-shirts—all colours. On top of that, she poured out miniature denim jeans and rompers, with press studs to allow for a change of nappies. "I am supposing that sour young girl, Tracy, said I tried to steal his shoes! Well, detective, I ask you how else would I know his size?"

So much for gut instinct. Bailey was annoyed with himself for allowing a fifteen-year-old girl's misgivings to distract him from the case. "Not at all Mrs de Graaf. I was simply driving by on my way to the office and I thought I'd stop to see how you were, plus assure you that we are doing everything we can to bring the perpetrator to justice."

"You have a suspect?"

"Enquiries are ongoing."

Mrs de Graaf had a portfolio of snorts that she used to good effect. She used one now. "Was there anything else?"

Bailey tried for a face-saving question. "Bram's father, Tom Watts. Is there anything more you can tell us about him?"

"He's a man without a conscience. Someone who can charm a young woman into bed then leave her pregnant with his child and not glance back. He is capable of anything. Such a person can mimic feelings, yet remain untouched. I believe he is a psychopath. I will be telling the child protection authorities that. They will not be wanting to give my grandson to him."

The lift was slow so Bailey walked down the stairs. Five flights. His heart didn't seem to mind. Going up might be a different story. Bailey shoved his hands in his pockets and slouched out of the foyer, acknowledging the receptionist by a lifted chin and a glance over his shoulder as he held the door open for an incoming guest. An odorous miasma emanated from the man who'd barged past him. Even from the back view of the smartly tailored navy sports coat, grey linen trousers and balding crown, he knew who it was. The distinctive odour was of something nameless but decidedly funky, a combination of garbage and fish, and could only belong to the owner of one of the more prosperous pawn shops to be found near the Burswood Casino. A shop full of anonymous Rolex watches and diamond engagement rings, some with dubious provenance.

Bailey let the door gently slip from his hand. He watched Bill Johnson, alias Stinky Bill, march to the lift. The Sheraton Hotel seemed an unusual place to find him so early in the morning. Curiosity roused; Bailey watched the light blink above the lift. It stopped on the fifth floor. Interesting.

"Many guests on the fifth floor right now, Sheila?"

The receptionist jumped and lifted her head. She'd missed his quiet return. She gave him the bright white smile once more. "In their rooms? How would I know that?"

"No. I mean booked in."

She checked the computer. "Two couples and one single. It's quiet right now."

"Their names?"

"I really can't give you those."

Bailey sighed. "Perhaps if you check with the manager. Otherwise, I'll have to call in some uniforms to stop all the guests leaving the hotel this morning to question them."

The smile vanished. "A moment," she said coolly. "Revealing a guest's personal information is above my pay grade. And I like my job."

"Go on then," said Bailey. "I'll be back in a jif."

He took Stinky Bill's lift, feeling rather like a K-9, except he was trying not to sniff the strong aroma left behind. Bill had explained his problem to him one day. The medical condition that made him smell so bad. The hereditary disorder was called TMAU, and was a disease that impaired the ability of an enzyme to metabolize the compound, trimethylamine. Bailey had tuned out, and stepped back, while Bill listed all the deterrents that he took to minimise the smell: vitamin B, a restricted diet, antibiotics, charcoal tablets. All Bailey had wanted at the time was the provenance of a certain jewel-encrusted watch, reported as missing from a body found floating in the Swan River after a rowdy thirtieth birthday party on one of the city's river boats. As so often was the case, the pawned article was brought in by someone with an excellent, but false, identity. The shop's camera was oddly faulty that day with more lines across the picture than those on Stinky Bill's well-worn face.

Bailey sniffed his way down the corridor. The smell was strongest near the three suites opposite the lift and virtually non-existent at the ends of the passageway. He put his ear against each of the doors but could hear no murmurs from within.

When he returned to the foyer he was intercepted by the manager, a fussy little man with a bouncing walk. After a token shrilling about the necessity of a court order, he handed over the sheet of paper listing guests′ names that he'd been waving around. Mixed messages there.

Bailey nodded. "I appreciate your co-operation," he said. "Anything I can do for you, sometime, let me know."

The manager appeared mollified. Bailey doubted he'd ever hear from him since he hadn't handed over his card. Joe Public rarely called the homicide squad asking for favours. Especially when they didn't have a name or the number of the direct line.

Chapter 9

Ignoring the *Do not disturb* sign, Bailey knocked on the door next to Ines de Graaf's suite. Suite 503 housed a young man with a heavy nine o'clock shadow and tousled hair. He was wearing pyjamas—blue pants and grey jersey top. Ralph Lauren. The shirt was inside-out.

Bailey consulted his sheet. "Mr McLean."

"Wha'? Who wants to know?"

"Senior Detective Bailey. Major Crime Squad. May I come in?"

The man threw a panicked glance over his shoulder. "You wearing any cloves, love?" He shouted. "Put summin′ on."

Bailey consulted the sheet again. The room was booked as a single. Even though the door to the balcony was open letting in a fresh breeze, he could smell the trace of marijuana. He couldn't smell the remains of Stinky Bill.

He heard a toilet flush, and then a peroxide blonde walked out of the bedroom. Hastily applied lipstick, leopard skin high heeled shoes and short, tight, form-fitting dress made it easy to guess her profession. Her nipples were misaligned searchlights, pointing east and north. "What now?" she said, grumpily addressing Bailey. Her head was large and in disproportion to her slim, lithe body. Large pores around an un-powdered nose patrolled lolly- pink lips pumped up with Restylane. She wasn't exactly young. Bailey figured she'd had plenty to do with the vice squad in the past.

"Looking for a man called Bill Holland. Owner of a pawn shop. Know him?"

"Wha' the fuck? Come bargin' in 'ere. Annoyin' innocent tourists. I came 'ere to get away from all the nanny-state business."

"You invited me in, Sir. I'm just trying to do my job."

The blond rolled her eyes. "I've heard that before. What d'you want with Stinky Bill anyway? Don't tell me he's missing? A bad penny like him always turns up."

Prostitutes knew Bill Holland and his pawn shop. It was where they sold the watches they filched from their customers. Customers who wouldn't want to make a police report about the theft. Although the Prostitution Act of 2000 made consorting with a prostitute legal in Western Australia, most wives still considered it a crime punishable by divorce. "Was he here?" asked Bailey.

"You woke us up, officer. Take a look aroun′. There's nothin′ to see."

Intercepting the look between client and prostitute, Bailey gathered the sound of the flushing toilet had indicated any illegal drugs were on their way through Perth's sewers. No doubt an expensive night for Mr McLean. To assert himself Bailey wandered into the bedroom while still keeping the open door to the passage in line of sight. It wouldn't do to miss Stinky Bill leaving one of the other rooms.

Messy sheets. Crumpled jeans flung on top of an open suitcase on the floor. A leopard skin bag hung over the door handle. He rifled through it, interpreting McLeans invitation to 'take a look around' broadly. A stack of personalised business cards invited the recipient to experience *Luscious Pink Lips* for themselves. Condoms. Lipstick. A wad of cash. Not much else.

"Sorry to bother you, Mr Mclean," he said. "Here from England, are you? On business?"

Mclean grinned. "Scotland—here for a lil' monkey business, which is none of your business!"

"—you didn't nick any of my cash did you?" The blonde gave Bailey a hard look. "Going through my handbag like that! And without a search warrant."

"Would I do that?

"It wouldn't be the first time," the blonde said.

Which gave Bailey an interesting insight into the current activities of the vice squad. He stepped out into the passage and checked his watch. Now he'd see what the occupants of suite 503 had to say. But if the scent led back to Ines de Graaf in 501 it could be a lead to her daughter's murder, no matter how slender. They were coming up empty everywhere else.

Suite 503 was vacant. The maid let him in. A couple from Singapore had already vacated and left it in spotless condition. The only trace the suite had been used were the damp towels in the bath and the duvet turned back on the king-sized bed.

Having heard no ping from an arriving elevator, Bailey presumed Stinky Bill was still on the fifth floor—and with Hannah's mother. He rapped on her door. No answer. He rapped harder, saying "Mrs de Graaf, it's James Bailey!" He left off his title. "I think I've left my wallet in your room." He slipped his wallet from his pants-pocket and tucked it safely inside his jacket. "Excuse me ma'am," he said raising his voice as if to a maid, "Would you let me into suite 501. I've forgotten my wallet."

The door opened a crack sufficient to expel a trace of Stinky Bill's presence. "Zair is no wallet here," snapped Mrs de Graaf, one gimlet eye on him.

Bailey gave her a deprecating smile, mouth turned down. "It must have fallen under the desk when I sat down. I'll just check." He thrust the door open, propelling Mrs de Graaf back several steps. He took hold of her arm to steady her.

"Why Bill," he smiled. "Fancy seeing you here!"

Bailey left the hotel mulling over the story he'd heard. How Mrs de Graaf had called the store to ask if anyone could appraise a diamond pendant that she'd like to sell to pay for her extended travel expenses, and Stinky Bill had offered to view it in her hotel room "in consideration for the circumstances, and for your safety."

The pendant had certainly been impressive. Two and a half carats set in platinum.

"My daughter, Hannah, had one that was identical," said Mrs de Graaf. "I also wanted to know if Perth's best-known pawn shop had seen one like it."

"And you didn't think to mention this to the police because…?" Bailey had asked, voice clipped, trying not to show his anger. "This is evidence that could lead us to the person who took your daughter's life?"

He was treated to one of Mrs de Graaf's portfolio of sneers. "Pffft. The police here are incompetent! Half of them are on the take, anyway. One of your men probably took the pendant. You have the worst Police Force in Australia."

Bailey twigged. The finding of the 2008 thirty-million-dollar Police Royal Commission had certainly indicated they believed this to be true. Mrs de Graaf had obviously been googling. He shook his head. "That was a long time ago, Mrs Graaf, and things have changed for the better I′m sure you are aware that in Western Australia, as everywhere else in the western world, we expect the mother of a victim to help, not hinder us. Withholding evidence is grounds for your arrest, which would give you a firsthand experience of how competent the Homicide Squad really is!" He certainly felt like putting her in handcuffs. And a gag wouldn't go astray, however he knew Langford would never go for something so damaging to the squad's image as locking up a international murder victim's mother. Imagine the lousy press.

Had Hannah really owned a diamond pendant that was now missing? Or was this something made up on the spot to explain Bill′s presence and throw Bailey off the scent. Why would a mother do that? What the hell!

As Bailey stepped out of the hotel, he called Evan back at headquarters, "Go out to *Hard Pawn* at Burswood, and get an inventory of all their diamond jewellery. Take a special note of anything that has been pawned, bought or sold in the last two weeks." All pawnbrokers were required to keep a transaction register and give details to the police if they were asked for it. Breaches involved heavy penalties in the five-figure range.

"Am I looking for anything particular? And would it be on the SPIRS register?" Stolen items of value were logged on the Stolen Property Identification and Recovery System. For a cadet, Evan was turning into a good detective. Steady. He didn't miss much. It was time they stopped thinking of him as the squad's novice.

"The piece hasn't been registered yet. We're looking for a 2-point-five carat diamond pendant set in platinum. I'll email a photo. The vic's mother says Hannah wore one that was identical. It wasn't recovered when we went through the room's contents."

"How much is it worth?"

Bailey checked his notebook. Mrs de Graaf had given him a short but succinct lesson on diamonds. "Around $38,000 retail. Depends on the four Cs—Carat, Colour, Clarity and Cut. Hannah´s was apparently cut in a pear shape, colour D, Clarity 1F"

"You can buy a lot of ice for that."

"Indeed." The amphetamine epidemic in Perth had led to soaring crime rates. Ice fuelled everything from domestic violence to robberies and murder. It was the modern-day scourge. Bailey wished they would bring back the death penalty for dealers. He wasn't as evolved as he'd like people to think.

"Why the fuck didn't the mother tell us before?"

Bailey paused a moment, "I'm not sure she'd recognise the truth if it bit her on the arse. Take it as read I could be sending you on a wild goose chase. Anyway, once you get the photo, put the pendant on SPIRS for me, will you? *Hard Pawn* isn't the only pawnbroker in Perth that's dubious."

Evan was the squad's go-to guy for IT. He could wend his way through tortuous computer programs like nobody else. Saved them all a heap of time and aggravation.

"Great name, *Hard Pawn.* Sort of like that TV program *Pawn Stars.*"

"I'm sure that's what gave them the idea. Where's Palfrey right now?"

"Search me. He didn't come into the office this morning."

"Don't worry then, Evan. I'll get onto him."

A blaring horn brought Bailey back to the street. He'd nearly walked in front of a dusty SUV. The kangaroo bar would have made a right mess of him.

"Dickhead!" the driver yelled. And Bailey had to acknowledge the truth with an apologetic wave. Just the previous week a kid had been killed when he walked across a train track while texting. The train driver was off work with PTSS.

The sky was hazed with smoke from the southern bushfires. They'd been burning since some firebug had splashed around gasoline and lit up. The fires had soon roared into the tinder dry bush and a strong easterly wind had fanned the flames into walls two metres high. He supposed the perp belonged to some godforsaken volunteer fire brigade and wanted to make a name for himself. Never mind the loss to wildlife and the property owners' desolation when they lost their homes with all their accumulated memories. To date there were no fatalities. One elderly widow had suffered a heart attack when dragging a suitcase of mementos to her neighbour's car. She was in hospital on life support. Three more people were missing.

At least memories were portable, unlike the small mill town of Yarloop where 95 houses had burnt

to the ground earlier in the year. Only the post office had been left standing.
Water authorities' lack of foresight and the neglect of sensible precautions in neighbouring properties surrounding the town had contributed to that disaster. No one had yet been held accountable. No charges had been laid despite 31,000 kilometres burnt out plus a lost vineyard. A bridge on the South West Highway had buckled and collapsed due to the intense heat.

Bailey was sick of the sheer waste of it all and hoped the latest fires would be beaten back. The air felt dense, like it was laden with tiny particles making it an effort to breathe. Under his blue chambray shirt his heart was ticking like a bomb. Today coughing didn't seem to regulate it. The state's firemen were deployed eighty kilometres south, and who knew how the skeleton crews would manage if some brainless, sociopathic wanker took it upon himself to light another fire in the suburbs.

Pedestrians around him had slowed to look over their shoulders as if pursued. The leaden air together with the hard-to-banish memory of the smell of Hannah's blood soaking the holiday apartment slowed him down to their pace.

The *ding* of his phone disturbed his train of thought. "Yeah?" he said, noting his partner's number. "Where've you been?"

"Just back home from King Edward Hospital with the family." Palfrey's voice sounded tight. Like he was speaking through a stocking mask and unable to move his lips.

"Why? What happened?"

"Remember I told you my son's ex and the children from that marriage came back to Perth from overseas?" The question was rhetorical; Bailey's memory was prodigious, so he said nothing, just waited. "The youngest, Jazz—Jasmine, was at a party last night. She was raped. Two perps apparently."

"Jesus. How old is she?"

"Fourteen."

"Bloody hell." They knew how that would play in court. "If she's a minor, why weren't you at Perth Children′s Hospital?" The Sexual Assault Resource Centre, or SARC, was housed at the King Edward Hospital but it only treated adults.

Palfrey sighed again. "Long story. Tell you later. It's a circus here. Lots of yelling and enough blame going 'round to sink a ship. Come by this evening when things have quietened down and I'll fill you in."

"She make a report to the Sexual Crime Squad?"

"Not yet. SARC doesn't oblige adult victims to make a report to the police. It is entirely their choice, unlike mandatory reporting for an attack on a juvenile.

"She using a fake ID?"

"Later. OK?"

"Diane all right?"

“Not really. That´s a no!”

“Take some leave. As long as you like. I’ll square it away for you with the boss without going into details, and I’ll bring a takeaway for us all tonight. For how many?”

“No idea. Give me a call from the shop.”

“Will do.” Bailey searched for something comforting to say. “See you soon. Anything I can do… you know I will.

Chapter 10

Bailey arrived at Palfrey's house with a selection of Asian take-away dishes balanced precariously on a cardboard tray: Samosas and Pork Bao buns side by side. A confusion of Sushi and Chicken Tandoori. Fried rice or noodles. Peking duck with pancakes. Popcorn shrimp and Black Bean Snapper. Broccoli with Cashews. It went on—a medley that travelled from Singapore to Japan.

"Something for everyone," he said.

"Jesus, JB, this must have cost you a fortune! How much do we owe you?" Palfrey was looking frayed, the buttoning of his shirt as mismatched as the cuisine. His lookalike granddaughters sat still and quiet on the faux-suede sofa, their hands linked. Diane was busy setting out platters on the table. Her eyes were red-rimmed, her face swollen from tears.

"You don't owe me a thing." Bailey dumped the tray down, gave Diane a hug, then he picked up one of the alfoil containers and emptied the contents onto a plate embossed with blue and white fish.

"Leave them in the containers, JB. Less washing up." Palfrey said. "This is Jasmine." he indicated the younger girl, "and her sister Fiona."

"Fi," she corrected, waving a hand displaying the snake tattooed on her wrist. "—
and we call Jasmine, Jazz."

Bailey nodded. “I hope there’s something here you like.”

The younger girl shrugged. “What, no pizza for the Orientals?” She flipped her silky black hair back and gave him a hard look out of bruised, almond eyes.

“Whatever,” said Bailey, discovering the girls’ Asian heritage and his potential gaffe at the same time. Palfrey hadn′t mentioned his ex-daughter-in-law’s country of origin. By the time Bailey had teamed up with him, the son’s marriage was well and truly over and Palfrey’s granddaughters were out of touch somewhere unspecified “overseas.”

“I like Asian food myself,” he responded to Jasmine’s dig, “it’s healthier.” He looked around for evidence of Palfrey’s son.

Used to reading his partner, Palfrey said, “Ian’s working the late shift. Not so much competition from Uber drivers after dark. They scare easily. He’s supporting two families now and needs the cash.”

“And Jasmine and Fiona’s mother? Where is she?”

“The girls had a disagreement with her, so they’re staying with us for the time being. We’re only too pleased to…”

Fiona interrupted. “She said it was all Jazz’s fault and that it served her right for never listening and always going her own way. Mum′s not exactly supportive.” She had a melodious voice—one that could soothe a baby. “It’s better here. Calmer. There’s not so much confusion.”

Jasmine looked like she would never smile again. “Does everybody have to know my business, Poppa?” she scowled, her mouth turned down.

“JB’s been my partner for ten years, Jazz. He’s family. We don’t keep secrets.”

“As if this family isn’t complicated enough!”

Diane forced a smile. “Dinner’s ready, darlings. Let’s not let it get cold.”

They collected plates and utensils from the end of the table, and perused the buffet in front of them. The girls each took a small quantity of the broccoli and noodles. Bailey was thankful he’d remembered to order one dish to cater for vegetarians. Why were so many young women against eating meat, he wondered? He took a hearty selection, as did Palfrey. Diane chose a few shrimp without much enthusiasm. The chopsticks the shop had provided proved to be a hit. Jasmine ate tiny amounts and visibly winced as she swallowed. Her neck showed the blue-black finger marks from her ordeal. Bailey wished he’d bought soup.

“Let’s have some Jasmine tea on the patio. It’s a lovely night,” said Diane. The buffet sat congealing, mostly untouched. “We’ll clear up afterwards.” They trooped outside and sat staring at the full moon.

“Anything new?” Palfrey asked about their case.

“There may be a burglary angle. The mother says Hannah had a valuable diamond pendant that’s missing. Stinky Bill is somehow involved.”

"No kidding? What…"

"What?" repeated Jasmine, her tone sharp.

"Just work," her grandpa soothed.

"Well get onto my case then!"

"You insisted you wouldn't report it to the police and lied about your age!"

"You're the police. You do something. Why the fuck should I tell some stranger."

"Don't be disingenuous, Jasmine," Bailey cut in, "You're an intelligent girl. I can see you want to be treated as an adult. But we're Homicide Squad—we don't deal with sexual assaults."

"Why are you calling it assault when it was rape!"

"Yeah, well…that's the way it's done these days."

They were quiet for a bit. The moon went behind a cloud throwing the backyard into a fuzzy umber. The lights around the bar-b-que were yellow to discourage the moths. Suddenly the high wattage motion-sensitive security lights flashed on as a shadow slunk down the driveway. Jasmine shrieked.

"It's just the neighbour's cat," said Palfrey. "Happens all the time."

"One time it won't be a cat," Fiona said quietly.

She was right. It didn't pay to get too comfortable and assume. The old adage, to assume makes an *ass* out of *u* and *me* came to mind. Bailey turned to her. "Why don't you girls start from the beginning? Tell us everything. Then we'll see what we can do."

No-one said anything. Silence reigned for a good five minutes. But Bailey and Palfrey knew how silence worked. They could usually outwait a witness and most always outwait a suspect.

The girls were sitting side by side, forsaking comfort for closeness. Co-joined twins could hardly have been closer. After another minute Fiona said in her soft voice, "I'll start, shall I?"

Jasmine looked down at her lap. Her dark lashes threw shadows on her cheeks. The two teenagers were extraordinarily attractive, with smooth, blemish-free skin and dark sheets of straight hair. Their lips were plumply kissable. The identical black tights with matching short skirts drew attention to their legs. Bailey could see how a man would be attracted. In counterpoint to their similar appearance, their personalities were poles apart. One came across as soft and compliant, the other angry and loud. An obvious renegade—in rebellion against advice or common sense. How did a parent protect a daughter like that? One who was determined to make her own decisions without the early warning system for self-protection? Teenagers with a rebellious streak dared bad things to happen to them. They were rarely disappointed.

But he was getting ahead of himself. "Go on," he said. He'd have preferred to hear from Jasmine herself, but perhaps Fiona would lead her into it.

Fiona nodded. “My friend, Alison, from work—I’m an apprentice hairdresser—heard there’d be a great new band at the nightclub *Jack Rabbit Slims.* Alison’s eighteen like me but she’s nearly qualified. Anyway, we watched the band on YouTube and the lead singer was so bad!” She stopped, and took a deep breath. “ --but in the end, I didn’t want to go.” She turned to Diane, “I had my period and got cramps,” she whispered, but the excuse drifted far enough for the men to hear. She paused, and turned to Jasmine, expectantly, but Jasmine just kept her head down, twisting her fingers in her lap. “You can’t dance when you don’t feel well,” Fiona shrugged, and stopped again.

Palfrey hummed a noncommittal “Mmm Hmmm.”

“So I decided to go in her place.” Jasmine said in a congested voice. “I borrowed Fi′s ID so I could get into the nightclub. All Asians look alike to bouncers.”

“Alison was pleased,” Fiona cut in. “She didn’t want to go on her own.”

“She’s blond and boys like that.”

“I warned Alison not to stay out late.”

“Well, we did. And it’s done now.”

The sisters had a moment when it looked like they would argue. “You tell the rest then, Jazz,” Fiona said peaceably.

“We met some guys. They bought us drinks. One was cute, and funny. He made me laugh. He said he'd borrowed his brother's ID to get in too. His name was David. I didn't ask his surname. You don't." She stopped and thought about this for a moment. "Why would you?"

Diane started sobbing and got up and went back inside. Palfrey shook his head.

"What's she got to cry about?" Jasmine demanded. "Nothing happened to her."

"It's called empathy," said Bailey. "Keep going."

Jasmine got up and began to pace up and down. "We went on to another nightclub and then the guys said they knew where there was a party where we wouldn't have to pay for drinks. Alison didn't want to go, and tried to make me leave with her, but David said he'd look after me. So the rest of us all piled into a taxi and took off. I had to sit on David's knee 'cos there was five of us."

"What kind of taxi?" asked Palfrey.

"Private, I guess but expensive, not like Dad's. It was a black SUV. The driver didn't say much. He was wearing one of those coloured berets like the reggae singer Dad likes. You know Poppa, Bob Marley. Dad has all his albums."

"Mmm Hmm," nodded Palfrey.

Bailey knew he was clueless.

"We headed towards Scarborough, and ended up in a big house by the beach. I could hear the waves but I don't know the name of the street. It was kind of up a hill with a palm tree out the front. There were coloured lights outside and loud music. Inside was a bit of a crush, so David said he'd get me a drink and we could peel off into one of the bedrooms and have a nice quiet talk and get to know each other."

She saw Palfrey and Bailey exchange a glance. "He was NICE," she insisted. We drank a few tequila shots, and then we made out."

Palfrey shifted in his chair and the iron scraped on the paving stones with the sound of a fingernail on a chalkboard. Bailey put his hand on Palfrey's knee to still him.

"I'm on the pill, Poppa. This wasn't my first time."

"Did you and David exchange phone numbers?" asked Bailey at his most neutral.

"Well I'm sure we would have but…"

Diane walked out carrying a fresh pot of tea. The screen door slammed behind her as she swore, "For Christ sakes, the bloody cat just sneaked into the house!"

"Leave it in for the moment, Pet," said Palfrey, "it won't do any harm. Just wants to get warm." But she slammed the tray onto the table and marched back inside. "Where were we, Jazz?"

"—but I fell asleep, and I guess David went back to the party. I didn't see him again. When I woke up..." A tremor shook her. "I was naked, and a man…he was…he was inside me." She gulped. "He penetrated me. That's what you say don't you? When you call it sexual assault and not…" she hiccupped, "rape?"

On the word rape she began to sob in earnest. Fiona moved in and hugged her tight. "You're safe now. Shshsh."

Jasmine pushed her away. "I called out for him to stop, but he slapped me really hard across the face. I hadn't realised, but another man was there too, behind me. He moved forward and I could feel his—*thing*—pressing on the top of my head."

"His erection," clarified Fiona softly.

"He put his hand over my mouth and said *shut up, bitch.* I couldn't breathe and started to struggle. The first man was rough and hurting me. Hurting me inside. And then. And then, I don't remember anything much until I was in the ambulance. I guess I passed out."

"Let´s have another cup of tea now, love," said Palfrey. "Then you can tell us a bit more."

Bailey took the lead. "Tell us what you remember about the men, Jasmine. Or should I call you Jazz?"

"Jazz is OK." She was sitting back on the lounger with her sister, twirling a piece of hair and then putting it in her mouth. "The man who raped me…"

"Let's call him man-one."

"OK. Man-one was tall. He seemed a long way above me," she frowned. "Taller than David who was about half a metre taller than me."

"Good—that's a good way to explain it. Was he one of the men you shared a taxi with?"

Jasmine seemed to gain confidence. "No. I'd never seen him before. It was dark. The light was off, but the moon was shining through the window. The curtains were open." She shut her eyes. "He had brown eyes and dark curly hair and he was wearing a white T-shirt with a football on the front. Underneath it said *Dockers rule*." She rubbed her face and swallowed with an effort.

"He had an earring in his left ear—just a gold stud, and some grey in his hair. Or maybe it was blonde streaks."

"Was his hair long or short?"

"Short but kind of," she searched for the word, "unruly."

"You have a good vocabulary, Jazz. I can almost see him. Did he speak?"

"No," her voice wavered, "He...he...grunted. As he, you know, came."

"What else?"

She expelled a long breath. "Man-two spoke. His voice was kind of clipped A bit, well, foreign I suppose. He leaned forward when he called me a bitch but I didn't see his face. He must have been jacking off while he watched, because he...he came in my hair!" She wailed it.

Palfrey coughed, a strangled sound. Fiona got up and checked the teapot. She poured the trickle that was left into one of the dainty Japanese cups and handed it to Jasmine, who blew her nose, then sipped until it was gone.

"I was kind of shaking my head from side to side, saying *No No No Stop please stop* and Man-two's hands were holding my shoulders down. He had a swatch watch on his left wrist with a Mickey Mouse face and above that, tattoos."

"What kind of tattoos?"

"Just… I don't know. A couple of them. Close together. I'm not a fucking robot you know!"

"Hey, hey, hey," Palfrey intervened. "You're the one who asked us to help."

"Never mind," said Bailey. "That's probably enough for tonight. It's hard. We understand that."

"You said you don't work in the Sexual Assault Squad so how could you understand?"

"We interview family members after a murder," said Bailey. Not inclined to give her a break. Sometimes sympathy in moments of stress made a witness break down completely and then they were no use at all.

Jasmine twisted her fingers, chastened.

"Tomorrow I'll go around to the house. See what I can find out." Palfrey said.

"I don't know the address."

"But the ambulance service does."

"Oh. Right. I didn't think of that."

Palfrey stood. "Pick me up?" he asked Bailey.

"I'll call you."

"OK. I think it's time for bed. Looks like I'll have to help Diane find that bloody cat."

"See myself out," said Bailey.

Fiona whispered, "Thank you."

Jasmine just sat there—eyes fixed on the distance—back at the scene.

Bailey gave Fiona his card. "You and Jazz can call me on my cell whenever you like, any time, day or night. Sometimes it's easier to talk things over with a stranger. I'm what you might call a professional listener. And," he paused, "nothing you say will shock me."

He hoped he was right.

Chapter 11

Palfrey was standing on the kerb with two steaming mugs of coffee when Bailey arrived to pick him up the following morning. He looked more together. Hair combed, shirt buttoned; his shoelaces tied.

"Girls OK?" Bailey took a large gulp of scalding coffee, immediately regretting it.

"Hard to say. Still in bed."

"Diane seems pretty upset." Bailey jammed the oversized mug into the car's holder, slipping right into the day's business and forgoing thanks.

"Women!" Palfrey threw his coffee down an asbestos lined throat and exhaled. "She's mad at Jasmine for getting herself into this situation. She's mad at our son, Ian, for going to work last night instead of giving his daughter some support. She's mad at me, because if we go after these two scumbags, I'm risking my job and the last two important years to sock away extra money for retirement; and she's mad at Ian's ex-wife for shunting the problem over to us."

"Well at least she's not mad at Fiona. She seemed like a sensible girl."

"Are you kidding me! She's particularly mad at Fiona for lending Jasmine her ID. Without it, she wouldn't have gone clubbing in the first place."

"Feel for you, mate."

"I'm in the shit and I haven't even done anything yet."

"We're not going to do anything to jeopardise our jobs, Palfrey. Just make a few enquiries. And the strange part is—we're going to make them in Scarborough, where Hannah was murdered, so we can argue we're on the case."

"Speaking of which, aren't we supposed to be on our way to interview Matey's father?"

"He doesn't arrive until late this morning. We should have plenty of time."

"You'd think he'd have been down here in a flash to see the boy."

"I guess since he wasn't there for the birth, Matey is just an abstract idea to him."

"Poor little chap." Palfrey shifted in his seat.

"How do you see us investigating the rape? We're not supposed to follow up family matters through official channels. Misuse of the police information system risks prison time."

"We're not going to use police computers. Who needs to when you can use social media?"

"Right," said Palfrey, sounding unconvinced.

"Hey—it's your call."

"Let's take it step by step. See if we can at least identify the scumbags."

"Exactly my thoughts."

"Jazz remembered something else last night. A tattoo that included a weird checkerboard pattern and the letters JNA or maybe ONA surrounded by a crown of thorns. She was busy trying to sketch it before she went to bed."

"Might help. Tough girl." He meant it as a compliment.

They relapsed into their normal silence, Palfrey drinking his coffee and looking out the window. Bailey weaving in and out of the morning traffic until they turned off the West Coast Highway and up a hill to the house Jasmine described, where there was a lone palm tree. The ambulance service had given Bailey the address first thing that morning. The coloured lights nailed to the fascia were turned off.

"Quite the palace," Bailey commented of the three-story stuccoed mansion looming over them. An empty, run-down palace however. No-one answered the doorbell, and when they peered through the uncurtained windows they saw the minimum of worn furniture with the only sign of luxury a giant flat-screen TV. At the back of the house, they found a below-ground pool showing evidence of more than a month's neglect, green algae forming on the blue tiles. The back door was locked and bolted, as was the front.

"Great," said Palfrey—always the more morose of the two.

"Let's ask the neighbours."

Neighbour One, a brick and tile bungalow, was vacant with a for-sale sign out the front. A red banner with "Price reduced" slashed across the sign. At Neighbour Two—on the righthand side— an elderly man with a bulldog in tow answered the bell. One of them was flatulent. The stink hit them like a missile.

"Yairs?" enquired the man, oblivious.

They introduced themselves as potential buyers of the bungalow. "We'd like to ask a few questions about the neighbourhood before we commit to making an offer."

"Come in. Come in. I can tell you a lot. I've lived here for thirty years and know pretty well everything there is to know. Would you like a cuppa tea?"

The old man was lonely. With the flatulence they could understand why. "The house next door…" began Palfrey. He could get no further. The old man—name of Quentin Blane—began a rant they had trouble stemming.

"It's on a couple of those wretched online sites. You stay in someone's house in some godforsaken part of the world, for days or months. Who knows. The owners have been away for more than three years, and in that time, there've been a number of different tenants. The last one is young. Parties all the time. Vomit on the pavement. Loud noise until the early hours. Upsets Churchill something terrible." he indicated the panting dog, "It's about time the authorities did something. I call and I call, and not a thing changes. The council won't do anything. I reckon it's devalued my property by at least $50,000. I thought my home would see me out. And I was happy about that until now. I should sue the owners. My real estate agent says they live overseas and only care about getting the rent. Couldn't give a pony otherwise. Until the tenant stops all this nonsense or the owners buck up, it'll cost me money plus many a good night's sleep."

Another blaring, noisome zinger was launched into the room. The detectives tried not to breathe. "Could you give us details of who owns the house?" coughed Bailey, a hand over his nose.

"—and what property sites it's on," chipped in Palfrey.

"You two a duet?"

It was the shortest sentence they'd got out of him.

As soon as they could extract themselves, the two detectives headed for an internet café to do a bit of non-police-computer sleuthing. Bailey logged into an account for Dick Lyons – an alias he used from time to time. Like a burner phone, or the throw-down gun so popular in American crime fiction, detectives often had secret lives online.

"I'll start with *www.rentwithus.com* and see what they have to say."

"Mr Blane said he'd done that, and got no response."

"He was complaining. I'm going to be helpful and say the tenants left the floodlights on. Who can I contact to get them turned off."

"That's complaining."

"That's helping. Floodlights are expensive to run. Plus, it sounds like an easy fix." Bailey clicked onto the site. Immediately a popup asked if a live person at the other end could help. After a little back and forth, Bailey was advised that the current tenant, who'd advertised the house, lived in Singapore, however the sister of the property's owner lived locally. Patsy Kelvin. She had a key. Bailey was given her number.

"Bingo," said Bailey after logging out. "And, apparently the house comes complete with a BMW, available for use at extra cost."

"So what?" asked Palfrey, unimpressed. "What happens when the sister comes and the floodlights aren't turned on? Are we supposed to go back into detective mode and identify ourselves? Not so keen on that idea."

"Step by step, like you said. Only do things by phone. Back out if things get tricky." Bailey entered Lyons' Skype account and dialled Patsy Kelvin's number. "Hello, Mrs Kelvin?"

"Ms Kelvin."

"It's Ajex Insurance here. A car registered to your brother's address in Scarborough was in a minor bingle last week. About $2,000-$3,000 worth of damage. I wonder if you have a contact number for the driver involved? I believe he is the tenant of your brother's property—What? Oh, don't you worry about a thing, we'll get it repaired and returned without any inconvenience to you."

Bailey wrote some details rapidly on a piece of scrap paper and rang off with thanks. He beamed at Palfrey, and held up the results. "Tenant's name and number. Minimum risk. Impersonating a non-existent insurance company employee without going on to commit a crime isn't unlawful as far as I know."

"Let's hope we don't have to argue that in court. Lucky there´s no CCTV in here."

"That´s why I parked two blocks away and came here in the first place."

Bailey simply introduced himself as Dick Lyons to the tenant in Singapore and said he'd been at his party and had a great time. If he wanted to throw a similar one at his own rental, how would he go about it?

"Where d'you get my name?"

"The guy who takes the money,"

"Al Gold?"

"Big guy," Bailey said, fingers crossed, figuring anyone in charge of cash in an alcohol and drug fuelled party would have to be able to look after himself.

"Those gold front teeth are a blast, aren't they?"

Bailey wondered if that was a trick question. "He wasn´t smiling."

The tenant, Steven Kee, had put the word out on social media with the expectation that *if you ask them, they will come.* And they usually did, filling the house. There was a cover charge to pay for the booze. He'd thrown parties like this in several different cities and usually made the cost of renting the house plus around

$3000. He always stayed the night of the party at a nearby hotel. He liked the Rendezvous Hotel. No way did he want to be at one of his own parties. Someone always found out who he was and came up to hassle him. He stayed in town long enough to pick up the cash, pay the cleaners, DJ and bouncer and fly out.

"Doing this isn't for everyone," he continued, "I'm in the entertainment business. I make a living throwing parties in various parts of the world. I use the same posse of DJs each time -Victor Vibes in the Perth house. He and Gold are reliable. Where's your property? Perhaps we could do something together"

Bailey thought quickly, "Cottesloe, near the railway line. Easy access plus quite a bit of parking nearby. I'd be willing to give you a cut."

"Sounds good. Call me again with the details and I'll see if we can get something going. I'm always interested in expanding. I've got a meeting now and have to run."

"Great. Thanks a lot. I appreciate it. I'll be in touch."

"What do you do for a crust?"

"I'm an accountant."

"It figures." Kee laughed and rang off.

"You are a bloody scam artist," Palfrey said in admiration.

"I'm not sure it really got us anywhere. But we could probably track down the bouncer and the DJ and ask them a few questions."

"How are we going to do that, JB – without it backfiring. If only Jasmine would press charges and get the sexual crime squad involved.?"

"Know any Hells Angels?"

"I hope you're joking."

"Back to work, eh?"

At headquarters, head down, Evan was still checking pawn shops for any sign of a 2.5 carat diamond pendant. A beam of sun through the window showcased dust motes dancing above his head. They advertised his incipient male pattern baldness. Bailey tried not to cringe. Only in his twenties and Evan was already losing his hair. Bailey's hair was one of the few things he liked about his own appearance.

"I went out to *Hard Pawn* to have a squiz," said Evan, looking up. "If Stinky Bill fenced the jewellery outside the books, there's not much we can do to find it. When I spoke to him, he was most indignant. Read me the riot act about how his business had always been law abiding. I wish I´d worn a gas mask."

"Yeah – what is it about this investigation?" said Palfrey. "Everything in it stinks."

Bailey looked around, Pamela and Tony were on their laptops, Hunter was nowhere to be seen. Before he could ask, Evan said, "Bob's gone to the airport to pick up Tom Watts. He thought you wouldn't get there on time. They should be back pretty soon."

"Initiative," said Bailey, secretly pissed off that Hunter hadn't run it past him. At last they'd get to meet Matey's father and see what sort of a guy could deny all responsibility for his son. Not that they were surprised. Deadbeat dads owed $1.4 billion Australia-wide.

Pamela walked over to join the conversation, ponytail bouncing. "Maybe Watts was more than a little worried by Hannah's reappearance in his life. She could apply for maintenance and cost him a pretty penny. The Netherlands are in a reciprocating jurisdiction for maintenance transfers."

Like Hunter, Pamela always spoke in complete sentences. The last sentence was a mouthful and a half.

"No need for Hannah to come to Perth for that. She could have applied directly from the Netherlands, either to the Department of Human Services here, or to whatever the equivalent is back there." They looked at Evan, who shrugged. "Hunter filled me in. He's on it."

"All the same," said Pamela. "The thought of years of payments looming ahead until the kid's of age can make some men do some pretty disgusting things."

"People," called Tony from his desk.

"What?"

"Can make some people do terrible things. Didn't you get the gender non-specific discrimination email?" Tony smirked. Usually it was Pamela who told them off for being non-PC.

Bailey sighed, sick of Pamela and Tony's bickering. Sometimes he regretted teaming them up together. "Let's not get bogged down in politically correct language right now. It's not progressing the case," he said. "Please, someone…people…" he grinned, "give me some ideas I can work with!"

"Who's down to interview Watts?" Pamela asked.

Bailey considered. "I guess Hunter has a head start so he can do it. Plus, he's the psychologist, and from Broome. Maybe he'll have an insight the rest of us won't. Since I know Matey, err Bram, I'll sit in. The rest of you keep doing whatever it is you're doing." Which wasn't getting them very far, he thought. They needed a decent break for a change. He looked at Palfrey.

"I'm popping down to talk to the Sexual Crime Squad about another matter. Something that came up from one of my snitches."

The team looked at Palfrey. He'd never mentioned snitches before.

He gave an ambiguous smile. "Won't be long."

Chapter 12

Tom Watts was a wiry, deeply sun-tanned man with sandy hair. His 1.8metre frame was kitted out in northwest standard issue: T-shirt, Docker shorts and flipflops. The fact he hadn't bothered to dress in city clothes for his police interview either indicated a man in a hurry or one who had nothing to prove. Hanging off one shoulder, his only luggage was a scuffed day pack with a pair of lime green running shoes dangling from a partially zipped compartment.

As he ushered Watts into the interview room, Hunter looked his usual immaculate, inscrutable self. "Detective Senior Sergeant Bailey," Hunter said, indicating the seat Watts should take, rather than turning to introduce Bailey, who'd entered the room behind them. They sat and Hunter intoned the usual phrase about the interview being recorded, the time and date, and who was present. The room had no windows and, save for a large one-way mirror for members of the squad to watch the interview from an adjacent room, there was nothing on the stark white walls.

Watts pushed his sunglasses onto his head and looked around at the vinyl floor and laminated table. He wrinkled his nose. "It's not like the TV series is it?" he said. He had Matey's deep blue eyes but his lashes were bleached white from the sun. "Aren't you supposed to caution me, or advise me of my rights. Should I have a lawyer or something?"

"It's just an informal interview to find out more about your ex-girlfriend." Hunter sounded uncommonly exasperated. Watts must have got up his nose on the drive in from the airport. "We're doing it at headquarters for convenience, then we'll drop you wherever you want to go. We record the interview in case you feel that something you've said is later misrepresented. It's for your own protection."

Watts nodded. "When do I get to see Bram?"

"The Child Protection Services will pick you up around 2pm and take you to see him in his current foster home. Bram will stay there while the custody arrangements are settled."

"No way am I allowing that bitch, Ines, to have him," said Watts referring to Mrs de Graaf, Hannah's mother. "My mum and dad said they could look after him."

"That will be for the Family Court to decide on the recommendation of the CPS," said Hunter. He paused, and then leant forward. "If you want a successful resolution, I'd advise you to avoid the language."

Bailey wondered if all Hunter's interviews would sound more like counselling sessions. Perhaps they could bring in a couch. But he let Hunter continue in his own distinctive way. Watts nodded again, possibly taking the advice onboard. Good cop Hunter.

Bad cop Bailey—if it became necessary. On the other hand, why wait?

"I believe your mother and father live in Newcastle, New South Wales. That wouldn't give you much time with your son, would it, since you work in Broome? Plus, both of your parents work full time in blue collar jobs that don't allow for much flexibility. Where does a little boy fit into this scenario?"

"My work's seasonal. I'd get to see him over the wet season, and if my parents say they'll do something—they do it, and without a lot of hoo-ha either. I′d think an Australian father and grandparents would trump Dutch grandparents in an Australian court."

"That's not your or our decision to make," said Hunter smoothly. "What we want to know about is your relationship with Hannah. Who you think could be responsible for her death? What was the aim of her trip, and so on."

Watts reached into his backpack and brought out his cell phone. He tapped on the screen and then handed it over. "This is the message I got from Hannah. She told me the dates she and Bram were coming over, and that she'd catch up with me in Broome. She didn't ask if the dates were convenient or check with me beforehand. Stupid…" he paused, "woman."

Hunter forwarded the email and Watt's response to both his and Bailey's phones, and they read through the brief messages as one. There was no salutation, no *Dear Tom,* nor was there any loving signature, just *see you then, H.* No line of kisses. Watts' response was equally as brief. *I can't send you any money towards the fare* seemed to be the gist of it.

"What do you do with your money, Tom?" asked Bailey. Money was always a contentious subject so the bad cop might as well have a go at it. "Your boss said you earn around $60 to $80,000 for a four or five-month season."

"What I earn depends on the catch. Living costs in Broome are high, plus I'm saving for a deposit on a house or a block of land."

Hunter jumped in. "Where d'you work in the wet season?"

"I go back to Newcastle and work as a mechanic. Free board and lodging with Mum and Dad. Mum does my laundry and cooks as well–you can't beat that. I did my apprenticeship in the mines—I'm a diesel mechanic/fitter— so I can always find work."

"Why not stay in Newcastle, I hear you can earn $150K a year or more there?"

"I got religion," Watts smirked at the detectives' dumbfounded expressions. "Coal mining," he explained, "it isn't good for the environment. I don't want anything to do with it. I'm a born-again greenie. Now I work in a sustainable workplace without leaving a footprint. I could stay in Broome and work on one of the pearl farms, but the money′s better in Newcastle."

Blah, Blah, Blah, thought Bailey. Save the planet with all the bullshit clichés copied straight off social media. Pretend to care about climate change and who signs the Paris accord but conveniently forget about paying for the maintenance of your own child. He didn't like the guy. He didn't like Ines de Graaf either. Who the fuck was going to care for Matey?

"How did you feel about Hannah coming over to see you?" asked Hunter,

Bailey almost shuddered. Now they were asking a POI about his feelings. Perhaps Bailey wasn't cut out for the new, or new-age, police force. What they needed for this case was evidence. And feelings weren't evidence, although to be fair, they could lead to motive.

"Well..." Watts paused, sighed, looked at the ceiling, considered, "I've been in a new relationship for about a year now. We were talking about moving in together. Maybe buying a place. I hadn't told her about Bram and Hannah. I was waiting for the right time."

"And how did she take the news when you eventually did tell her?"

"She wasn't overly impressed. Said I should have told her at the beginning."

"Where does your girlfriend work? What's her name?" Hunter asked.

"Lizzie Tang, she manages the retail shop for *1699 Pearls.*"

Hunter turned to Bailey, "*1699* is the year William Dampier came to Broome and named Roebuck Bay after his ship. Apparently, the crew found some natural pearls in the shell, or so he wrote in his book *Voyage Around the World.*"

"Is information about my girlfriend, or her workplace relevant?" Watts asked, shifting in his seat.

Bailey wondered the same thing. Sometimes Hunter tried too hard to impress. "Everything is relevant in a murder enquiry. Just answer the questions."

They continued but learned little they didn´t know already.

Watts had chosen to stay at the Blue Seas Apartments where Hannah was murdered. Both Bailey and Hunter thought it a weird—almost perverse choice. As they drew up in front of reception they could hear the surf pounding on the beach and the seagulls' raucous cries.

"Did you recommend this place to Hannah?" Bailey asked.

"Me and the crew always stay here when we come down to Perth. Maybe I mentioned it to her in the past. She must have made a note of it."

"How many times have you stayed here?"

"No idea, really. A few times. We bring the boat to Perth for annual maintenance."

"Why not stay in Fremantle closer to the fishing boat harbour?" asked Hunter, obviously more versed in the ways of the pearling industry than Bailey.

“It’s cheaper here and closer to the surf. We don’t get much surf in Broome. Plus, our job is just to bring the boat down, not to do the maintenance. The shipyard does that.”

“We′d like a list of people who’ve stayed here with you.”

“You’re kidding! The crew don’t actually shack up together. It cramps our style.”

“Well, give us the years and dates you’ve stayed here, any names you remember, and we’ll check with the office for the ones you’ve forgotten.”

“What? Now?”

Bailey adjusted the rear-view mirror to better view Watts. The reflection showed the portrait of a carefree, ordinary Aussie. Mr Normal. How often had the squad been misled by that? “Yes now! Your little boy is breaking his heart for his mother and you don’t seem to give a shit. We have a job to do catching the killer, and it’s time you fucking well put some effort into helping us.” Bailey was sick of the sight of him. The only question Watts had asked about Matey was when he could see him—as if he was trying to fit him in before he hit the waves.

The trio got out of the Camaro and trod the overgrown path towards reception. To Bailey’s surprise, considering the overall lack of maintenance prevalent in the complex, the shattered glass on the office door had been repaired since their last visit.

Watts registered without Beverley recognising him from his previous visits. She did however remember Bailey and gave Watts and Hunter an extra careful look.

"How long do you keep records of guests, Beverley" asked Bailey.

The receptionist looked gratified to be addressed by name. She no longer had the green, shocked complexion; instead sporting pink dyed hair and a ruby nose ring to match. "Five years, in case we're audited by the tax department."

"We may have to look at the records a little later. I assume they're digitalised?"

"Yes, for sure. If you let me know what months you want, I'll copy them onto a flash drive for you."

Bailey gave her an extra special smile, thinking of the time they would save by not applying for a warrant. Thank goodness for a rare member of the public who actually wanted to help the police. Perhaps she didn't watch police procedurals like Watts and had never heard of a warrant. He hoped Malcolm Birch, the manager, wouldn't give her hell. "We'll let you know shortly."

The detectives followed Watts up the stairs to his second story apartment. It was on the first floor but identical to the apartment in which Hannah had been murdered minus the bloodstains. The blinds on the aluminium framed window by the entrance were open displaying a typical Scarborough Beach autumn day.

Brave swimmers were being sandblasted by wind as they trudged to and from the waterfront. A few surfers were still out, pirouetting through the waves, but mainly the surfers came early and then went on to their more mundane jobs.

Bailey, who had taken back the lead after the interview, waved at the desk in the bedroom and said, briefly, "Write!"

Watts threw his backpack on the double bed and sat down.

Later, back at headquarters, Evan stared gloomily at his computer screen. "So, I'm supposed to look at people staying at the Blue Seas Apartments within the dates Watts says he was there, plus check names against the dates Hannah was there. See if any stays correspond. Also check the guests against criminal backgrounds."

"That's about the size of it."

"No one told me joining the force would simply be another IT position."

"Don't complain. Who made the breakthrough last year and got all the Kudos for it?"

"Yeah, Yeah. You can't eat glory, and what's more, it doesn't last."

"Well, that's the trouble about being good at something. You're bound to be in high demand."

"—and I suppose I'm to do this while you three go across the road and have lunch?" He glared at Bailey, Palfrey and Hunter ranged in front of him.

"We'll bring you takeaway."

"Bring me some too,' said Pamela, joining them from her desk by the window. Her perfume washed over them, tart and sassy like Pamela herself. "I'll give Evan a hand."

Evan gave her a grateful look.

Bailey sighed. Another good cop won over and under Pamela's sway. His days as Senior Investigating Officer were numbered for sure. Favours given demanded reciprocity. He wasn't great at granting favours. His father used to say *Neither a borrower nor a lender be—and that means not ever being in anyone's debt.* Whereas his advice was usually solid, his father hadn't had to claw his way up in the Major Crime Division hierarchy and then cling on. Why did Bailey care about his position anyway? The extra money wasn't all that significant, and if he needed a better salary he could get a job in private security. Perhaps he should consider retiring when Palfrey left the force. His superannuation was pretty healthy, plus he had the portfolio of shares his aunt had left him on her death and which he'd grown with dividend reinvestment schemes.

"Plum duck and fried rice, OK?" he asked, knowing Evan's preferences. "Popcorn shrimp for you, Pamela?" Apparently, he wasn't so bad at courting favour after all. He looked around. "Where's Tony?"

"Checking all the Scarborough Beach recordings in slow motion again." A horribly tedious job. They'd obtained the videos from commercial premises near the Blue Seas complex in the hope they'd see a person of interest.

"Lemon chicken for him, then."

The trio headed off towards the lift. Bailey couldn't think of a job to distract Hunter from lunch, which meant he wouldn't be able to ask about Palfrey's visit to the Sexual Crime Squad. He hoped the discussion hadn't put their futures in jeopardy.

Chapter 13

Tracy's mother sat on the sofa with a blanket clutched around her. Her hands were shaking and she'd spilt most of the tea that Tracy had made after her mother's screams woke her. Another nightmare, or maybe delirium tremens. She hadn't given up alcohol or pills as far as Tracy could tell.

"Get you another cuppa, Mum?" she asked.

"And some toast, love. With honey. Honey is soothing."

Tracy cut the toast into soldiers so her mother could dip the slices in her tea. How many other teenagers had to look after their mother like this? None that she knew.

"What was it this time?" she asked as she placed the tray on the coffee table.

"I dreamed I was driving. Reversing and not looking in the rear-view mirror. I heard a bang, and when I looked back there was blood…" she shuddered, "blood all over the road."

"You're having a lot of nightmares lately, Mum. Maybe you need to see someone."

"Like who? A psychiatrist? No thanks!"

"A counsellor, maybe. Or your GP. Someone sympathetic."

"Nobody is going to tell me how to live my life, thank you. I had enough of that when I was growing up."

Tracy had to agree that her grandparents were hard to get on with. "Suit yourself. Be your own worst enemy. I'm going for my run now. I'll turn on the TV for you. You can watch the news." That would hardly soothe anyone. The world seemed to be getting shittier and shittier. Sometimes she'd like to follow her mother′s lead and pull the blankets over her head. One more month and Tracy could actually move out and into that big bad world. She'd be sixteen. Old enough to qualify for a government stipend to help her live independently. She wouldn't mind packing up right now.

She pulled on her socks and orange trainers and headed out on her bike. It was 2 kilometres to JB's house where she would leave the bike in the backyard and pick up Shooter. She and the dog would then jog another 5kms before she headed home to get dressed for school. By then she expected her mother would have dozed off again and be snoring her head off.

But when she got home, her mother had showered, dressed and was fully made up. "If you could back the car out of the garage for me, love, I'll drive you to school."

"Make sure you stand well clear then, or it will be your blood you dreamt about!" said Tracy. "You do realise I am too young to drive! Where are you off to anyway?"

"The CPS are taking Bram's father, Tom Watts, to see him this afternoon. Norma called yesterday and asked if I could be there too. Bram still says a few things in Dutch and she'd like a translator, plus another opinion about his reaction to meeting his father for the first time. I think she's hoping the CPS won't find either Watts or Mrs de Graaf suitable guardians, and then she'll be able to adopt him."

"I'll come too. And we'll take Shooter. Matey will like that. It'll make him more relaxed."

"I think I can manage this on my own, Tracy!"

"I'm sure you can, Mum. But I'm coming regardless, and if you won't take me, I'll cycle there myself."

Her mother looked her up and down. "You're growing up."

"—and soon I'll be gone," said Tracy. "So, let's make the most of what little time we have left together. I'd like a few good memories to take with me."

"That's rather harsh."

"Don't pretend it's any different. That's just how it is. I'll get the car and bring it around. It won´t hurt to miss a day at school. Write a convincing note."

They arrived a good half an hour before Watts and the woman from the CPS were due. Shooter was a big hit, although at first, houseproud Norma was loath to let him inside.

"Dog!" shrieked Bram. "Big black dog!" He rushed forward and threw himself on the dog, tipping it sideways onto the tiled floor amongst much scrabbling of paws. Together they slid down the passageway and bounced off a wall.

Thank goodness for Labradors and their good nature, thought Tracy. Bram lay back, his head on Shooter's stomach. Shooter twisted his head up and around and tried to lick him on his forehead, which made Bram giggle in delight. A cunning look swept over his face.

"My dog!" he said, with a sly look at Norma.

"No, he's not your dog, darling," she said. "He belongs to the nice policeman."

Tracy liked the way Norma spoke to Matey— she never thought of him as Bram— in complete sentences. It had obviously worked wonders for his English comprehension.

Her mother obviously agreed as she said with a frown, "Well, I can see I'm redundant. I can't see why you wanted me to come." That was her mother all over. Everything was about her. She'd win a gold medal for narcissism.

Norma smiled, "Joanne, I've found it's always good to have a neutral witness when officialdom calls. Come into the kitchen with me while I prepare a tray of tea and biscuits."

Tracy saw her mother was only partly mollified.

"Where's your husband, Norma? Why isn't he here?" she asked as she followed close on Norma's heels, not one to beat about the bush.

"At work...and you can't describe him as a neutral witness, can you?"

Tracy guessed that Mrs de Graaf had bought the little boy's outfit. He was dressed in a sailor suit and denim shoes with the ubiquitous Velcro ties and animal soles. This time any footprints would leave a trail of wombats. The clothes were cute in the European style but overdressed for a casual Aussie boy. "What happened to his old clothes, Norma. They were a bit more relaxed."

"Mrs de Graaf said they might hold bad memories, so she took them away when she brought the new ones."

"I wonder what his father will make of him. He looks like a proper little Dutch sailor right now, not a rough and tumble Aussie."

It didn't take long to find out. The Child Protection officer, a woman dressed entirely in mauve to match the perm in her short wiry hair, bustled in with a reluctant-looking Watts in tow. She introduced herself by waving the lanyard around her neck holding several photo with the assurance that she was a genuine child specialist. Norma ushered them into the lounge where Bram was pretending to ride Shooter while keeping his feet fixed firmly on the floor. Tracy was yelling, "Giddy up cowboy. Yahoo!" and the dog was making pretend growls and yips, adding to the clamour.

"Hello, son," said Watts, lifting him off the dog's back. Bram opened his mouth to bellow an objection, but Watts deftly lifted him onto his shoulders and stood there swaying from side to side, and saying "I am a mighty elephant," while holding tight to his legs.

Tracy liked that. She liked that a lot. It was obvious that Bram liked it too.

He held onto his father's hair and called, "G-up."

They all laughed, then distributed themselves around the room on the available chairs. Norma hurried to the kitchen to bring in the afternoon tea, her face downcast at the realisation the boy might quickly bond with his father.

Fostering children and then giving them back must be the hardest job in the world, thought Tracy. Fat chance the CPS would find neither the father nor the grandmother suitable.

Her mother was in an unusually reflective mood on the way home. "He's a lovely little boy, isn't he? Norma's heart is going to break when they take him away."

"She knew what she was getting into when she volunteered as a foster parent," said Tracy, playing devil's advocate. "Foster parents must know that it's not permanent."

"Knowing and believing are different."

"I thought Tom was nice."

"Did you?"

"Didn't you?"

"A man who doesn't make an effort to know or spend time with his son until the mother is murdered isn't my idea of a good parent."

Tracy was amazed. All the same she said, "You're the expert."

Shooter seemed to sense the tension in the car, and peered between the front seats, giving a little whine. Tracy tousled his large black head. "Good boy!"

"He doesn't want a wee, does he?" Joanne asked.

"He's completely house trained, Mum. Your car's safe."

"Shall I drop you back at school?"

"No, there's only an hour and a half left and it's PT, which I hardly need with all the exercise I do each day. Drop me at JB's with Shooter. I'll walk home."

"You see rather a lot of that policeman. I hope there's nothing going on between you?"

"Mu-um! He's old enough to be my father."

"Well, since your father pays very little attention to you, it's not unheard of for a young girl to fall for a father figure. Detective Bailey is a very attractive man and young girls are a huge temptation to single men."

Tracy hoped so. "I only stay in touch with him to find out what's happening with Matey. Plus, it's safer to run with a dog. Shooter and I are great mates now. He'd miss me if I stopped running with him. JB has a girlfriend so you needn't worry." She didn't say the girlfriend was a uni-student, not much older than she was and currently in Singapore. "Anyway, I've been thinking of trying out for the police academy when I'm eighteen and he could help me with the application process."

"What happened to your plan to go to university?"

"Well, it depends on my matriculation scores. And if I do well, I'd do a degree that would help me become a detective. Law, or something like that."

Her mother swerved to avoid a murder of crows on the road. "Hope that's not your cat!" she said of the roadkill.

"Misty," Tracy rolled her eyes, "My cat's called Misty!" She noticed that whenever her future came up, her mother disengaged. Talk about her father being a disinterested parent.

Tony was hunched over his computer and had the videos from a Scarborough Beach shop and the bank's CCTVs on split screen, comparing them frame by frame, when Bailey delivered his somewhat congealed lemon chicken.

"Something?" Bailey asked.

"Maybe. Look at this." He froze the picture of a man in a dark hoodie, his back to the camera, and then advanced the right-hand side photo. The same man, his face still hidden, was with an older man dressed in a suit. They were standing a distance from each other but the black and white CCTV had a high resolution in low light situations and the second man's distinctive profile was in plain view.

"Fuck me! It's Stinky Bill."

They continued to watch the brief exchange, frame by meticulous frame displaying both time and date. The hooded man had waited a considerable time until Stinky Bill arrived. He then made expansive gestures with hands and shoulders as if explaining the unexplainable. Stinky Bill's profile turned away and his shoulders slumped. At 18:20 both men turned in separate directions and were gone. The exchange was on camera for no more than 30 seconds. "Not long after sunset on the day of the murder," Bailey said. "Can you pick either one of them up on any of the other cameras?"

"Not so far."

"Hard to believe it's a coincidence."

"Remind me what time Hannah bought the kid's dinner?"

"Five fifteen. Kids eat early. Which camera is this from?"

"The corner ATM"

"A bit casual of them."

"The bank installed two additional hidden cameras a couple of metres from the actual cash machine. There have been a few instances of bully-boys waiting to prey on pensioners."

Bailey was mentally trying to figure a timetable that included following Hannah from the fast-food outlet back to the Blue Seas Apartment, threatening and killing her, and then getting back to the bank in time to liaise with Stinky Bill.

Tony read his mind. “It’s just about doable. But why?”

“That’s the question.”

Tony took a large forkful of lemon chicken and gulped it down. “It’s about money, obviously. It’s always about money—and/or sex.” He wiped a trickle of sauce off his chin with a checked handkerchief. “But would her missing pendant be worth killing for?”

“Even at half retail It could be worth as much as $20,000.”

“Definitely worth it!” Tony said

“But he’d have to fence it to Stinky Bill, and only get about 10% of the value.
There was nothing on the video to show an exchange of goods or money?”

“You saw what I saw. Do we pick Bill up?”

“Let’s go through all the videos again. Stop lights. Car parks. The lot. I’ll rope Evan in to help. It won’t be so tedious now that we have an idea of who we’re looking for. Be good if we could get a partial vis of Hoodie’s face or his car’s registration, assuming he arrived by car. Let’s get all our ducks in a row. Put Stinky Bill and the shop under surveillance, and tap his phone.”

“If Hoodie’s the perp, I imagine he’s been warned to stay well clear.”

“If he’s a druggie. He’ll have his hand out.”

"Let's hope so."

Bailey threaded his way to Evan's desk to find the youngest member of the team unhappy at the thought of spending the rest of the afternoon looking at CCTV footage.

"Wouldn't my time be better utilised getting the surveillance warrants?" he asked.

Evan was starting to mark out his territory, thought Bailey. It was a good and a bad thing. Good to understand where your talents were best used, but bad if you were going to question the SIO's every direction.

"...and we´ll need the warrants to include confiscation of all smartphones when you decide to pick him up. Even if he's destroyed the SIM card there'll be a lot stored on the phone's internal memory. To delete everything, you need to employ multiple reset commands. Most people don't do that. One Android I looked at required ten different commands to delete all data, including text messages, phone numbers, call timers, and logs."

"Bill's probably got burner phones." Bailey said.

"All the more reason to bring him in early."

"I bet he uses the phones people have pawned. Have you any idea how many he'd have access to!" Bailey grinned. As the squad's known anti-nerd, whose IT proficiency didn't extend much past googling, it wouldn't be his job to trawl through them.

Evan groaned. “We’d be going through them for months. Let’s hope the videos provide some info then,” and accepting the lesser of two evils. “I’ll go help Tony.”

Chapter 14

"Why didn't the guy in the hoodie take Hannah's Cartier watch?" Palfrey was stomping around Bailey's patio tossing back a can of beer. Bailey knew he was avoiding going home. The two granddaughters and Diane would be straight on his case. The girls would be hoping he had done something about the rapists without divulging Jasmine's name; and Diane would be concerned that he had put their retirement into jeopardy by doing just that. Meanwhile the two detectives were batting theories back and forth about both the rape and Hannah's murder.

"I don't know. Maybe the watch is too easily identifiable or Hoodie freaked out."

"Seems strange. Usually, addicts are pretty focussed on stealing anything they can fence to feed their habit. The watch screamed money. It would be pretty hard to overlook."

"And why all the blood, and the frenzy if it's just a burglary to get your next fix?"

"Yeah. I don't get it." Palfrey slumped down onto a wrought iron patio chair. "Hard to imagine you′d find that type of emotion if he was stealing to order. You know. If Stinky Bill sends him out to specifically steal the pendant for a client. I'm guessing that happens often enough. But how did he know about the pendant in the first place?"

"Maybe Hannah tried to pawn it and didn't like the offer he made?"

"Could it be that it's just a distraction. Maybe there is no second pendant, and Mrs de Graaf made up the second pendant as an afterthought, to explain why Bill Holland was in her hotel room. It's a safe lie. Impossible for us to find a non-existent pendant...and since the parents deal in diamonds, they could always dummy up evidence that there were two."

"Then why was Hoodie there in the first place? It's too complicated. We need to find out who Hoodie is before he's on the wind, and without alerting Bill. He's like Teflon. Nothing ever sticks."

Bailey went back inside to get two more beers, Shooter at his heels. When he returned he saw Palfrey staring at his phone. "It's a text from Diane," he sighed, "wants to know when I'll be home."

"One more?" Bailey held up a can of Victoria Bitter.

"She'll smell it on my breath."

Times like this Bailey thanked his lucky stars he was divorced. He popped the top of his can and took a slug. "So, getting back to your meeting with the sex squad. Run it past me one more time. What did the guy say?"

"I gave them a copy of the drawing Jazz made of the perp's tattoo. Said I had an anonymous tip that a bloke with a similar tattoo was messing with underage girls. Asked if they might have an idea who it was and if they'd had any other information like that."

"And they asked who the snitch was, but you said you didn't know."

"Then they told me it was an ex Slovakian army tattoo."

"Why couldn't we find that out ourselves without involving them? We could have googled it."

"Using police resources for personal reasons. Remember? Cause for prison time."

"But it's all right to use an actual policeman?"

"No, you know it's not. But this doesn't leave a digital trace."

"Except the policeman will log in the information and you'll be the source."

"Unlikely."

They contemplated each other. Snitching on colleagues was frowned upon, but not as much as in the past—before the enquiry into police corruption. "Did you ask him not to log it?"

"Just said I'd owe him one if he could tell me anything about the guy. I´m guessing he read between the lines."

Bailey put his head in his hands. "Jesus! This was exactly what we weren't supposed to do. Diane will kill you!"

"Well, I'm not going to tell her, am I? And this way you're not involved."

"Except I'm your partner."

"And a pretty shit one at that."

They laughed. What could you do? There were two fuckers walking around thinking they'd got away with raping Palfrey′s granddaughter. It was personal. Bailey and Palfrey knew they had to find them and pay them out. One way or another, and the sooner the better, so they could get back to the job at hand.

Shooter's ears pricked up and he bounced to his feet and began prancing around like the pup he used to be. "What the…?"

Tracy waltzed around the side of the house, swinging a fringed shoulder bag. Tight denim jeans. White midriff top. Red hair out of its usual pony tail flowing down her back. "Thought you had a date, JB?" she said, frowning at Palfrey.

"Didn't your mother ever tell you to wait for an invitation?" asked Bailey.

"Can you lend me twenty bucks?"

"Am I your bank now?"

"My bank card's not working. The ATM ate it. Mum's out. Dad's not answering his mobile. Apparently, I'm bankrupt because someone didn't deposit money in my account. There's no food in the house, discounting cat food, and a girl's gotta eat! You owe me anyway, for training your dog."

"My dog was already trained before you came on the scene."

Tracy laughed at the obvious untruth. "Your dog doesn't do a bloody thing he's told." Shooter pawed her leg and left a swatch of red dirt on her trousers to verify this truth. "Bloody hell, now look what he's done! I just washed these jeans."

"See! Your training isn't worth a dime."

"Hi darlin'," interrupted Palfrey, amused at the back and forth. "I've been wondering when we'd meet?"

"And you are, who?"

"JB's partner in crime. Detective Ian Palfrey at your service."

Tracy gave him a close look. "I'm Tracy. You look nice. Like somebody's grandpa."

Palfrey, who'd unconsciously sucked in his gut, let it out with a sigh. Bailey laughed out loud and slapped Palfrey's shoulder. "Just what you wanted to hear, eh? Grandpa!"

"Here's an idea," said Palfrey. "Why don't you and the young lady come and have dinner at our place."

"Great!" said Tracy, eyes alight.

"You'd do anything to postpone the inevitable, wouldn't you?" asked Bailey. "Diane will still want to know what you've been up to."

"What have you been up to?" asked Tracy.

Palfrey winked at her. "Fish and chips all right?"

A wind suddenly blew up from the west. Leaves from the neighbour's gum trees whirled around their feet and swept into the pool. The automatic pool cleaner coughed and then, with a murderous gurgle, stopped its relentless circling and slowly turned over and rose to the surface.

Palfrey peered into the pool "Looks like a dead fish."

"Oh, please don't tell me," said Bailey. "Not another breakdown! I've already had a technician around to fix the air conditioner. If it's something I can't fix with duct tape it always costs a fortune. House repairs are leaving me dead poor."

Tracy knelt down and pulled the head of the cleaner out of the pool then cleared a gum nut from the intake valve. She flipped it back over and dropped it back in the water where, after a pause, it slowly sank to the bottom of the pool to recommence its circling.

"As effective as a Heimlich manoeuvre," said Palfrey in awe. "What a girl!"

"Maybe I should plan to be a mechanic, not a policewoman."

"Not a policewoman," said Bailey and Palfrey in unison. Bailey reached for the jacket slung over the back of his chair. "You want to borrow something warm, Tracy?"

Tracy caressed the cavorting dog before getting back on her feet. "I'm fine. Can Shooter come to dinner as well?"

"Palfrey has a cat," said Bailey.

"It's the neighbour's," protested Palfrey.

"Shooter likes cats."

"He likes to eat cats," corrected Bailey.

"The cat's a damned nuisance," said Palfrey. "Do come, dear. The more the merrier. It might help defuse the atmosphere."

"Talk about delusional," said Bailey.

Diane stood at the end of the passage looking like thunder and wasn't mollified when Palfrey proffered an armload of fish and chips. "Save you cooking," he said.

"I've already cooked."

"Warm up whatever it is tomorrow?" he suggested gingerly.

"When I send a text, I expect you to answer."

Bailey had never seen Diane in anything but welcome mode. This was a different person. He could see why Palfrey was worried.

"On the job, love. I can't have my phone buzzing and stop chasing a perp to phone home. Wouldn't be good for our success rate, plus the lads would laugh at me."

"Were you chasing a perp?

"Metaphorically speaking."

Diane frowned at Shooter who was creeping past Bailey and Tracy on his belly, pretending to be invisible in the hope no one would notice and put him outside. "—and who do we have here?" she waved a hand at Tracy.

"I hope it's not an imposition,' said Tracy stepping forward and offering her hand, "I ran out of money to buy food and your husband said I'd be welcome. That one more for dinner wouldn't make much difference."

"Tracy's a friend of mine," added Bailey. "She's my dog whisperer. Looks after Shooter for me." Shooter gave a short ruff, to show he was following the conversation and recognised his name.

"How old are you, Tracy?"

"Nearly sixteen, Why, is there an age limit for exercising dogs?" She looked at Diane's face, which if anything, looked even darker. "Don't you think the batter on the fish will be getting all soggy while we talk? I'm starving. Let's serve it while it's still hot."

"I'll call the girls," said Palfrey.

Jasmine and Fiona slouched into the room, rearing back when they saw Tracy. Fiona gave Palfrey a look that mirrored Diane's. Not happy. How dare he introduce a wildcard into their family dynamic. Bailey was acceptable, but only because he might be of use.

Bailey introduced Tracy, trying not to react to the sisters' closed faces, but Tracy seemed unworried by the obvious resistance to her presence in the room.

"Great to meet you both. Nice of you to include me. Shall I help lay the table?"

Bemused, they followed her into the kitchen where she opened cupboards and stacked plates and then knives and forks at the end of the benchtop. Bailey thought Tracy was like a cuckoo. She made herself at home wherever she went. It was a talent not many had. The others were so dumbfounded by her confidence they simply watched. She unwrapped the paper from the fish and chips and dumped them on two large platters, then filled a glass jug with water from the tap and took out some tumblers. Tearing off paper kitchen towels to make serviettes, she asked,

"Shall we help ourselves? Where do you keep the tomato sauce?"

Diane dumbly indicated the pantry. Tracy came back with a handful of condiments.

"This is nice," she said. "Mum is out most nights so I usually eat on my own."

Bailey thought Joanne was 'out cold' most nights. Tracy was a good kid not to mention that. She didn't whine about her lot like many teenage girls. He hoped his own daughter would have been the same.

They lined up and served themselves then went into the sunroom to eat. Shooter sat by Tracy in the knowledge she would feed him her chips. Tracy attempted to chat but the lack of response eventually cowed even her habitual self-confidence.

"Lovely room. It's so comfortable." She tried again, after cleaning up her plate. She looked around at the wicker furniture and the lush green plants thriving under the glass solarium. "Have you lived here long?"

"Forty years," said Palfrey. "Since we were first married."

"Oh…so Jasmine and Fiona aren't your children?"

Diane's face lit at the implied compliment, "Our grandchildren."

"You must have had your own children when you were very young."

Bailey thought Tracy would actually make a good detective. People relaxed around her and opened up despite themselves. He'd seen that when she was with Norma and Matey.

"Where do you guys go to school," she asked the sisters.

Fiona replied, "I'm an apprentice hairdresser. Jazz goes to Scarborough High."

"What year?" asked Tracy, and then suddenly they were talking. Jazz quietly explaining that they'd only come back to Australia with their mother eighteen months before; Tracy asking about Thailand and sounding envious that she hadn't travelled more; Fiona saying what lovely hair Tracy had, could she practice a new style on her. And before Bailey, Palfrey and Diane knew it, the teenagers had repaired to their bedroom to do just that.

"Well," said Bailey, stacking the plates to take them back to the kitchen, "That went better than expected."

"She's a nice girl," agreed Palfrey.

"We still have some talking to do," said Diane. "You make the coffee, JB."

When Tracy and the sisters re-emerged, Tracy gave a twirl and a curtsy to show off a cluster of red curls. "Nice or what?" she beamed. "Fiona is really talented."

Bailey thought the hairstyle added ten years, and not in a good way. He preferred the pony tail. He suspected Tracy did too.

"You ready for home?" he asked. Palfrey's airy explanation about his off-the-cuff conversation with a colleague to try and track down anyone with the tattoo Jazz had drawn had led to more thunderclouds and had reminded Bailey that marriage was not for the faint hearted. Diane, to her credit, pretended to forget her bad humour when she kissed Tracy goodbye, saying she was welcome any time. Bailey felt that could be a mistake, based on the frequency Tracy dropped in on him unannounced.

"That was awkward," he said as he slammed the door to the silver Camaro and accelerated away.

"Oh, it wasn't so bad…and I got to talk to Jasmine about the rape."

"What?"

"Yeah, yeah. You don't think I'd let Fiona touch my hair without some sort of trade off, do you?" She shook her head and red curls whirled around her like strawberries in a blender.

"I hope you encouraged her to report it to the police."

"No. I didn't. I'm pretty sure the whole experience was traumatic enough without telling a stranger about it."

"You're a stranger! And the Sexual Assault Squad are specially trained to be non-judgemental and respectful. Jazz could have a support person with her during the interview and ask for a woman police officer, if that's what she prefers. No action would be taken unless she gives her permission, but the crime would be recorded which might help in future cases."

"You mean these guys have done it before and are going to do it again."

"Most likely. Especially if there are no consequences."

"That's what I thought." Tracy stared out the window at the highway lights flashing by. "Anyway, I'm sure you and Ian told her exactly the same thing you just told me. If that didn't convince her, nothing I say will."

"Except you're her age. Apparently, teens listen to advice from other teens."

"Well, if I were raped, I wouldn't go to the police either. I'd kill the guy myself."

Bailey shook his head. "Unfortunately, we don't have the death penalty for rape, or anything else for that matter."

"More's the pity," said Tracy, sounding older than her years.

"If you see Jasmine again, maybe you could put in a word for the police. It would help Palfrey and me. And don't forget—you want to be a detective so you have to uphold the law."

"If you say so."

"I do!" said Bailey, thinking what a hypocrite he was.

Chapter 15

Bailey looked around the conference room where some eighteen detectives and detective constables were assembled. It was unusual for the three teams to congregate. Usually, they were widely spread out on different investigations. They had arrived that morning to find one of the general administration pool assistants standing at the door advising them there would be a meeting first thing. She didn't know why. Nor did anyone else. They helped themselves to coffee and waited, making increasingly unlikely guesses about what was going on.

"Anything happening with the surveillance team?" Bailey asked Evan, taking the opportunity to get an update. The warrants to tap Stinky Bill's phone and put him under observation had been granted the day before.

"So far Bill hasn't left his house except to go to the shop."

"Nothing unexpected then," The pawn store opened at 9:30 a.m. but Bill usually didn't front until late afternoon. He was a night owl. Addicts who frequented the shop with stolen goods, didn't get up until well into the day.

The door opened and a middle-aged woman in a charcoal grey suit walked in. She had short dark hair with a streak of white over her right ear; a pale neutral lipstick on thin lips, currently pressed together.

1.7metres or thereabouts, she wore sensible black court shoes with kitten heels but her tan stockings showed the legs of a younger woman. There were no signs of nerves at addressing a room of seasoned policemen. Her blue eyes scanned the room.

"Good morning. My name is Marcia Odell. As you know, the Major Crime Squad has recently been renamed the Homicide Squad, and I have been appointed as Officer in Charge to replace Detective Inspector Langford and to oversee this division." Head tilted to one side, she watched the shuffling feet, frowns and questioning looks. "DI Langford has taken medical leave for the foreseeable future. He has been diagnosed with stage 4 cancer and will be undergoing treatment at the Sir Charles Gardner comprehensive cancer centre. At this difficult time, his family have asked for privacy and thank you for your understanding."

Bailey cast a quick eye at Pamela but her expression was stony, giving nothing away. He wondered how many in the room knew of her extra curriculum relationship with Langford. Palfrey, who was standing next to her, patted her back. Typical non-PC move. She took a step to the side, quickly shrugging off such a public gesture of support.

"I've been recruited from the Melbourne Police Force where I was the Detective Superintendent. This is my first appointment outside of Victoria. I've heard good things about what was the Major Crime Squad based here in Perth and I look forward to getting to know you all. My focus is to come quickly up to speed on the state of current investigations. With that in mind, the three senior sergeants in charge of teams are invited to stay behind while the rest of you get on with the job. No doubt I will start putting names to faces in due course."

Palfrey raised his eyebrows at Bailey and joined the exodus. Bailey backed behind the other two senior sergeants, and began to gather his thoughts. He'd miss Langford. He'd been a good boss, rarely second guessing the team. He hoped the new woman would be similar, but somehow doubted it. Women in positions of power usually had to prove themselves and be twice as good, twice as involved, as a man. Was it sexist to think like this, or realistic?

Odell finally got to him. Bailey had listened to the two other senior sergeants make their reports and appreciated her incisive questions about the future investigative directions each team should take. No bullshit. Straight to the point, and respectful of each man's point of view. Looked like it could work out OK.

"So, summing up," she said after his spiel, keeping eye contact with him without blinking, "finding out the identity of the man in the hoodie is your best, and only, lead?"

"We could bring in Stinky Bill, and interrogate him, but judging from past experience he'll simply lawyer up and say nothing."

"What about showing him the video?"

"He'll say it was some random guy asking for directions, or a fag. I believe it's best to continue surveillance."

"How about the victim's mother? Is there anything there, do you think?"

"A double surveillance? Langford didn't want to order the overtime?"

"I'm new. That should be good for some extra leeway until such time I crash and burn." She smiled. "I think the mother's link to the pawn shop owner might prove some added traction. It's too much of a coincidence that he's linked to both the mother and the location where the victim was found."

Good instincts, thought Bailey, nodding. He appreciated her self-deprecation, but he suspected it was used to hide a great deal of ambition. "There's something not quite right about the mother."

"Do you have a magistrate or judge, who," she paused, "—is usually on board with issuing warrants under the TIA act?"

The Telecommunications Interceptions and Access act allowed the police to examine stored communications—emails, SMS or voice messages. It was certainly a good place to start. "I'll have the team's IT specialist, Evan, apply for the warrant," said Bailey. "So far, he's been lucky and hasn't had any pushback."

"Good. It's amazing how often people convict themselves by keeping sensitive data."

“Let’s hope so,” said Bailey, taking her proffered hand and shaking it.

“Good to meet you, Detective Bailey.”

Evan stretched, and blew his newly grown fringe off his forehead. “The problem is, I’ve been through all the interviews and we don’t have Mrs. De Graaf’s mobile number. The Dutch police said they’d email it, but to date haven’t. We can only contact her at the hotel.”

Bailey was annoyed with himself. “Sorry. I missed that. I guess Greta Meer, the Netherlands’ consul will have it.”

“OK – I’ll give her a buzz.”

Bailey thought about Palfrey’s comment—and that Greta was without a wedding ring. Had he sensed some type of rapport with her, or was that wishful thinking? Maybe after this was all over, he could ask her out. Someone nearer his own age. More appropriate than Sarah. “No, I’ll do that. You get on with filling out the warrant, and I’ll give you the number ASAP.”

In the end, Greta was harder to track down than he expected. He left two messages, and it was over an hour before she got back to him.

“Mrs de Graaf thinks you may be interfering in the child custody arrangements?” she said, after giving Bailey the number, an enquiry in her tone.

“Matey’s future isn’t in our hands. It’s the Child Protective Service who make the report to the family court and gives it their recommendations regarding placements. They're trained to spot potential problems."

"All the same, you were first on the scene, and she said you seem to be favouring the father, despite him never showing an interest in the child."

"Ms Meer…"

"—Greta," she interrupted.

"Greta, the CPS took Watts to see his son, as is normal. They need to see how the child interacts with both his father and grandmother, independently. It may be that they won't find either party suitable. Our interest is to find and convict Hannah's killer, and to keep the family informed of progress," or in this case lack of progress, he thought. "That's our brief."

"You've been very understanding, Detective Bailey. When this is all over, I'd like to invite you for a coffee. My work as the honorary consul doesn't usually involve a police presence, and I've been pleasantly surprised by your openness and courtesy."

Bailey grinned. He guessed Pamela wouldn't be invited. The two women had locked horns. "I´d enjoy that, Greta."

Tracy tried on a tiny gold mini skirt and paired it with a gauzy black, fitted top. For a bit of whimsy, she wore high-top tennis shoes that she'd sprayed with glitter to match the skirt. She shook her booty, then twirled. Hmm. Yep, despite the rubber soles she could dance in them and they'd be perfect if she had to run.

Hair plaited, she wound it tightly around her head. No loose hair for someone to grab and hold. You never know what might save you in an unsafe situation. She poked her head around the bathroom door to where her mother was showering.

"Mum, I'm going out tonight. Meeting some friends. We're going dancing."

"Is Liam going with you?"

"Yeah. We're meeting up with him and he'll drive us home. And don't worry—he doesn't drink. He doesn't like alcohol. He's into Coke."

"I hope you don't mean cocaine!"

"Coca Cola, Mum. Get a life. No-one uses cocaine these days. The drugs are all synthetic, like Ice." Her mother stepped out of the shower. How she maintained her body with all the alcohol she drank Tracy didn't know. Only a slight puffiness around the eyes and cheeks gave her away. "Mu-um! Put a towel around you. Children shouldn't see their parents naked."

"How do you know so much about drugs?"

"School, Mum. We get lectures. Visiting doctors. Recovering drug addicts. You name it. They don't want us to go out into the world without being prepared. It's called a preparatory school for a reason."

"Don't get smart with me young lady! We pay a lot of money for you to attend a private school and you should appreciate it." Her mother slowly towelled her hair dry, squinting at Tracy's reflection in the bathroom mirror. "You're looking pretty fancy. Where did you get that skirt? Is it new?"

"It was yours. I found it in the back of your closet and took up the hem. Looking fancy is what I'm aiming for."

"It's too early to go dancing, isn't it? And don't you have to be eighteen and have an ID to get into a night club?"

"I have to be with an adult, and Liam is 20. I can't drink alcohol and since I don't, it's no problem." Well, she did take a sip, but only now and then. Not after seeing where that had led her mother. Tracy twirled just for the hell of it. "We're going for a bite first. You did put more money in my bank account, didn't you?"

Her mother nodded. "I called your father. He put in a few hundred. Said he was sorry he forgot this month. He's been a bit preoccupied. Business hasn't been good."

"Great. I'm set then. See you later."

"Your father…"

Tracy slammed the door before her mother could finish the thought and headed for the

bus stop. Her father was big on excuses. Why it was he couldn't do this or that. She didn't want to hear about it. No point expecting either of her parents to be responsible. There were too many disappointments in the past for that. A girl just had to get on with it.

The bus dropped her a street from the hairdressers where Fiona worked. The plan was to go to a movie, then to meet up with Liam, have a burger, and around ten-ish hit a few night spots. Fiona was bringing her a fake ID. The salon had a drawer-full, for blondes, brunettes and red heads. They were going trolling for men with ex-Slovakian army tattoos. If successful, they could help JB and Palfrey to identify the men who'd attacked Jazz. Nothing ventured, nothing gained. Tracy felt a stirring of excitement. This is what undercover detectives did. She was pretty sure she was born for it.

Fiona was waiting under the salon's tattered awning, long hair twisted into a multitude of ringlets. Tracy couldn't help but think that her shiny straight hair would be best left in its natural state. The platform shoes with ankle straps she'd opted to wear gave her a good extra 3 inches. They'd be no good for running. Unlike her, Fiona wasn't focussed on self-preservation. Strange really, considering what happened to her sister.

"Hi – you ready for this?" Tracy greeted her with a hug.

"Sure. Anything to help Jazz – and Poppa."

"What did you tell them?"

"That we had a styling session after work, and then the boss was going to take us all out for dinner. I told Jazz the same. I didn't want her to worry about me."

"Good one!"

They beamed at each other.

“Is your boyfriend handy with his fists?”

“Not really, but he’s smart, and has a car and a mobile phone, that’s the main thing. Think of this as a reconnaissance mission.”

“What?”

“You know – Mission Impossible.”

“If it’s impossible, why are we doing it?”

Tracy sighed. “Never mind.” She peered through windows that needed cleaning at the rather rundown salon. Three basins. Dog-eared magazines. Unimaginatively called “Curls,” and shoehorned between a tattoo parlour and an Asian takeaway that smelt of reused deep-fried oil. It didn’t look very salubrious. “D′you like working here?”

“It’s not too bad. It’s hard to get an apprenticeship so I’m lucky, really. My Mum says being a hairdresser is a very portable profession. People always need a haircut.”

“D’you get on with your Mum?”

Fiona waggled her head. “You know how it is.” Tracy did. They linked their arms together and set off towards the cine-complex.

“Rom-com?” she asked.

Fiona nodded. “Absolutely.”

Chapter 16

Tracy pulled the duvet up over her head as Misty snuggled closer. The cat's deep throated purr lulled her back to sleep and it was 10am before she threw the covers off and went in search of breakfast. "Mum?" she called.

The kitchen was spotless, so her mother hadn't had breakfast either. No coffee pot. No dirty dish in the sink. She must have slept over with her latest beau. Ron something or other. Slim. Balding. Late forties. Worked in mining up north. Six weeks on. Six weeks off. Tracy doubted her mother could be faithful for six weeks at a time, but maybe she could for someone who wined and dined her so assiduously.

She opened a tin of cat food and winced at the strong fishy smell. She held it at arm's length—cringe. Thankfully her own breakfast of Weetabix didn't smell of anything much. She'd had a few Bacardi and Cokes the night before, and whereas she'd tried to make them last, she didn't really have a head for liquor. Liam hadn't been happy with her, even though she'd ordered half tots and topped the glass up with his Coke. He'd opted to drop her off first, and had gone on with teetotal Fiona to say his goodnights.

They'd started at *Mint* nightclub. If you got there before 9pm there was no cover charge. At around midnight, after checking out three more venues including *Villa* with its huge dancefloor, they ended up at *Jack Rabbit Slims*, an edgy nightclub named after the 1950s diner in Pulp Fiction. Fiona said they'd met the guys who invited them to the party there. For some reason, even though it was Friday, it was a quiet night and Fiona didn't recognise anyone. The three of them danced together, with Liam taking rather more interest in Fiona than Tracy would have liked.

Since Tracy had met Liam, it had been hard holding him off with promises. In a months' time, on her sixteenth birthday, she would finally reach the age of consent. But Fiona was already eighteen, and from what she'd told Tracy, she'd had her share of experience.

"Waiting is for your own good," Tracy had told Liam. "You'd be the one going to jail for having underage sex!" However, apparently libido has no common sense. In a way, she wouldn't regret losing Liam—only his ability to drive her wherever she wanted, whenever she wanted, in return for a bit of harmless pashing in his highly uncomfortable Mini. Until she got her driver's licence, her bike certainly limited sleuthing. Was she ready to go all the way with Liam? She wasn´t sure. With no experience how could she know?

After last night´s bust, this morning she´d take the bus to visit the tattoo parlour next to Fiona's hair salon and show them Jazz's sketch of the rapists' tattoo. Pretend she wanted one like it. What was its history? Had they ever made one or seen one like that? Known anyone with it? Of course, there must be hundreds of tattoo parlours in Perth and the suburbs. Google said there were twenty-two top rated parlours in the northern suburbs alone. And of course, the guys might have had the tattoo done overseas or in the eastern states—or in a cheap low-rated parlour. LOL. Still, it was somewhere to start. She absentmindedly poured the rest of the milk from her cereal into the cat's bowl.

"There you are, sweetie," she said. "This should hold you until I get back." Misty didn't look grateful. She lapped the milk up and turned her back to look out the sliding glass door at the magpies warbling and poking in the grass for worms. Cats were like that. If they could talk, Tracy bet their first word would be, "whatever!"

"We've run out of kitty litter, so I can't refill your box. I'll let you out to terrorise the birds and poop outside. OK?"

Misty paced, eyes on the Magpies. She knew 'out.' Outside was her domain.

The door to the tattoo parlour rang as Tracy entered. Spotlights highlighted framed designs on the rough plastered walls in the dark interior. She leaned on the scratched wooden counter.

"Think Ink is a pretty good name for a tattoo parlour," she said to the heavily inked man in front of her. "A lot more appropriate than some names I've seen."

“Glad you approve.” The man flexed his biceps so the improbably blue and rose- coloured snake drawn on his arm writhed and bared its fangs.

“Amazing!” she said, hoping the snake wouldn’t enter her dreams.

“Here to have a tattoo? I’ll need a photo ID and proof of age.”

“I wanted to look at some designs first.”

“Have you an idea about what sort of tattoo you’d want, and where?”

“A rose? A crucifix?” She fiddled with the gold cross on a chain around her neck.

“But will you always follow a Christian religion?” asked the man—Bluey, he said his name was. His spiky black hair was dyed blue at the tips. “You have to keep in mind that a tattoo is with you for life. You and your beliefs may change. You might become a Buddhist—or an animist. How old are you anyway?”

With a haughty look, Tracy slapped the ID Fiona had lent her the night before down on the counter. “For God´s sake. I’m so sick of people asking me that.”

“Number one. If you’re religious, don’t blaspheme. And for seconds, don’t insult me by giving me an ID from *Curls* next door. Who do you reckon supplies them with the damn things?”

Tracy giggled nervously. “OK—you got me!”

“Let’s start again. The name’s Bluey. I have a master’s degree in art. Don’t underestimate me because there's a fucking snake crawling up my arm." He flicked his shirt up to display a taut six-pack and a drawing of two men in medieval costume. The design was intricate with the men appearing to be illuminated. He contracted his abs and the men shook hands.

"Jesus!" said Tracy, "It's the Night Watch."

"Language!" warned Bluey, "but I'm impressed that you recognize it. Painted by…?"

"Let me think," Tracy screwed up her face and tried to remember her art history class.

Bluey frowned. "I'm disappointed. One guess, or you're out of the shop."

"Harsh!" She pulled her nose in thought. "Vermeer?"

"Rembrandt. Sorry, no cigar." He bustled around to her side of the counter and she noticed one leg in the skinny black jeans was shorter than the other, giving him a limp. "Now what′s a smart cookie like you doing here? Really. No bullshit."

Tracy pulled the crumpled sketch that Fiona had supplied out of her back pocket. "I want to know about this tattoo, and if you know anyone who has one like it?"

Bluey smoothed the paper out on the counter next to a stack of tattered *Urban Ink* magazines. He gave it his full attention, nodded, and kept nodding as he grasped her upper arm and drew her towards the entrance. "Little girl," he said, "go home and come back when you really are eighteen, which I estimate will be in a good three- or four-years' time."

Pulling her arm away, Tracy warned, "No touching!" She thought a moment. "It's important, and if you won't tell me, I'll go somewhere else. Somewhere the owner might not have a fancy art degree. Where they won't care how old I am, and they'll take advantage of me." She gave him the look that usually worked with older men, face cast down, eyes peeping up through her fringe. Bluey must be at least fifty no matter how hard he tried to be with-it.

"Behave!" he growled, but he gave in as she knew he would, "It's a Croation army tattoo. You don't want to mess with someone who has one of these."

"Can you give me a name? A person who′d know more."

"I can't, and if I could, I wouldn't."

"They raped my friend."

Bluey looked sad. "You should tell the police."

"She won't—it wasn't me—so it's not my story to tell."

"Then knowing who they are won't help you."

"She's only fourteen. There were two of them. And why should they get away with it? What if it was your daughter next?" She didn't give him time to reply. "I'm Tracy, here's my cell number. If you could find out a name, I know a policeman who might..." Might what? Tracy asked herself. "—do something about it," she said, feeling lame.

Bailey was catching up on bookkeeping when Shooter started barking. It was the friendly sort of barking, not the *unknown intruder* type. What now? Couldn't he have one Sunday morning to read the paper without being interrupted? He planned to later check online to see how his stock portfolio was going. He'd bought some shares to add to his aunt's small inheritance. Mainly banks and miners. Supposedly blue chip but not doing too well right now. Maybe he should have used the money to buy a rental property. Negative gear it and get some tax benefits. Hard to know which way to go. He'd signed up for dividend re-investments and hoped by the time he retired, when the shares were added to his superannuation, his retirement capital would provide him with income to travel around Australia, then maybe overseas.

He looked up to see Shooter at the front door, whining up a storm, tail wagging. Sighing, he stood up and strode to open it.

"Where've you been?" he asked Tracy, who was sitting on the step looking at her mobile. "Shooter's getting fat without your daily runs together."

"It's voluntary, remember," she said, face downcast.

This wasn't like her. "What happened? You normally barge straight in." He held the door open and waved her in." Come and grab a Coke from the fridge and tell me all about it."

Bailey closed his laptop and pushed it out of the way while Tracy took two Cokes from the fridge, gave one to Bailey then had a long swig of her own. "That feels better," she said, uttering a loud burp. "I had a couple of Bacardi's last night."

"Since when have you been drinking alcohol?"

"I was trying to blend in."

Bailey thought it would be hard to get lost in a crowd with her good-looks. "Why? And where?" he said, trying to keep it simple.

Tracy pulled Jazz's sketch out of her pocket, screwed it into a ball and tossed it across the table, nearly upending Bailey's mostly empty can of Coke. He was glad he'd thought to move the laptop out of harm's way.

As he unravelled the paper, Tracy said, "We went out clubbing to see if we could find anyone who might know who the two guys who attacked Jazz were."

"We who?"

"Fiona, my friend Liam, and me. Fiona copied Jazz's sketch on Diane and Ian's scanner and gave us a copy each. We asked around at the bars of a few clubs, but no-one knew anything."

Bailey decided not to waste his time telling her it was a stupid, and dangerous, idea. It was done. Kids made mistakes. Hindsight wasn't particularly helpful. Rather than say *you shouldn't have done that,* it was better to ask them not to do it again.

Noting that Bailey wasn't interrupting with protests, Tracy continued, "So today I went to *Think Ink,* the tattoo parlour next to Fiona′s work, to see if they could tell me anything." She smiled. "Guess what? It's a Croation Army Tattoo!"

She waited for signs of approval. Instead, he took the last mouthful of his Coke, rubbed his unshaven chin and finally said, "There's a reason why we don't want civilians to involve themselves in police work. We already knew it was a Croation army tattoo—and now after your efforts, they probably know that we know."

"How would they?" argued Tracy.

"Someone you talked to will tell them."

Tracy's mouth turned down, and she looked like she was about to cry. "We only wanted to help."

"I know. But it's best to leave it to the professionals." Bailey thought as criticisms go, that was pretty mild. Tears slid down Tracy's face all the same. "Hey. Cheer up. I was thinking of taking Shooter to Floreat dog beach for a run, then going on to Scarborough for an ice-cream. Wanna come?" Shooter heard his name and pushed his snout into Bailey's hand.

"It's a long walk over the dunes to the beach and I'm wearing sandals. They're hopeless for walking in sand."

"But it's perfect for Shooter and you can go barefoot."

"The waves will be up with the wind—and sometimes snakes are on the path."

"Well, aren't you a happy little camper today!"

"Okay. I'll go. But if I get snake-bit, you have to promise to suck the poison out."

Bailey nearly said *my pleasure* and then remembered Tracy was fifteen. A dangerous age and not to be encouraged. "Let's hope it won't come to that," he said instead, standing up and turning to take his car keys off the kitchen counter, "—and anyway, they say not to do that anymore. Just tightly bind the wound until you get to hospital. I'll bring a roll of masking tape. I can use it on your mouth if you get too cheeky."

"Ha. Ha." Tracy rolled her eyes, back in form. "I'll get Shooter's lead."

Shooter wasn't the best-behaved dog on a lead. It was fine to take him to the dog beach where he could run in and out of the waves unfettered. He'd even stand under the doggie shower so the sand could be washed off before he jumped in the car; but take him for a stroll along the Scarborough Beach shopping precinct when you were eating an ice-cream and bedlam ensued. He wrapped the lead around Tracy's legs. Tried to make friends with any child walking the other way, often making them cry, and jumped up on a pusher and licked a toddler's chocolate smeared lips, which to be fair, seemed to go down well with the toddler but the mother nearly had hysterics and threatened to call the police. Tracy was in favour of Bailey showing his badge, but Bailey apologised instead and offered to buy the mother a coffee at the Rendezvous Hotel.

"Excuse me! My husband wouldn't like that." The woman bridled.

Tracy giggled, and whispered *sotto voce*, "She stopped listening at Rendezvous."

Bailey had to laugh. They watched the woman saunter away swinging her ample hips. Bailey thought women of that size should avoid athletic wear, which tended to emphasize cellulite. He kept this to himself. Janet, his ex-wife, had given him the lecture about how men's expectations, based on years of reading Playboy magazine, pushed women towards anorexia.

"You've made her day, JB. She probably hasn't been propositioned for years."

Bailey requisitioned Shooter's lead and shortened it, ensuring Shooter walked close to his left leg. Tracy sashayed along wiggling her hips in parody. "Where to, Handsome?" she said throatily. "Shall we check out the Rendezvous Hotel?"

An elderly woman walking the other way gave them a worried look.

"You'll get me into trouble, Tracy."

The idea seemed to cheer her up no end. The mobile on her hip buzzed. She looked at the screen. "Wait up. It's Liam."

Bailey wasn't listening. He was watching a man in a hoodie on the opposite side of the road. He handed her Shooter's lead. She handed him the mobile. He took a quick look.

The text read, *We've got your number and we know where you live, Bitch.*

Chapter 17

Bailey gave back Tracy′s mobile and took out his own. "Tracy, we have to follow that guy in the Hoodie across the road."

"What? But something's happened to Liam. The text came from his phone!"

"The most likely scenario is someone stole his phone and is trolling all his contacts. I can only handle one investigation at a time."

"No-o. I'm sure it's more than that!"

" I'll contact Evan to see if his telecom friend can find the location of Liam's phone on a weekend. But—be quick now. Cross the road!"

Tracy looked like she would argue further, so Bailey dragged the dog across the street. Tracy followed reluctantly. Bailey thought they were giving a good impression of a family. Put-upon father, unhappy daughter and unwilling dog. Arguing. Nothing unusual in that if Hoodie turned around.

"What's Liam's full name and address, and his mobile number?" he asked, tapping and activating the speech app and holding the mobile to her mouth. "Does he live with his parents?" When Tracy confirmed that he did, he sent the email with a short explanation to Evan, then called Palfrey. "Any chance of hot-footing it to Scarborough?" he asked when he heard the gruff voice answer. "I think I've found

Hoodie. Tracy's with me, but we're following. If he jumps in a car before we get to him, we're stuffed."

"On my way."

That was what Bailey liked about his partner. No unnecessary questions. Action when it was needed. "Stay on the line," he said. "I'll give you a running commentary."

"What makes you think he's the one?"

Bailey could hear keys jingling, then the sound of Palfrey's SUV engine turning over.

"Grey hoodie. One shoulder higher than the other."

"See his face?"

"Not yet." Bailey held up his phone and snapped a shot of Hoodie's back. "Nike running shoes. Black." The Nike distinctive tick showed on the heel of the shoe. "Heading down the Esplanade towards the car park."

Tracy had been listening to this. "I could jog past him and tangle him in Shooter's lead. Stop him in his tracks."

"Let's close in on him first." They picked up their pace. Shooter for once behaving.

"Only 50 metres now," said Tracy. She slipped off her sandals, hopping from one foot to another. "Just in case. It wouldn't look right to run in my sandals." She took off. Sandals in one hand, she held her mobile in front of her as if she was running on Facetime. As she passed Hoodie she started gabbling, pretending to talk with a friend, "—and then he said he'd dock my allowance, so fuck him. He's only my step-father and he can't tell me how to live my life." She stopped and stepped into the entrance of a shop, the mobile angled towards the passing Hoodie. "Oh well, you're right. He does all right by Mum. Maybe I'm being too hard on him. She has to have a life too." Hoodie glanced at her. White face. Heavy stubble. Nose that had been broken and badly set at one stage. Mirrored sunglasses didn't allow for eye colour. "I guess I could give him the benefit of the doubt. What d'you think of my new lipstick?"

Bailey caught up to her. She put her hand on his arm to stop him for a moment. "Has to look like we're making up!" She showed him the phone. "I got him on video, I'll send it to you." They walked on; fifty metres behind. Bailey kept Palfrey on the line, filling him in about the threatening message sent to Tracy from Liam's phone.

"The kids went out clubbing, and asked around about the two guys who assaulted Jazz. Unfortunately, they were specific about the Croatian Military tattoo. Looks like Liam may be in trouble. I asked Evan to check with his parents, and see if he's actually at home or if he's been in touch since last night. If not, maybe Telstra would triangulate the mobile. Evan has good connections there. They've helped him before on the qt without a warrant." He could hear the roar of Palfrey's SUV and the distinctive intermittent squealing from its worn brake pads.

Palfrey groaned. "Bloody hell. It doesn't rain it pours, never one thing at a time. Getting Evan involved puts us in the shit."

"Yeah." They contemplated this for a moment in silence. "Hoodie's turning right towards the car park. At least we have a decent shot of his face on record now. Where are you?'

"Maybe five blocks away."

Bailey turned and saw Tracy talking on her phone. "What are you doing?"

"Talking to Fiona. She said when Liam dropped her off, he was going back to the club. See if there was any action."

Bailey shook his head. Could it get any worse?

Shooter smelled the sea beyond the carpark and began to tug on the lead. Bailey quickly bent to let him off, then ran after him calling, "Here Blackie!" which he knew would be white noise as far as Shooter was concerned. He was a dog who knew his name and even then he only came back when it suited him. Hoodie reached his car, a beat-up red Mini. As he slid into the driver's seat, Bailey stopped and called "Here boy!" as he memorised the registration number. Shooter pranced to his side and Bailey reclipped the lead to his collar. Tracy, gasping for breath, joined them.

"Bacardi makes you puff!"

"Don't drink it then." He watched the Mini pull out of the car park and turn right. "Red mini turning south into West Coast Highway," he relayed to

Palfrey. "Rego 9LZ812. Repeat Niner Lima Zulu eight one two."

"Right," said Palfrey, ever laconic.

"We'll follow," said Bailey.

They ran to the Camaro and piled in, Shooter scrambling over Tracy's bare legs, as usual, leaving scratches. "This bloody dog needs a pedicure!" she said.

Bailey didn't worry about answering. He reached out to put the magnetic-mount, blue light on the roof and accelerated away. The blue strobe would just get him some room on the road.

"We're a pretty good team," said Tracy.

Bailey let that comment lie. She was right, but if his new boss got to hear of it—that a fifteen-year-old teenager was with him while he was following a suspect—he'd be in deep shit. He passed two more cars then slowed down. Dragging Tracy along on a high speed chase was a definite no-no. Palfrey's black SUV soon overtook them. A more common car than the Camaro, it would likely blend into the traffic. "I've got eyes on the Mini," Palfrey reported.

"I'll hang back," said Bailey, reaching out to take the blue light off the roof. He turned to Tracy and—reciting Evan's phone number from memory—said, "Tell him you're with me, but I'm on another call. Also, who you are, where you live, where you, Liam and Fiona went last night, and that you possibly pissed off some men who are threatening you."

Tracy's thumbs were lightning fast passing on the information. Bailey wondered if he should let Tracy and Shooter out of the car. They could walk home.

"Don't even think about pulling over. I'm safe enough in the car," she said, as if reading his mind. "It's good to have two mobiles. We can track two things at once."

She was right.

"Is this about Matey and his Mum's murder? The guy in the hoodie?" she asked.

"He's someone we want to identify and interview. Nothing more than that."

"You seem pretty wound up."

"This is the first live sight we've had of him. We need a name and an address."

"What did he do?"

"Maybe nothing. He's just a person of interest who might have some insight." Bailey overtook a 4wheel drive towing a horse trailer. There were three or four cars between him and Palfrey. "OK?" he asked Palfrey in their normal pared down speech.

"Yeah. He's just tooling along. Not looking in his rear or side mirror. Must be listening to music. I can see his head nodding and his shoulders moving in time to it."

"What station?" Bailey joked.

"It's not the ABC."

They laughed.

Tracy was reading another text on her phone.

"I've got another message. It's an address," she said to Bailey. "*14 Pleasant Grove, Falcon, Mandurah.* That's all it says. From *unknown phone number*, like the last one."

"Send it to Evan as well. Tell him to contact the Mandurah police and ask them to drive by in an unmarked car and report back." He didn't like how this was escalating.

"What if they want a ransom? You know—pay us $5,000 and don't tell the police."

"Did they say that?"

"Well, no – but they might when I answer. I should send a text back. They'll expect me to be checking my phone all the time, like most…" she hesitated.

Bailey was sure she'd been about to say "kids."

She swallowed, "—people."

"I can't think about that now. Just send the text to Evan. He'll get onto it." Evan, the youngest and latest member of the squad, was becoming indispensable with his varied list of contacts and unmatched IT knowledge. He was young, single, ambitious, and wouldn't care that his Sunday had been interrupted. More than that, he'd relish it.

Palfrey butted in. "What's going on?" he asked. The open line between them allowed him to hear Tracy's as well.

Tracy ignored him. "What about my Mum? They said they knew my address? What if they go there and hurt her?"

"Call her. Tell her to go out for a bit until I drop you home," said Bailey. He overtook a semi-trailer advertising a well- known logistics company. When did they start calling transport companies logistics, he wondered, before dragging his thoughts back to the matters at hand?

"JB," said Palfrey – a note of warning in his voice. "How will you explain sending a car to the address in Mandurah. Jazz didn't report the assault. We're not supposed to be involved."

"Ah fuck." They drove. Tracy tried her mother's mobile to no avail. Finally, Bailey said, "this is about Liam now, not about Jazz. That should make it all right."

"I can see this going belly up as we speak. They'll interview Tracy, and Liam if he's OK, and someone will talk to them about Jazz. The PCIU will be on us like fleas on a dog"

"What's the PCIU?" asked Tracy.

"Police Conduct Investigation Unit,"

Palfrey swore. "There goes my pension. I knew this would blow up in my face. Maybe yours too, JB. Hope your shares will be enough to give you a comfortable retirement."

Bailey noticed Tracy's sidelong look. It was evident that she'd never thought of him and a pension in the same sentence—which could only be a good thing. Mind you, it wouldn't be human not to regret his loss of status as a desirable boyfriend. Being a teenager's hero gave him a certain cachet that he normally felt was missing.

"It'll be fine. We'll just try to keep a finger on the pulse and tamp down any speculation." He turned to Tracy. "When's your birthday?" he asked.

"Soon. June. Why?"

"No reason."

The sound of a siren interrupted. An ambulance was approaching fast. Bailey pulled to the side of the road. A minute later he said, "Palfrey? You still on it?"

"Shit shit shit. No! He didn't pull over. He's gone."

"Well, take off after him. Fast."

Tracy put her hand on Bailey's knee. "What about Liam?"

"Palfrey, I'm going to turn into Ocean Drive. You keep on the West Coast Hwy. If either of us don't catch up to the Mini in ten minutes, we'll have to concede we've lost him."

Ten minutes later, Bailey had to admit Hoodie was gone. He pulled into the car park of the Floreat Forum shopping centre. "I'm done," he said to Palfrey. "I'll see what Evan has to say and get back to you."

Tracy and Bailey looked at each other.

"Mum's OK. She's staying over at her boyfriend's. He's new, so there's no way they can find her there. I didn't even have to ask. She told me not to expect her home."

"Where will you stay? I don't want you to be on your own."

"Can I stay with you?"

"I'll ask Diane. See if you can bunk in with Jazz and Fiona."

"OK. But tell me what Evan says first!"

He'd expected more resistance. "You're not to do anything about Liam. We've got that covered. Or we will have." But Evan's mobile was engaged, and when Palfrey checked in with a similar lack of success at locating the car, they agreed to head back to his place.

"Can I stop by home and pick up some clothes?" asked Tracy.

"Best not to. I'm sure Fiona will lend you something. No point in going home if they—whoever 'they' are—follow us back to Palfrey's."

"And to Jazz!"

"Yes. And to Jazz. They probably think she's reported the assault."

"How many women report rape?"

"How would we know? We can't count the ones who don't. I can only tell you that only thirty percent of reported rapes lead to an arrest or to legal action. It's not a wonderful percentage shot."

"I bet if men were raped there'd be more effort in getting the rapists behind bars."

"I'm sure you're right. The whole subject is bloody depressing."

"More than that. It's…" she struggled to find the right word. "—unconscionable." She stumbled slightly over the word. "People know that murder's wrong. They expect to be punished if they're caught. But it seems like assaulting women is just fair game."

Bailey had nothing to add to that. It was why he worked in the Homicide Squad. At least with a murder, there was a higher likelihood of a successful resolution. If his own daughter had lived, he wondered if he'd be having this same conversation with her. Not that it was a conversation. There was nothing he'd have been able to tell his daughter, except to be careful. And look how that had worked out.

They pulled into Palfrey's driveway and as Tracy opened her door, Shooter once again scrabbled over her bare legs.

"Your fucking dog!" she said.

And Bailey had nothing to add to that either.

Chapter 18

As it turned out, Diane and the girls were out, leaving a note that said simply *Gone shopping*. Where and for what or for how long didn't seem to matter these days when everyone carried a mobile and could be in constant touch. Instead, the page torn out of a notebook had lots of hearts and kisses and they'd all signed their names in different coloured pencils. Palfrey surreptitiously folded it and slipped it in his wallet while Bailey walked away to smile at the show of sentiment. His partner was a secret softy. And a lucky man to have a family who cared so much about him.

Palfrey showed Bailey and Tracy into the kitchen and then rattled around filling the kettle and demonstrating his unfamiliarity with Diane's domain by opening all the cupboards to find mugs and tea bags. Finally, taking over, Tracy said, "Sit down, Ian, let me do it. I remember where everything is from last time."

Tracy's tendency to assume control when others faltered was a trait that could be equally annoying or endearing.

She placed the mugs in front of them with a jug of milk, sugar and teaspoons, then opened a packet of shortbread biscuits and poured them onto a plate. "I've had an idea," she said. Palfrey bit into two biscuits at once and crumbs exploded down his shirt where they took over the folds above his substantial stomach. "I know JB from finding Matey. If I bumped into him in the street, wouldn't it be normal to stop him, and show him the text and ask what I could do about it? Jasmine wouldn't have to come into the equation at all. Liam's my boyfriend, after all."

Bailey raised his eyebrows at Palfrey who slowly nodded. "Duh! It's obvious when you think about it. I'm over complicating things. With Tracy in the picture, we can be totally upfront about it."

Palfrey stood up, brushing the crumbs from his shirt onto the floor. "Tracy, why don't you make up your bed for the night. I'll text Diane that you'll be staying. The bedding's in the linen cupboard at the end of the passage and there's a pull-out truckle bed in the girls' room."

Tracy put her head into the cupboard under the sink to look for a dustpan and broom then flourished them indignantly before scooping up the crumbs on the floor. "Why can't I stay and listen to what Evan says first?"

"It's against regulations. We'll tell you about it later."

"You only follow regulations when it suits you," she said, but she left all the same.

"She's not wrong, the cheeky devil!' said Palfrey.

Bailey shook his head. "She's fifteen going on twenty. It's hard to keep up."

"A dangerous age, JB. Be very careful."

"She's like my daughter. Or how she would be, if she'd lived."

"She's somebody's daughter – but not yours!"

Evan's phone rang a good ten times before he picked up. "Boss," he said, "I'm still waiting for Mandurah to get back to me. The address is in a street of warehouses and workshops. 14d is at the rear. There doesn't appear to be any surveillance cameras fitted in the complex. They've driven in and parked. One of the units is a tech repair shop and if anyone stops them, they're going to say their phone has packed up and needs fixing."

"On a Sunday?"

"Well at least that way the premises will be shut! I guess they'll play dumb."

"Hope they play dumb but act smart. Seems a bit too cloak and dagger to me."

"I'll call you back."

Bailey thought Tracy's comment about having two mobile phones to do two things at once wasn't such a bad idea. Although they usually worked in pairs, maybe the whole team should carry two phones for times when they were on their own. Marcia Odell seemed to think that as a newbie she'd have access to funding. That is, until she stumbled, which she was bound to do. No one's perfect. But in the meantime, she was a new broom sweeping all before her in the hope she'd bring the solve rate up.

He sighed. Waiting. Always waiting for information before they took the next step. It was the part of the job he disliked the most. Long stakeouts were the worst. But going off half cocked and messing up an operation was infinitely worse. Patience.

Fifteen minutes later, with Tracy back in the room and hanging over his chair, the return call came. "Bailey," he said.

Evan loudly exhaled, as if he'd been running or holding his breath. "The door wasn't locked, so they went in. They found a young man on the floor, unconscious. No injuries evident so probably suffering from an overdose. They put him in the recovery position and checked for ID but otherwise haven't touched anything. Just called for an ambulance. He had no wallet on him but his phone was in his back pocket, so it seems it's Liam."

"Any photos from the scene?"

"I'll send 'em on."

Tracy put her mouth to Bailey's ear, "Liam doesn't even drink alcohol. No way he'd take drugs," she whispered.

Bailey nodded, although he'd heard a version of this belief more times than he could count—relatives and friends saying a victim would never take drugs. "The drugs may not have been self-administered," he told Evan. "Tell them to secure the premises; and ask where the ambulance is taking him. Find out who owns, and/or rents the place and then, if you can, who has keys and access." Bailey looked at

Tracy, who was ashen, "If I leave now, I should be there in just under an hour."

"*We* should be there! We're on our way." Tracy said emphatically.

Bailey put his hand over the receiver. "No! You're staying here with Palfrey. He's going to track down Hoodie's motor vehicle registration and address. You can help him with that. He's shit at IT."

Palfrey gave Bailey a look that was meant to wither. "Tracy can look after Shooter and make sure he doesn't eat the cat. I'm pretty sure I know how to negotiate the motor vehicle registry by now."

"Shooter loves the cat, man. The cat just doesn't understand him," said Bailey. He ended the call with Evan and headed for the door before Palfrey got the last word in.

"Dogs and cats shouldn't mix!" Palfrey shouted after him.

Bailey knew he wasn't talking about cats.

Bailey had barely got as far as Rockingham when his phone buzzed. "Bailey," he said economically, putting it on speakerphone.

"Sorry, Boss," said Evan. "Better turn the car around. They're sending him on to St John of God Hospital at Murdoch. And,He's comatose so they can't ask him what drugs he took, and they need toxicology to narrow it down. He has a slow arrhythmia that depressed his myocardial function."

"In English!"

"He has a slow, uneven heartbeat. Most overdoses are from methamphetamines which speed up the heart and disrupt the brain. Make patients disinclined to co-operate if they're conscious. But Liam's case is likely caused by calcium channel-blockers and is much harder to treat. Beta-blockers are the main suspects, but it can also be caused by a massive overdose of local anaesthetics or cocaine."

Bailey was glad they had a nerd on the team. Diversity. They weren't wrong about that being helpful. "Assuming he didn't take the drugs himself, I can't imagine anyone's going to fritter away their precious cocaine to make a point."

"Exactly. Anyway, if you turn around now, you should get to the ER about the same time he arrives in the ambulance."

"Any chance he'll be conscious?"

"None, from what the Doctor at Peel Health Campus said. Not to mention he's intubated."

"I won't waste my time then. You better inform his parents?"

"Will do."

Bailey drove on to the next exit, then headed back the way he'd come. He turned the radio to 96fm and listened to Diane Krall croon smooth jazz while thinking about his Dad's legacy— the old Camaro. It had been worth every penny he'd spent restoring it, although he rarely got to enjoy driving it without interruption. He'd installed new speakers and the sound was great. Something about cruising along a highway seemed to release endorphins like those he got at the gym. No answer when he pressed Palfrey's number. With the petrol gauge nearing empty, he swung into the next gas station to fill up, buying an ice-cream to savour in the afternoon sun. May had been a strange month weather-wise, without much of the normal pre-winter rain. An Indian summer. Why did they call it that? Something he'd have to google.

He watched a small flock of pink and grey galahs settle in the grove of golden acacia trees that separated the service station from the Kwinana freeway. They began to decimate the malformations on the branches. called galls, which contained insect hives. Leaf buds scattered in all directions. A white Cockatoo called to them from a ghost gum tree. He felt strongly in the moment, but at the same time nostalgic for an Australia that no longer existed. Or if it did, not in his neighbourhood. His life was rife with suspicion, gore and murder.

When he retired, perhaps he'd move to the country. Buy a bungalow in the middle of a few acres. Plant trees, watch birds and become a recluse. Become a twitcher? Wouldn't that give the squad something to talk about. Detecting birds instead of perps. Twenty plus years to wait. Would his investments in the stock market allow him to retire earlier? He couldn't see himself persevering until he was 67. And if they took him away from frontline duties because of his age, he didn't want to retire to desk duties either. With superannuation, even a cop could retire as a millionaire these days—which just goes to show that you had to be a multi-millionaire to be worth anything.

The ice-cream seemed to be turning him maudlin, so he threw the rest in a bin, and slid back into the car. This time Palfrey answered after the third ring.

"What's happening?" Palfrey coughed.

"Liam's been transferred to Murdoch in no state to interview so I'm on my way back. What's up with you?"

"The girls are home. There was a 50% off, sunday sale. They rushed home with a dozen shopping bags, tipped everything onto the sofa, and now there's a pink explosion. Why do girls think they have to wear pink?"

"You wore a pink shirt to my last barbeque!"

"I didn't buy it."

"You could tell Diane you don't like pink."

"You think? I can see why you're divorced." He paused and coughed some more. "Anyway, I could barely hear the mobile for all the screaming and now they're modelling new outfits. Diane thought a little retail therapy might cheer Jazz up and give her something else to think about. Apparently one size fits all, so Tracy's trying things on too even though she's a good head taller."

Bailey thought that fourteen-year-olds were more resilient than most people expected. Good for Diane.

Palfrey had a paroxysm of coughing then said, "I was just going to escape and drive out to the registered address of Hoodie′s car. It's in South Fremantle. Wanna meet me there?"

"Text me where to go."

"What shall I tell Tracy?"

"Just say Liam is still unconscious—but being well looked after, and his parents are on their way. No need to say he's being transferred closer to home. I don't want her jumping in a taxi and rushing to his bedside. She's safer at your place."

Bailey waited for the text to arrive then dialled the address into his GPS. It looked like it would be one of the old worker cottages that rented for far more than it was worth. Since South Fremantle had gone from down-and-out to up-and-trendy, prices had exploded. Half an hour to get there.

The radio station morphed from jazz to hip hop, so he turned it off to better hear the twin exhausts as he accelerated away. The V8 engine was music to his ears. It brought back happy memories from his childhood—plus a few memories of his parents′ arguments. His highly-strung mother complained about how unsuitable a two-door coupe was for a family. She often ripped into his father about that, but for once his father was undeterred. "It's a classic, love, same as you," he'd say, giving her a hug or a smooch, always adding, "can't beat a classic."

It had come to this. His idea of a great Sunday was to drive his Dad's old car, listen to jazz and ruminate on the past or dream of the future. All the same, his mind was automatically tracking leads in two cases. One strictly official and one, off limits. He had to admit, that right now he wouldn't change a thing. It was exactly where he chose to be.

Chapter 19

The red Mini was parked in a narrow street of worker cottages. These were built in the early 1900s and over the years they had been haphazardly modified, extended or run-down. The path to the front door of the registered address was overgrown with weeds. The only sign of habitation was a faded BMX bike thrown into the dandelions that constituted the pocket-handkerchief front garden. Would Hoodie be there?

Bailey saw Palfrey's SUV halfway down the street. Its nose was apparently saving a parking space for him while its rear blocked a driveway. Palfrey stuck his hand out of the window, signalling him to wait, then backed up. He then turned off the ignition and slapped a *Police Business* notice onto his dash. This usually kept complaints to a minimum. He and Bailey knew from bitter experience what would happen if the same notice was displayed through the Camaro windscreen. Someone would kick in a side panel or scrape the car with a key. As far as Joe Public was concerned, the police had no right to drive a decent car and if they did, they could pay.

"Thanks," Bailey said as he met up with his partner on the pavement.

"What now?" Palfrey asked.

"Got a name from the DOT?"

"Yeah – site said the car belongs to a Fred Butcher."

"Not keen on the surname."

"The right-hand tail-light's broken." Non sequiturs being Palfrey′s usual currency.

"Might be an opening. There's no guarantee the car belongs to Hoodie, but we know what he looks like now, so we'll soon see."

They strolled down the street, body language relaxed. Bailey felt his partner always aced this part of an unannounced interview. He was overweight and not a natural athlete. Slow and casual described his body to a T. It came nowhere close to describing his mind or the ability to think outside the box. Suspects were taken unawares. Palfrey personified everything they thought about *the Pigs*. Slow and stupid. Only he wasn't.

The two front windows of the cottage were covered by what had obviously been satin sheets. Although black, they were stained with something Bailey didn't want to think about.

Palfrey gave an exaggerated shiver. "Makes me want to wear gloves to ring the front doorbell."

"There is no doorbell."

Palfrey pounded on the door then he stepped behind Bailey.

"Thanks a lot!" said Bailey.

They waited. Then Bailey pounded. They heard footsteps and the door opened to the same face Bailey had seen on Tracy's video: Broken nose, shoulder length hair, bloodshot-blue eyes. Knowing the eye colour was new.

"What?" Hoodie said.

"Are you Fred Butcher, the owner of the red Mini outside? The one with the broken taillight?"

"What's it to you?"

Bailey produced his ID. "Yes or no?"

"No."

"Could we have your details. Name and address?"

"There's absolutely no need to tell you that, since I´m only visiting."

"Where's Mr Butcher?"

"No idea!"

"Not co-operating with a police investigation is an offence."

"Bullshit."

Bailey nodded to Palfrey, who mumbled, "It is a requirement to give the police your personal details when asked, and it is an offence not to do so. Your personal details include your full name, date of birth, current address, and the address where you usually live. If the police believe your details are false, you can be requested to produce evidence of your identity."

"All this for a broken taillight? You're fucking kidding me." He began to shut the door. Bailey stuck his foot between the door and jam.

"Name and address," he said.

"John Smith. Salvation Army hostel."

"In another life. Try again," said Bailey, straightening up to his full 1.9metres in order to look his most menacing. "The correct name, ID and details NOW."

As Bailey spoke to Hoodie, Palfrey drifted down the side of the house to cover the back door. Hoodie turned as if to go back down the passage, then barrelled past Bailey, grabbed the bike and, one leg thrown over the seat thrashing around to finally find the other pedal, was out the gate heading the wrong way down the one-way street.

"Bugger!" said Bailey, running after him. "Palfrey!" he yelled.

Palfrey charged to the street and ran for his car, jumping in and reversing to the crossroad. With a quick look, wheels squealing, a neat 3point turn allowed him to accelerate past Bailey.

Hoodie, with local knowledge of South Fremantle's layout, turned left and left again cycling down one-way-streets. The neighbourhood was a maze that defeated many a visitor to the area. Palfrey paused briefly to slam a blue light on the roof and set off the siren to warn oncoming vehicles, but then with unexpected athleticism, Hoodie jumped the bike over a front fence and pedalled past a surprised homeowner who was out watering his roses.

"Gone," puffed Bailey when he caught up. "I'll head back to the house and see what, or who, I can find."

"See you there," Palfrey agreed.

The front door was still open. It looked onto a warped linoleum lined passage, a door off both sides. "No consent to enter," warned Palfrey.

"Person of interest fled the scene. Someone inside might need help."

"Anyone there?" called Palfrey. There was no answer. "Police! We're coming in to render assistance."

"Render?" queried Bailey.

"Just popped out of my mouth."

They entered, knocking on the doors to what turned out to be bedrooms. The first, on the left, opened to display charity-shop scuffed furniture and a single bed with a Micky Mouse bedspread thrown over the top. A child's bedroom. There was an old-style, cathode ray television on a low stool, and a soccer ball, a small pair of sandshoes stuffed with dirty socks and a poster of the movie *Frozen* taped to the wall. In the corner a crumpled striped football jumper was tossed over a pink tutu.

"Two kids, sharing the room?"

"Only one pillow. Could be a girl or a boy. Maybe a bit of both. These days they can't make up their minds."

Bailey frowned at him.

"What? Tonto never speaks with forked tongue."

"Tonto means crazy in Spanish."

"The Lone Ranger didn't know that."

They opened the door to the opposing bedroom. Again, there was nothing much to see just an empty water glass on the cardboard box that made do as a bedside table. The bed was two double mattresses, one over the other. The striped cotton cover was rumpled and thrown to one side. No shelves or drawers to search, not that they were able to under the law. They could only observe what was out on display, and even that would be questioned if their entry ever made it to court. A chair stood in for a wardrobe and was festooned with a pile of T-shirts, jeans and trackpants some of which had spilled onto the floor. A rag rug of the type Bailey's grandmother used to make covered part of the same scabby linoleum. There was an unplugged two-bar electric radiator in the corner. Winter was coming.

Palfrey sniffed. "A lot of Mary Jane has been smoked here."

"No butts in an ashtray though. Can't take a smell to court."

"No women's apparel."

"Apparel?" said Bailey.

"Diane makes me play scrabble with the girls."

"Ah. That explains it."

"Take the water glass for prints?"

"Tempting, but illegal." They reluctantly left it where it was.

Moving on to the back of the house they found a kitchen-diner-lounge displaying similar sad furniture. Calling it second hand would be extravagant. All the same, the room was semi clean. Someone had swept the floor and washed the dishes that were draining by the sink. The only surprise was the 55inch flat screen TV.

"Expensive," said Bailey who had recently priced one.

"Probably got it from Stinky Bill for services rendered."

Bailey looked at him and nodded, "Could well be! See any serial numbers?"

"On the back. No can touch."

Bailey stumbled, his shoulder catching the edge of the TV and turning it on its wall mount. "Hmm – perhaps I should take a photo back and front to prove I didn't damage it."

"Maybe put it back to how it was afterwards. It's the right thing to do. We don't want to cause the occupant undue stress."

There were no pictures on the wall, and no notes on the kitchen counter. These days people used their cell phones for their secrets and didn't have a landline. In a few years pens and pencils would be redundant. There was no computer and no marijuana butts in the scrupulously clean ashtrays.

"Doesn't smoke in front of the kid..." was Palfrey's take on it, "even scumbags can be OK fathers."

"You reckon? Then where *is* the kid?"

"Mother has custody of a weekend?"

It was as good a guess as any.

They walked out of the sliding glass door to the back yard. A fibro bathroom and toilet unit had been tacked on at some stage. The door was open and the ablution block was empty aside from a battered scuba tank hanging next to a neoprene wetsuit, fins and mask. No washing machine or Hills Hoist were evident, which generally meant the occupants used a laundromat. The wooden back fence had a gate that led onto a lane. Up until the 1950s, horse-drawn wagons had used the lane once a week to empty the toilet pans of the outdoor dunnies.

"He'll come back this way," said Bailey.

"No point stayin'. Could be gone a while. We'll get him eventually. Wanna head home?"

"Might as well." They locked the sliding door and let themselves out the front, making sure to latch the lock. "—sorry to foist Tracy on you, mate."

"She's actually a lot less trouble than Jazz and Fiona. Lightens the atmosphere."

"Good to hear. I'm going to stop for a beer. Join me?"

"Nah. Gotta show willing and get home to the trouble and strife."

"Ok. See you tomorrow."

The lobby bar at the Rendezvous Hotel was quiet, with just the one elderly couple drinking coffee, their service dog at their feet. It was a black Lab like Shooter, and its mournful look seemed to say, *Save me.* Bailey gave it a sad shake of his head. The barman suggested the bar and band, poolside, was a better bet. Tossing up between sitting alone in air-conditioning and listening to live music was an easy decision. Music won hands down.

Most of the tables and chairs around the pool were occupied, so he sat at the bar and ordered a light beer. The band was just finishing their set. The woman singer was pretty good, but not as good as Annabelle Miller had been. The mother of a murder victim, before losing her daughter she'd belted out cover songs with her own special verve. Later she'd left to sing on European river boats. Bailey thought it gutsy to reinvent her life after losing her only child. Most parents of victims were so destroyed it was like the murderer had killed them as well.

A hand touched his shoulder and he turned to see Greta Meer, consul to the Netherlands. Her diaphanous linen shift covered a yellow bikini that matched her bright blonde hair. Damp from a recent swim, the hair was held back with a tortoiseshell band. Wow. She looked more like a model than a civil servant. She was only a centimetre or two shorter than him. He'd read that the tallest people in the world came from the Netherlands. The tallest women, however, came from the Ukraine. Why trivia like this stuck in his mind he had no clue. He'd always remembered miscellaneous stuff.

Greta's husky voice interrupted his thoughts. "Detective Bailey, I didn't expect to see you here."

"JB. I'm JB when I'm off duty." He shook her hand. "Good to see you again. I didn't pick the Rendezvous as one of your haunts."

She smiled, showing off her perfect teeth. Expensive dentistry. It certainly added to her outstanding looks. "Some friends from home are staying here. They invited me to meet up by the pool for a swim and have now gone off to change and meet some distant family members for dinner. I begged off and was just on my way home when I saw you."

"Buy you a drink?" asked Bailey.

"Sure," she said. "I'd love a mojito."

Bailey gave the order to the barman along with another light beer for himself and asked for the bar's menu. He hadn't eaten all day.

"Sorry mate – the outdoor kitchen closed at 4 o'clock. The hotel tries to minimise paying double time to kitchen staff on a Sunday. We have packets of chips and nuts. Or if you want to be fancy, a tin of olives."

Greta said, "Olives—I don´t mind fancy."

Bailey didn't consider himself to be at all fancy. Just a regular guy with an irregular job. One that was difficult to share with civilians. "Let´s have a packet of each, I´m starving."

Greta waved her arm towards the pool. "I've still got a table over there with our wet towels on it." They made their way over to it, skirting patrons' bare feet and shucked flip flops.

"Looks like you're a keen swimmer. Does that make you a Pisces?" asked Bailey, searching for an opening gambit. He really needed more practice with topics not based on blood-drenched murder cases.

"Good try, but I'm a Scorpio."

"Ah – here it comes, the sting in the tail."

"We are honest, brave, loyal…"

"—ambitious, secretive and resentful!" added Bailey.

"You got me," she laughed. "How do you know so much about Scorpios."

"My ex-wife is a Scorpio."

"Ouch!" She laughed. "Maybe it's time to give Scorpios another chance."

"I'm nothing if not flexible," which as far as he knew was a total lie.

The band came back and played their last set. Cat Stephens, the music far too loud to allow much in the way of conversation. They sipped their drinks, smiled and kept eye contact. "Since there's no food here, I thought of going to The Wild Fig for dinner," said Bailey when he was able. "Would you like to join me?"

"It closes early on a Sunday," said Greta, "and I'm hardly dressed to go out!"

"Well, my place is just down the road. I have a fancy, all singing and dancing bar-b-que—and a pool. I can offer barbequed lamb chops or a mean pasta dish with home-made sauce. Not mine. One of my colleagues, Tony Caravelli, makes it. His family comes from Sicily and they get together once a year to make a huge batch from their backyard vegetable patch. I can't run to a Mojito, but I have a pretty decent red, or an average white?"

"A Pinot Grigio?" she guessed.

Bailey gave a shamefaced grin. "I don't drink white and just buy what's on special."

"Pasta and a good red wine sound perfect. Plus, I'd love another swim. I can't believe how hot it is for May. Climate change. Or are you a global warming denier? Don't say you are!" She touched him on his shoulder and didn't give him a chance to respond. "Give me your address and I'll punch it into my GPS."

As Sunday nights go, this one was shaping up better than expected.

Chapter 20

Bailey was beating half a dozen eggs for breakfast but looked up to smile at Greta. She sat, slumped at the table and rubbing sleepy, mascara-smeared eyes. His blue cambric shirt looked good on her. It was 6 a.m. and she'd complained rather grumpily when he'd left the bed, telling her that on a Monday morning duty called early.

"Would you like some herbs with your omelette?" Bailey asked, indicating the vertical herb garden that Sara had given him before she left for Singapore.

"Sure – I didn't take you for a greenie. Whatever you think would be good"

"It was a gift, hydroponic so it doesn't take much care. Chives and parsley with cheddar?"

"Sounds amazing. There's nothing sexier than a man who can cook."

The night had given him another occasion to bless Sara. She'd begged him to get rid of his old futon and replace it with a decent bed and mattress. Greta's enthusiastic athleticism certainly warranted a sturdy bed and a mattress with inner springs.

Greta's thoughts were elsewhere. "—and a pink shirt. I love a man who's secure enough in his masculinity to wear a pink shirt."

He thought of Palfrey. What was it with women and pink? Was it some sort of a test? Wear pink to show your complete devotion? He didn't much like the thought and said, "I come up short in that department. No pink shirts in my cupboard."

"I'll buy you one!"

"Trying to make me over? I am only moderately biddable."

She laughed, "So far I like you how you are. You're honest, a very attractive trait."

"In women too. Takes out a lot of the guesswork!"

"You're a bit of an enigma though. You don't share many of your private thoughts."

"That's why they're private!"

They'd had a good evening. Eating, lolling about in Bailey's pool sporadically rejecting Shooters attempts to join them while they got to know each other. Their political alliances. What it was like living in the Netherlands. Why Greta had moved to Australia. Sport—she followed golf; he followed the AFL (out of no particular interest but so he could bond with colleagues over a beer in the pub). They told deprecating stories about themselves, trying to outdo each other. Bailey had forgotten how easy it could be with the right person. Being over fifteen years younger, Sara had brought a youthful exuberance to their relationship, but they hadn't shared the same memories or aspirations. Sara had yet to launch herself into the grownup world outside tertiary education. Bailey was stuck, midway through his professional journey. Sometimes he felt Sara was psychoanalysing him for a chapter in her thesis. Would a senior policeman have more insight into behaviour than anyone else? Perhaps he'd been as much subject as boyfriend. Sara however, had said straight out what she wanted and expected from him, which was a relief after his tortuous marriage. He'd loved that about her.

"Tell me one private thing about you."

"I'm allergic to nuts, so if you ever cook for me, that's my weakness."

"Well, my secret is that I don't cook. I don't want to, rather than can't. I pretty well live on *stamppot,* which is mashed potato with any vegies that happen to be in my fridge thrown in." She looked around. "Is there coffee? And it better be full strength." Bailey picked up a dented coffee percolator from the cooktop and poured her a large mug. "What no expresso machine?" Greta said, sniffing it and taking an approving sip.

"If I were a greenie, I wouldn't believe in aluminium capsules and landfill."

She nodded, "regardless, you're a Capricorn so we should get on all right."

"You do realise astrology isn't really my thing. It was a desperate opening line."

"I know. All the same…"

Bailey's cell chirped. It was Palfrey.

"Tracy had a text from Liam's parents. He's conscious so we should head over to the hospital and find out what happened to him. Visiting hours for non-family members are from 3 to 8 p.m so Tracy & Fiona are going to head over there when Fiona knocks off work. Diane said she'd drive them. But we can interview him from 8.30 a.m after he's had breakfast and the specialist has done his morning rounds."

"OK. While we do that, since the photo on Butcher's licence matches the guy we saw, and Tracy′s video corresponds to the ATM video with Stinky Bill, Tony and Pamela can go out first thing, to intercept and interview him."

"Theirs is a combustible partnership!"

"Well, the team have got to learn to work together. And lately those two have been complaining that I don't give them enough latitude to work independently."

"You going to suggest they ask a few local uniforms to watch the back exit?"

"Does that sound like micro-managing to you?"

There was a pause, while Palfrey considered this. "See you at the hospital," he said.

That's the problem with being DSS, Bailey thought as he hung up, how much latitude is enough and how much is too much? Perhaps he'd mention the back exit and leave it to them to show their initiative. The two had plenty of experience. On the other hand, he didn't want a fuck-up. He sighed. Cutting the omelette in half, and trying to be in the moment, he flipped it onto two plates. "I'll put on another pot of coffee."

St John of God Murdoch Hospital was one of the leading private health campuses in Western Australia and a major healthcare hub serving the southern region. With room service and three cafes, it followed the modern model of healthcare, offering a hotel-like ambience. Liam however, was in a shared room. Like Liam, the other occupant was connected to several monitoring devices. Unlike Liam his head was bandaged and he was strapped to the bed.

The swarthy male nurse with the five o'clock shadow who had accompanied Bailey and JB indicated the other man and said, "He was brought in around 3 a.m. Are you here to interview him about the attack?

"What attack?" asked Bailey.

"Northbridge again. We're sick of seeing the mayhem. More and more people attacked after attending nightclubs there. We get the overflow when the closest emergency rooms are overwhelmed. It's time you guys sorted it!"

When did nurses start to resemble Greek wrestlers, Bailey wondered? "Tell that to the politicians. We need more feet on the ground and much more funding."

"This fellow took a king hit, plus he was chock-full of amphetamines."

"It's not our case. We're here to interview Liam, so if we could have some privacy?"

The nurse gave him a hard look. "I'll be back in five minutes."

Liam squinted at them. He appeared dazed and rubbed the hand that wasn't connected to an IV over his face.

"I'm Jazz and Fiona's grandfather," said Palfrey. "D'you feel up to telling us what happened to you?"

"I'm not… It's hard to say. Lying here trying to work out… I dropped Fiona home. Then I went back to check more clubs. Super hero, Liam… not sure what happened next."
Liam´s voice was slurred and his eyes unfocussed. "Anyway, I went to the Axial. Been there before. They had my fingerprints so I skipped the line. No need to scan my ID. Busy. Crowded." He stopped, closed his eyes and swallowed. "Water?"

Bailey held the glass under his chin and helped slip the straw into his mouth. After a few sips, Liam's head fell back on his pillow. He rested a while and gathered his thoughts.

"I got a Coke. Wandered around. It seemed a lot harder without Tracy." Bailey helped him to another sip of water. "The place was packed. I asked one of the bouncers about the tattoo and talked to a bunch of other guys. Someone handed me another Coke – and really, that's all I remember. Guess they slipped me a Mickey Finn." He moved restlessly in the bed. "Mum said I could've died. She was pretty upset."

Palfrey nodded. "Do tell," he said succinctly. "Anything else?"

"How'd I end up here?"

Palfrey took him through it and asked if he could remember anything else. Liam slowly shook his head as if the movement was the most painful thing he'd ever experienced.

"Sorry."

Palfrey exchanged a look with Bailey. "Wanna head to the Axial? Check out their CCTV?"

Bailey shrugged "It's too early. Maybe later."

Palfrey patted Liam's hand. "Hang in there," he said. "The doc says you'll be fine."

Liam gave them a thumbs up.

Palfrey and Bailey were heading out the door when the stroppy nurse returned. "I hope you haven't upset my patient," he said.

Bailey leaned closer to read his name tag. "Certainly not…Mr Spagos. Wouldn't dream of it."

"The last thing on our mind," added Palfrey.

They walked down the passage breathing in the smell of disinfectant and body fluids.

"Race you to the car. Last one there buys lunch." said Palfrey.

"I don't feel like lunch!"

"All the better."

As it turned out, before heading to South Fremantle, Pamela had bumped into Bob Hunter. The newest member of the Homicide Squad, he was making his way to SCS—the Special Crime Squad investigating missing persons and cold cases—to do a profile. The squad had said the likelihood of the profile leading to a solve was remote and showed their desperation. Hunter was more than keen to postpone that job and get out in the field.

The way Pamela told it to Bailey, Bob had waited at the back exit to Hoodie's house and when, as expected, Hoodie had done another bunk and shot out of the gate, Hunter tackled and cuffed him. Tony and Pamela arrived to find Bob standing back without a crease or a smudge of dirt on him. "How does he do it?" asked Pamela, who was no slouch in sartorial elegance herself.

Bailey laughed. "Good to know he can handle himself, anyway."

"—and then some! Butcher's in the interview room cooling his heels. Want us to take it from here?"

Bailey would have preferred to do the interview himself, but after the successful collar they should get the opportunity. His and Palfrey's investigation of Jazz's rape, and now Liam's enforced overdose, was interfering with what should have been their focus. He hoped Pamela and Tony would be able to discover what Hoodie had been up to with Stinky Bill. Would the bet pay dividends?

"The serial number you sent from his TV matched a stolen set," said Pamela. "We're getting a warrant to search, and discover it all over again. Legally. Evan's on the job."

Bailey grinned. Why did he underestimate his team? They were brilliant—especially with Pamela's overarching ambition on display.

"I'll watch from the observation room," he said. Was this the breakthrough they needed to find who had killed Hannah and left Matey's future torn in the hands of the court? With two entities fighting for custody, his choice veered towards a third. The more deserving parent would be the foster-mother, Norma. Not a blood relative, but someone who would always put Matey's needs first.

Pamela lent forward towards Butcher, her shirt pulled tight against well-endowed breasts. Did she do it on purpose? wondered Bailey, watching through the one-way mirror. It was certainly drawing the POI's eyes lower. Interesting that Tony, with more years under his belt, was allowing Pamela to conduct the interview. He was sitting with his chair tilted back against the wall. Lids lowered over sharp eyes to give the impression of boredom.

"—and your name is Frederick Butcher, currently residing in Strang St, South Fremantle?"

"Fred."

Pamela nodded. "Well, here's a to do, Fred. My colleagues came to ask you some simple questions and you bolted. They identified themselves as policemen but you pushed one of them out of the way. That's assault. What was that about?"

"No comment."

"I see you refused the presence of the legal aid solicitor."

"Useless bunch of cretins. Heard they were telecommuting these days. Can just imagine the two or three minutes they'd give to my ridiculous case."

Pamela opened a manila file that she'd hastily stuffed with pages of small print torn from an outdated file. "You do seem to have been through the wringer. Three convictions in the past ten years for B&E. Theft. Assault. GBH. Dealing."

Bailey smiled. Scrolling down a tablet in front of a suspect didn't have the same effect as thumbing through sheets of past misdeeds. Well done, Pamela. A good start.

"Poor lawyering." Butcher tried a smile in her direction. "Those hyenas who represented me never did me any good. One of them even breached a client's confidence—mine—to speak to the prosecutor about me. Got me an extra 10 months. I was a lad led astray and could´ve done with some help. There´s not a thing on me for the past few years. You have to understand that bad company and a lack of maturity played its part."

Pamela suppressed a shudder at his nicotine-stained teeth and general lack of dental hygiene and smiled back. He was a surprisingly coherent suspect. His choice of words clashed with his air of disorder. Butcher was both more and less than he seemed on paper. He spoke like an educated man but had the usual chip on his shoulder that all perps displayed.

“What do you do for a quid now you’re clean then, Fred? I don’t see any mention of a job in here.” She riffled through the pages as if they had everything else on him.

“A bit of this and that.”

“Specifically?”

“Home repairs. Removals. Stuff like that.”

Bailey thought the removals would likely be Butcher removing goods from houses he’d broken into, in order to take the goods straight to the pawn shop. He tried to envisage the slight man in the interview room lifting a sofa. Failed.

“You don’t look all that strong to me,” said Pamela. “That must be hard work. How’s your back coping,” idly riffling through the file again.

“Yes – well. I’m on compo plus the single parent’s benefit at the moment. Can’t work. My back’s stuffed. There´s no money to replace the Mini’s tail light. Arresting me for that is a bit over the top, isn’t it?”

“Assaulting a police officer…” Pamela began.

Tony tipped his chair forward with a thud. “Where were you on May 13th?”

“Wha ? How the fuck would I know?”

Palfrey entered the observation room and lent on Bailey’s shoulder. His breath smelled of the peppermint gum he’d taken to chewing ever since Jazz had been raped. Said it calmed his nerves but it was actually to stop Diane realising that he was back smoking again. “How’s it going?

“Good cop. Bad cop. Tony’s the bad cop.”

“No kidding. I would have put money on Pamela being the bad cop. Guess now she doesn’t have anyone higher up the ladder to massage her career, she’s on turbocharge.”

“Can’t imagine either of them will be getting close to Ms Odell.”

That was true. Pamela’s liaison with the homicide squad′s previous chief had bitten the dust with his unforeseen cancer diagnosis and his equally quick return to his wife and home comforts. The new boss, Marcia Odell, was a woman and since Tony was gay…

“Say no more,” said Palfrey – who usually had plenty more to say. “There’s a woman with a kid in tow downstairs in reception wanting to see you. Good looking in a beat-up sort of a way. Wouldn’t give her name, but says it’s about Hannah de Graaf. I showed her into one of the free interview rooms and gave her a cuppa tea. She wouldn’t talk to anyone but you.”

“Stay here and give me an update?” He didn’t wait for Palfrey to reply.

The woman downstairs was around mid-thirties with dishwater blond hair scraped back into a ponytail. Her finely sculptured face wouldn’t have disgraced a fashion model were it not for the bruise on her left cheekbone. She’d applied makeup but the blue still shone through. She had a child, who Bailey estimated to be around two years old, on her knee. He had a dummy in his mouth and the edges of his nappy showed underneath his tiny denim shorts. Bailey didn't approve of dummies. Or nappies for toddlers once they were walking, however he also didn't approve of screaming children so the dummy seemed a reasonable trade-off. Mind you, the kid seemed pretty relaxed, unlike his mother who hadn't stopped fidgeting.

"Detective Bailey," he introduced himself, "I'm the senior investigating officer of Hannah de Graaf's murder. You wanted to see me?" She nodded her head.

"—and you would be…?"

"Just call me Brianna, Bree." Her voice was soft and breathy. The child looked up at her, green eyes bright and knowing. Satisfying himself she was all right, he made a move to get down from the comfort of her lap. Whether she'd been comforting him, or he comforting her was hard to decide. The boy slipped to the floor and trotted over to Bailey.

Good coordination, thought Bailey. "Your son? What´s his name?" he asked. Mostly informants needed to be gentled along before they came to the point of the visit.

"Peter," she said, short and to the point.

The boy lifted his arms to Bailey, asking for a lift onto his knee. Bailey complied, settling him on one leg and jigging him up and down. The child leant towards him and sniffed, then settled against his chest. Bailey raised his eyebrows at the woman before him.

"You smell safe," she explained. "No odour of alcohol or gunja."

Bailey was sad for them both. No need for further explanation. He knew what sort of life they lived. One constantly on the edge, with a partner whose temper would be set off by the slightest infraction. A partner who drank and smoked marijuana and probably took amphetamines and God knows what else. It was all too common.

"The boy. Hannah's son. Bram. Is he OK?" Brianna's eyes were cactus green.

"Yes, he's fine. At the moment he's with a foster family until the family court sorts out custody. How do you know him?"

"I don't. Just followed the story on TV. Made me think about Peter. What if anything happened to me."

Bailey thought the chance of something happening to her was above average. One woman was murdered each week by her partner or former partner. Forty percent of women who'd experienced domestic violence continued to be harassed even when separated. The statistics were appalling.

"You have some information for me?" His voice gentle.

"Saw you on the news. One of the journalists said you'd used your own T-shirt to use as a nappy for Bram when you found him. I liked that. Didn't expect it from a policeman." Her eyes teared for a moment. She took a deep breath. "I heard Fred was here. Word gets out." She sniffed and wiped the mark on her cheek. "I was in a relationship with him for a while until we had Peter." She raised her chin toward the toddler, who had nodded off. The dummy had scraped out of his mouth when he leant against Bailey's shirt and he was now leaving a long spool of drool to mark his acceptance. Bailey had stopped his jiggling. "Fred still visits. Sometimes he brags about what he's been up to." She looked around the room. "Are you recording this?"

"No, I would have to advise you and ask your permission before we did that. Would you consent to being recorded?"

She shook her head. "No! I can't be identified as a…" she paused while she thought of the word, "—source. If my name is in any record, I'm bound to end up dead with a heroin overdose injected between my toes. They'd make it look like an accident." Bailey must have shown his surprise, because she added, "I'm a sex worker. I know all about drugs and convenient suicides. I stopped using when I fell pregnant and I haven't relapsed once, although it's a hard life, being a single mother." They were silent for a long moment.

Bailey knew that addiction recovery statistics were low. The fact Bree had done it while looking after a child showed considerable mental strength. All the same, relapse rates were between forty to sixty percent. For Peter′s sake, he hoped she would be one of those in the forty percent success rate.

He worried about scaring her off. The case was barely staggering along and her information might be crucial. "I promise your name won't be revealed. We have anonymous tips all the time. Lots of tipsters phone Crimestoppers from a phone box, or make a report online." Why hadn't she done that? If she'd looked, she would have seen that the site explained how it protected the source of any information in great detail. It used Tor, an extremely sophisticated VPN, or virtual private network. With Tor the signal was routed through a series of randomly selected global nodes and encrypted multiple times so the IP address was never known. All information generated an 'action' in the computerised case management system called VIPER.

All the same, there was always the human factor. He hoped he could keep his promise to her and superstitiously crossed his fingers. Promises often brought bad luck and soured the chance of convictions.

"Fred's pretty mouthy. He went to Scotch College and has wealthy parents. After high school he couldn't go on to university because he was already using and getting into all sorts of trouble. His parents eventually threw him out and disowned him. After that he went downhill. Married young. Had a daughter. The wife took off and left the kid with him." She touched her cheek. "I can understand why."

Bailey nodded. He kept silent in case any wrong word stopped the flow. An informant could be talking up a storm and suddenly the whole atmosphere would change and they bolted out of the interview room without a backward glance. Mind you, with the toddler on his knee, Brianna had limited options.

"When I first met him—he was a regular client—I felt sorry for him. Should've known better!" She looked around again, up at the cornices as if to spot any recording device. Eventually she said flatly, "He did it. He killed her. Hannah."

Bailey nodded, "Go on."

"He came to see me for sex. I told him since we're not an item anymore he'd have to pay. After all, he wasn't giving me maintenance for Peter." She pushed her sleeves up and Bailey saw that her arms were a story in themselves. Names. Places. Birds. Rainbows. Dolphins. All tattooed on her arms with barely a centimetre space between them. She touched one of the black oblongs, things blanked out that now only remained as dark memories. Bailey assumed it had formally said *Fred.* "He told me to never say no to him again. He'd killed women for less."

"Women? Plural? More than one woman?"

"I know what plural means!"

Bailey cursed himself for his occasional slip in gender politics. Gender misconceptions were a minefield. Just because Brianna was a sex worker didn't mean she wasn't intelligent, or educated. He nodded again. Not sure how he could apologise and keep her on track.

"I kind of mocked him. Yeah, yeah sort of thing. He hit me and then asked if I'd seen the news about the kid you found walking down the highway. Same age as Peter, he reminded me." She looked over at Peter who had stirred at the sound of his name, then settled back into Bailey's chest with a sigh. "*I killed the boy's mother*, he said. He could see I didn't believe him." She stopped. Looked at her son, so comfortable on a policeman's lap, and then looked at the door.

"Did he say why or how?" Bailey asked. Plenty of men kept their women in check with lies. He knew that the 'how' of Hannah's death had mainly been televised, but the why might help them close a case. Motive. Sometimes they never knew what the motive was, but if they did it certainly helped to get a guilty result in court.

"He'd been told she had diamonds from Amsterdam. He was searching the apartment when she came back with a drink from the reception vending machine. He threatened her, but she said she'd swallowed the diamonds to keep them safe. That's what all the stabbing was about."

Bailey swallowed. "He was trying to get the diamonds from her stomach or intestines?"

"That's what he said. He was high on ice. A fence asked him to get the diamonds. I assumed it was *Hard Pawn* out at Burswood. They have an arrangement from way back. Thieving to order."

So it was Stinky Bill and Fred Butcher. The bastards. Bailey took a mental step back, "and the other woman or women he killed? Did he say anything about them?"

"His ex. Said it was no coincidence she wasn't around asking for custody."

Chapter 21

The bright yellow Hyundai pulled up at St John of God´s hospital entrance. One of the things Tracy had learned about Palfrey's wife, Diane, is that she liked to lift the spirits of everyone around her. Whether it was the marigold colour of her car, or her ever-present welcoming hospitality, Diane strove to bring happiness with her. Tracy joined Fiona by the driver's side and Diane buzzed the window down to say "Jazz and I are having a pedicure if the salon can fit us in, and then we'll stop at the supermarket. Call me when you're ready to be picked up."

Fiona and Tracy nodded in unison. Yet another non-threatening activity to distract Jazz. She was slumped in the passenger seat, one hand holding onto the edge of Diane's cardigan as if to stop herself from floating away. She'd told Tracy the assault had made her feel smaller than she did before. The new haircut didn't help. Jazz had begged Fiona to buzz cut it. The memory of the man ejaculating onto the hair she'd delighted in growing since she was ten years old had been one that she couldn't stomach. Now her features appeared pinched and older than her years. Tracy supposed Jazz would always think of her life as *before the rape, or after.*

"You sure you don't want to come and visit Liam?"

"—and that would cheer him up, how? He's in hospital because of me."

There was no answer to that. For such a petite girl her voice was loud and angry, so they simply waved and said, "OK. See you later."

Despite an initial feeling of friction when Liam showed interest in Fiona, Tracy and Fiona got along well. Staying with Palfrey and Diane had cemented her friendship with the two girls. With three of them sharing a bedroom, Tracy had unsuccessfully tried for a pyjama party mood; but Jazz's life had changed forever and there was no point in pretending otherwise. Each night Jazz crawled into bed with Fiona and sobbed until she fell asleep. Fiona had, in turn, then slipped in with Tracy for comfort. Tracy wasn't one to show her emotions. She waited until both girls dozed off before her own tears fell. It was just so unfair. Jazz was a year younger than she was. Something in the world was broken when grown men preyed on children. Before she dozed off, a frisson of fear made her wonder if the men who raped Jazz would find them? Hurt them? She was glad she wasn't at home, alone.

There was a line waiting to consult the hospital receptionist. "Thanks again for making me feel welcome," Tracy said to Fiona as they queued for attention. "Jazz is my sister, but when I try to talk to her, I have no idea what to say. Your being there makes it seem more normal."

"Whatever normal is. How come you're staying with your grandparents anyway?"

"Mum's in a new relationship and says it's her turn to have a personal life and that it's Dad's turn to look after us. He works the midnight to dawn shift driving a taxi. Diane thought we shouldn't be on our own at night. Like that made any difference in the long run!" Fiona´s frown was becoming permanent, etching worry into what was previously a carefree face.

"I´m nearly always alone at night," Tracy said. "Mum sleeps through the day and stays out to party most nights." She was silent as she thought about their similar circumstances. Mothers seemed to be focussed on themselves these days. Fathers too. Good fathers were the ones who signed the monthly maintenance cheques. Better still if there was a monthly bank transfer. Bad fathers didn't even do that. She barely knew a school friend whose parents were still together or whose dad took an interest. One girl mentioned her father was teaching her to play golf. That was pretty cool. Tracy's father mostly remembered to pay maintenance. That was something. No wonder so many people associated love with money.

"You´re lucky you have Diane and Ian," she said at last.

Following the directions of the receptionist, they trailed a thickly-set man in green hospital scrubs along a corridor and into the lift.

"Third floor," they said as he pushed the button.

"Who are you lovely young ladies visiting," he asked, and when they replied, "Liam O'Neil" He said, "I'm just about to check his drip. You've come at a good time. The drugs are wearing off and he'll be able to talk sensibly to you." He gave them an admiring glance. "Sisters?" he asked.

"Hardly! Note the big difference in height, race and hair colour?"

"His sisters, I meant. No doubt you've heard of mixed families and hairdressers?"

Fiona laughed. "Who hasn't? Actually, I'm a hairdresser, and I can tell you Tracy is a natural redhead. No hairdresser had anything to do with that gorgeous colour."

Tracy wished Fiona hadn't said that. He′d be thinking she had red pubic hair. No doubt male nurses watched porn and imagined women naked like most men. She leant forward and read the nurse's nameplate, *Nick Spagos.*

"We're just good friends of Liam, Nick. How's he doing anyway?"

"Follow me and you'll find out."

Liam was sitting up in bed finishing off what looked like a healthy serving of Shepherd's Pie.
He smiled up at them and said, "the hospital has room service. I get to order whatever I want. It beats what I get at home—but don't tell Mum that!" The bed next

to him was newly made up and empty. He nodded at Nurse Spagos and said, “The cops came and took him away in a wheelchair.”

“Good,” said Spagos. “I didn’t sign up to work at a private hospital only to discover it was actually a de facto public one. There´s not nearly enough funding for the so-called Australian universal health system.”

Tracy realised how little she knew about politics. She should remedy that if she wanted to work for the police. She knew enough to realise that law and order was related to politics. She bent over to kiss Liam on his cheek while Fiona walked to the other side of the bed and took his hand.

Spagos smiled. “Look who’s in the pink now. The meat in a gorgeous sandwich.”

Tracy rolled her eyes. Mothers should teach their sons to relate to women without mentioning their appearance? The conversation should come up so frequently it became embedded in their DNA. “I thought you were going to check his drip,” she grumbled.

“All in good time.” Spagos made a show of increasing the flow of the drip. “Just finishing this one off and then I’ll give him a new one.” His sleeve had slipped back, showing an impressively muscled bicep.

“Interesting tattoo you have there.” Fiona’s eyes widened and her hand tightened on Liam’s.

Spagos turned to her and flexed his bicep. “My army tattoo?”

"Is that what it is? What battalion? My dad was in the army too."

"Wrong army, dear. I did a couple of tours with NATO in the Middle East, then immigrated here from Slovakia when my active duty was up. I trained as a medic."

"Oh – how old were you when you emigrated?"

"Too old for you, I expect. More′s the pity."

"Are there many Slovakian ex-army men here in Perth?"

"More than you'd think."

"So, do you have a club or something? My Dad's always off to the local RSL club."

"Not a club, but we do meet up at a pub for a beer now and then. Review the mistakes of the past. But I rarely go. The past should stay in the past."

"A bit like what they say about Las Vegas?"

"Exactly."

They smiled at each other.

Tracy interrupted this moment of unity. "Isn′t Spagos a Greek name."

"My father was Greek and my mother Slovakian."

"Your English is pretty good."

Spagos sighed. "Unlike Australians, most Europeans are polyglots. We speak a lot of different languages from an early age."

"I didn't know that," said Tracy.

Fiona chipped in. "Where do you ex-army guys go for that beer? Maybe I'll see you there one day." She flipped back her long hair. "Don't worry, I'm eighteen and I've got a ridgy didge ID. I can have a beer."

"Why not give me your phone number and I'll let you know when I'll be there."

Tracy chipped in. "Maybe I'll come too."

Spagos shook his head. "Two good looking girls having a beer with me? One who looks like she's underage. No thanks. That's a disaster waiting to happen. Although being seen with two gorgeous chicks would boost my street cred, someone would want to fight me. They think of women as the spoils of war."

Liam pushed his tray aside. "Hey! I'm the patient here. Talk to me! And by the way, Fiona, would you do me a favour and pick up the Mini. It´s still in the car park by the nightclub. You can use it until I get out of here. There´s a spare key taped under the right-hand front mudguard."

"Really? You´d trust me with your precious car?"

"Sure. Mum offered but she´s the worst driver in the world, and Dad´s too busy."

Tracy shrugged. Looks like Liam was transferring his affections to a more likely suspect. She couldn´t blame him really. Who wanted to date jail bait; and she wasn´t at all sure that she was ready to stop holding him off when she turned sixteen.

"You′re a star, Liam!" beamed Fiona.

He beamed back.

Spagos winked at Tracy. Game on.

Bailey walked Bree and her son to the street and asked if they'd like a lift home. "No way!" she shook her head vehemently, a haunted expression on her face. "I can't have anyone see me being dropped off in a strange car. The bus is fine for us."

Peter leant out of her arms towards Bailey, green eyes twinkling. Bailey felt a tug on his heart strings. Against his better judgement he cupped the toddler's face in his hand. "Be a good boy for mommy."

The child waved, then kissed his own pudgy hand and threw him a kiss. I'm losing it, thought Bailey. Sentimental. Not good for a policeman. "You have my personal mobile number, Bree. Call me any time."

"Does that make me your snitch?" asked Bree, a half-smile hovering on her lips. "Any money in that?"

"I care what happens to you and want you to be safe. Peter as well."

"Well then. I'm not sorry I came. Well – not very sorry anyway."

"Don't worry. We protect our sources." Human Sources, in shorthand HS, were protected by legislation. The first step would be to determine if Bree was simply going to provide, or 'download,' information; or if they could task her with obtaining something useable to convict Butcher. A recorded threat in a phone call? His mind was racing ahead to various possibilities and scenarios. How they could use her without endangering her life. "Give me a call or an SMS." It would give him a contact number and save him having to track her down another way.

"My first pimp warned me to never put anything in writing and to stay off the grid. Not to even use social media."

Peter sat up as if galvanised, "Queen Bree!" he said, patting his mother's arm.

Bailey watched her walk quickly away. Slightly dingy tracksuit bottoms dragging on the pavement but cradling a very neat bottom all the same. She'd be popular at her work. He sighed and headed upstairs to check how the interview was going.

Palfrey had an unlit cigarette in his mouth. "Just counting the minutes," he said. "This isn't going anywhere. Butcher seems quite unfazed by the CCTV photo. Said he has a girlfriend who lives near there that he visits now and then. Went to the ATM machine to get money to take her out for a few drinks and bumped into Stinky Bill. Asked him about buying a new TV on the never never. Now Tony and Pamela are trying to pin him down to times and dates. How often does he see said girlfriend? Her name and address. Where they went for a drink. They're getting his so-called every move so we can check it. The usual hard graft to come."

"Good work then," said Bailey. "Meanwhile we've got an informant. The woman downstairs was Butcher′s ex-girlfriend. Says he told her that he killed Hannah."

"No shit? On the record?"

"Not at the moment."

"Think she's on the level?"

Bailey didn't answer at once. There were always informants who seemed legit but who were playing their own game. Cards held close to their chest. It may well be in Bree's interest to have Butcher locked up, away from her and Peter. But in the end, he nodded, "I'd say so—but not put any money on it until we find out more."

"Cynic," said Palfrey.

"Back to you!"

They shared a wry laugh. So many cases together. Regrets about the ones that got away. There were always surprises waiting to trip up a successful investigation and prosecution.

Bailey stretched his shoulders back and turned his head from side to side to get rid of a crick in his neck. "I've got a few things for Evan to chase up for me. The HS said Butcher claimed to have offed his ex-wife as well. I want to see what we've got about her death. Maybe we can get him for that one as well—or at least use it to rattle him. Say we're reopening the investigation, if in fact there was an investigation. Was there anything about that in his file?"

"Can't even remember reading he had a wife."

"Well, we know he has a kid. I guess we can find the ex through the birth records."

"Anything you want me to do?"

"No. You're shit at IT."

"Starting to think I'm shit at everything."

Bailey buffeted his partner's shoulder and noticed how beat up he was looking. His day-old stubble had patches of uneven grey and there was still a gob of toothpaste on the side of his mouth. "Diane a bit preoccupied these days?"

"Too worried about Jazz to have time for me as well."

"Well, I'm starting to worry about you. That must count for something."

Palfrey frowned at him. "Don't get sentimental."

"I was just having that same conversation with myself."

"Take your own advice then."

Bailey would. It seemed like it had been a long day. "You staying?"

Palfrey shrugged. "Nicotine calls. Tony and Pamela will fill us in if they come up with something. Maybe I could go on to the Axial. Look at the nightclub's footage and see if I can get any closer to who hijacked Liam."

"Not our case."

"Yeah – but now that Liam's involved and on the record, I can start looking in earnest. Out in the open. Not jeopardising our retirement by using my position to follow something personal."

"Not sure I follow, but if that´s true Diane will be pleased."

"Yeah. That would be a change."

"You're a lucky son of a gun to have her," warned Bailey. "It's only natural she has less time for you at the moment."

"Yeah, yeah, JB. For a single guy who knows nothing about women, you do go on. She's mad at me because I've done nothing about the men who raped Jazz, and she's mad at me if I do something, and she's mad at our son and daughter-in-law as they seem to have abandoned responsibility for their own children and expect us to look after them. And—well that's just for a start. I could go on."

"Sorry I said anything." Bailey had heard it all before but knew that his partner needed to get it off his chest.

"You should be."

Chapter 22

Tony and Pamela entered the squad´s room looking as dark as the threatening sky outside. They'd let Butcher go with a warning that he was lucky not to be charged with assault after pushing a detective whilst on his lawful business. They may need to interview him again.

"Blah blah, and so on and so forth," was Tony's take on it.

"Ditto," agreed Pamela, arching her back and giving a pretty good idea why their former boss had been so keen on her. She was covertly sexual, if there was such a thing. Seemingly unaware of the attention she got, but really? She was a detective; she knew full well how she distracted the rest of the squad. Except Tony of course. One of the reasons Bailey had teamed them up together. And after the initial friction, it now seemed to be working out OK.

"Anyway," Pamela said, "we've got a lot of blather to check on."

Evan looked up from his desk, "Does that happen to include the name of his ex-wife? It'd save me searching for her in the registry of births, deaths and marriages."

"We're nothing if not thorough," said Tony, riffling through his notebook until he came to the name. "*Amanda Croydon.* Didn't change her name to Butcher when they married. A bit of a feminist apparently. Died four years ago. Drowned at Cottesloe Beach."

"Butcher didn't seem too bothered about it," said Pamela, "except to say it was traumatic for the kid. A girl, now ten years old called Quinn. Apparently, they were going to name the baby Quinn whatever the sex was. Yeah, Butcher can blather to distraction. He'd win a gold medal for it. The kid's currently with her maternal grandparents, who give him a break every now and then."

"Well done. Sounds like you got the full bio. Can I suggest a break? Maybe a beer?" said Bailey. "My shout."

Tony checked his watch. "Sure. Nothing like celebrating diddlysquat."

"You taking elocution lessons from Palfrey?" They all laughed. It did seem the whole squad were taking on Palfrey's shorthand lingo and current hangdog demeanour. "Where is he anyway?" asked Pamela, looking around.

"Helping the locals in Mandurah get some info on a weird abduction. The vic's a friend of his granddaughter. He was found drugged in a warehouse down there. It may involve the Axial.

Evan pushed his chair back from his computer and stood up. "Heard the nightclub's going down-market now with new owners."

"Oh yeah? Who'd that be?" Bailey rubbed his eyes, hoping a coldie would push back his sudden weariness.

"Some Slav name. I can look it up when we get back if you like? Just add it to the list."

The great thing about Evan was that he actually liked to do his sleuthing online, rather than out in the field, and so rarely grumbled about his workload. "Sure. Let's go. Plain Street Bar OK?"

The Hyatt Hotel was an easy stroll from Police Headquarters. Pamela's sister was the hotel's concierge and one of their long-time employees—a bonus because she made sure they were looked after. The staff were instructed to always seat them in a corner where their usual bloodthirsty conversation wouldn't upset other patrons. Employees were also cautioned about media presence. Keep any journalists well away from the murder squad. Another unforeseen bonus was the fact that Bob Hunter's new girlfriend, Claire Foy, worked the Plain Street Bar as a sous chef. Hyatt was transferring her from café to restaurant to bar to give her a broader work experience. The squad now moved with her.

Bob Hunter was a constant source of mystery to the team. All they knew about him was that he was single, came from Broome and he was the first indigenous member of the homicide squad. Plus, his degree in psychology was useful in working up a profile of a potential suspect when facts were short.

Claire was visible in the open kitchen. She lifted her chin in their direction in acknowledgement but didn't come over to chat. Like Hunter, she was always focussed on the job at hand. Something to prove perhaps.

"Shall we have a few snacks as well?" asked Bailey.

"Hummus or guacamole?" suggested Hunter.

Evan nodded. "Salsa and nachos would be good with a cold beer."

Bailey beckoned the waiter over and they gave their orders. Pamela stuck with soda, lime and bitters whereas the rest of the team had low alcohol beer.

"What's your take on Butcher?" Bailey asked Hunter, realising he hadn't given him any particular job to do that day although, in fact, he'd been the one to apprehend Butcher. Hunter was like a ghost. Even when he was present Bailey tended to forget he was there. "Did he say anything of interest to you in the car on the way to the interview?"

"He's smarter than he looks. Talks a lot but says nothing. Typical spin doctor. He was waiting for a clue as to what it was all about. Just because he's down-at-heel doesn't mean he's not intelligent. He's from a good family. Knows how to behave but chooses not to. My take would be that he prefers to be underestimated."

Bailey wondered if Hunter punctuated his text messages. When speaking he rarely used abbreviations. "No easy confession from him then."

"DNA or a witness would be the best bet for a conviction."

"How's the processing of the DNA from the murder scene going, Evan?"

"There's a huge backlog at the lab. Apparently there's around 40 different samples to test, but they have hardly started yet. Too busy working on the kidnapping."

A five-year-old girl had been taken from a house known for drug dealing. Finding a live child was more important than tracing the perpetrator of a dead woman. No one in the squad had a problem with that.

They all nodded; resigned to the plodding work ahead. Bailey hadn't told them about the new witness, Bree. Her information would come through the Tor network where she'd be assured of anonymity. Although he trusted the team, a thoughtless remark could always derail an investigation. He'd like to develop a relationship with Bree and task her with getting more information from Butcher. A drowned ex-wife didn't sound like a murder – but one never knew.

"We'd better look into Amanda Croydon's death," was all he said.

"Using the royal we, I presume," said Evan.

"I could do that," volunteered Hunter.

"Great!" Evan grinned. And they left it at that.

Small tapas plates began to arrive and they tucked in. "Some chicken wings?" asked Evan to general nods of approval. He lived alone and ate cereal for dinner most nights.

Bailey was heading to Palfrey and Diane's for dinner but since he was picking up the tab he could hardly demur. "Go for it, you've earned it," he said.

There was a general hullabaloo at Palfrey's house when Bailey arrived at the open front door. It seemed like everyone was trying to talk over the top of each other, and so only unconnected words shot towards him, like deviant missiles that had missed their target.

"Hello!" yelled Bailey.

Not ever again! My business! With Tracy! Eighteen years old! Not with Tracy! I'm of age! Not in my house! – I'll leave then! Go where? For Godssake! Be quiet! Listen to me!

"Anyone home?" tried Bailey again. "Can I come in?" Nobody seemed to be listening to him, or to anyone else, so he walked down the passageway towards the family room. There he found Jazz and Diane confronting Fiona. All were red in the face. Palfrey sat in the corner, his head in his hands, raising it in time to see Bailey, then shaking it with an eye rolling grimace before putting it back in his hands again.

"I brought sushi!" Bailey proffered the takeaway plate from the hotel's bar. He didn't think he'd mention that although he'd ordered it, none of his fellow squad members would touch it. Tony had said "Real men don't eat sushi!" which had the rest of the squad hard pressed to speak from laughing.

Whether it was the entry of another person, or the sushi, the cacophony abruptly ceased. Diane, remembering her manners, said “JB—sorry you had to witness that.”

“No worries,” said Bailey, wondering what in fact he had witnessed. “What’s going on?” He turned to Palfrey, “This anything to do with you?”

“Not guilty,” said Palfrey. “Let’s have a beer and leave them to it. Things to tell you.” He stood up and the two men walked from the room into the kitchen. “Police business!” Palfrey threw over his shoulder like a Molotov cocktail. The arguing started again, so he carefully shut the door.

Bailey got two low alcohol cans of Carlton Dry out of the fridge while Palfrey hefted his bulk onto a kitchen stool. “Fiona and Tracy went to visit Liam in hospital. The orderly, or nurse, or whatever you call ‘em, is ex Slovakian army and has a tattoo similar to Jazz’s attacker. Off duty he drinks at a bar where the other ex-Slovak army guys go. He’s asked Fiona to meet up there with him.”

“What?”

“—or maybe Fiona asked if she could go with him. Tracy wanted to go too?”

“No way. She’s under age. Where is Tracy?” asked Bailey,

“Your place. Said you’d warned her not to go home. She left in the middle of the argument.”

“How long has it been going on for?”

“Months. Years. Generations” said Palfrey. “Let’s go outside. Bring the sushi. Diane hasn’t even started on dinner yet. She may have forgotten you were coming.”

They went out the sliding door to the backyard and slumped into the wicker chairs. Both reached for the sushi garnished with tuna then tossed down a mouthful of icy cold beer. “Hmm,” said Palfrey in appreciation. He’d taken to eating sushi with low-cal beer when his doctor warned him that he was heading for a heart attack if he didn’t moderate his diet. “How did it go with Butcher?”

Bailey could see Palfrey wanted to switch gears and transfer his attention to their case and to authentic police business. It didn′t surprised him. Palfrey was usually a conscientious partner, but catching Jazz’s attackers had overtaken his interest in the current case.”

“Lots of follow-up work for Evan, and now Hunter.”

“Really? Hunter is finally invested in a case?”

“Yeah, He volunteered. Tony and Pamela did a thorough job with the interview. Lots of unconnected dates and facts to check. Enough to muddy the waters. That’s how we’ll get him. Inconsistencies. Slowly, slowly catchee monkey.”

Palfrey nodded, “Nothing I could have done to help then?

Bailey laughed. “This isn’t like you. Where’d the guilty conscience come from.”

"It's not that. It's Diane. I'm worried she'll leave me if I jeopardise our retirement."

"You don't give her enough credit, mate. She's a stayer. She'll stick with you through thick and thin. But she's your devil's advocate. She makes you examine the big picture and see what you may have overlooked."

"You reckon?"

"I do."

Palfrey looked unsettled. "I thought I was the big picture guy."

"Tell me about the Axial," said Bailey, knowing a conversational dead horse.

"First let's order something from Deliveroo so Diane won't have to cook. We'll stick to Asian." Palfrey leaned back and hit the speed dial for yet another takeaway delivery. Then looking up he said, "Security at the nightclub were very co-operative. They downloaded the video from the night Liam was there onto a flash drive. There's a partial scene of him chatting to a group of Middle Eastern looking guys." He checked Bailey for any protest about racial profiling and found him nodding for him to continue. "I emailed it to the locals at Mandurah but also said I'd run the faces to see if any of them had form."

Flash drive? Running faces for form? Bailey's eyebrows shot up. "You've finally dropped a couple of generations and leapfrogged into the current century. I didn't know you had it in you."

"Granddaughters," explained Palfrey succinctly. "All the same. I sent it to Fenton Farrell at IT with the case number from Mandurah. He'll get onto it tomorrow."

Bailey's ex-wife had been briefly married to Fenton. Despite this, Bailey and Palfrey had a cautious working relationship with him. "Any chit chat?" asked Bailey.

"Had to sweeten the request with some small talk, JB. Ask how he was doing. Seeing anyone?"

"And?"

"He's not seeing Janet, if that's what you're wondering."

"I wasn't," lied Bailey.

"D'you ever hear from Janet these days."

"Not if I can help it. She's moved on, and that's how I like it."

"So—back to the Axial. There was nothing on tape showing anyone giving or buying Liam a drink. The general chat around him seemed friendly enough. Liam wandered off and was leaning on the bar asking for a refill and that's all she wrote. We'll just have to see what Fenton comes up with, but I can't see any of the staff being involved, as they have to be vetted for form before they're hired. Maybe one of the other fellows he was talking to on the video will come up tops." He chugged down the rest of his beer and tossed the can a metre into an open rubbish bin.

"He throws. He scores. Today's renaissance man," Bailey laughed.

“Steady on, JB. You’re getting a bit too literary for my taste. Anyway…” he took a deep breath and shook his shoulders as if someone was walking on his grave. “Fiona seems to want to do a bit of sleuthing at the Slovakian Army’s bar of choice. Diane and Jazz are vehemently against it.”

“Me too,” agreed Bailey.

“Try to stop her,” said Palfrey grimly.

They heard a vehicle pull up. Lights flashed down the driveway. Bailey gave Palfrey a hand to get up from the deep-seated lounge chair, but when they reached the kerb, they saw taillights disappearing down the street. “Not Deliveroo then,” said Palfrey.

Standing under the street light, they waited until a motorbike with Deliveroo’s distinctive logo pulled up. The kid bringing the order that night looked about twelve. Bailey felt like he should ask to see his licence, however Palfrey pulled out his wallet and gave the approximate amount they owed plus a generous tip.

“Have a good night, sir,” chirped the teenager before throttling away.

“You know people use Deliveroo or Uber Eats when the night’s too dirty to go out themselves. And then someone else’s kid gets to go out and risk life and limb.”

“Yeah,” said Bailey, who actually hadn’t thought about that until now. He preferred to cook for himself. It was a therapeutic decompression stop after a day of murder.

They swung back through the backyard to pick up the remains of the sushi and entered the kitchen to find Diane and Jazz on their own.

"Where's Fiona?"

"Took an Uber to your place to join Tracy." Diane's tone severe.

"Jesus Christ. Sometimes I think I'm running a halfway house for wayward girls," said Bailey.

Opening a cupboard, Diane shrugged and laid out some plates on the counter top, "When they get to that age you can't tell them anything. Let's eat!" she said gloomily.

Chapter 23

The day′s weather forecast of thunder storms had later brought a violent wind that whirled the gum leaves down the street and into the gutters. When a blast of dust obscured his vision Bailey activated the windscreen wipers. The chilli prawns he′d eaten at Palfrey′s had left him with indigestion. When he pulled into his driveway, his house showed only the weak porch light. The windows were dark. Where the hell were the girls? Maybe around the back by the pool? Unlikely in this weather. He whistled for Shooter but there was no answering bark. The dog was AWOL again.

"Anyone home?" He called as he unlocked the front door. A scribbled note, left on the shelf where he normally dumped his keys, said, "*We′ve gone to my place and taken Shooter for protection. It seemed a bit of an imposition for the two of us to stay here. Plus, a woman called by. Said she was in the neighbourhood. She seemed pretty surprised and not very happy to see us. You should call Greta.*" Both Tracy and Fiona had signed the note with their names and lipstick kisses.

Of all the fuckups! Shooter for protection? The dog would follow the postman on his rounds and refuse to go home. There had never been a person he didn't bond with. Typical Labrador. Bailey could just imagine what Greta would think, finding two gorgeous teenage girls settled down in his house. It wouldn't look good. Wasn't there some kind of rule to prevent a new girlfriend popping around without an invitation? He'd never do that. When he was married, he could barely go home unexpectedly in case there was another man in his bed. He'd called Greta in the middle of the afternoon and left a message saying he hoped they'd get together soon. He hadn't issued an invitation to join him that evening.

Tracy had turned off her mobile and taken out the SIM card at his insistence so he couldn´t call her. Fuck! He didn't have Fiona's number. He called Palfrey instead who said to his surprise, "OK Evan. I've got it in my notebook in the other room. I won't be a tick." After said tick he whispered Fiona's number and swore liberally. "I can't tell Diane about this. The whole scenario's gone to hell. Want me to come over?"

"No. Stay home and mend some fences. I'll let you know if I need you."

Fiona's mobile went to voice message. Better to drive over there. Bailey stomped out of the house, jumped in the Camaro and reversed onto the street with a screech of tyres. He´d told Tracy not to go home. Why were teenage girls so boof-headed. They didn´t listen to a damn thing. Foot down, he burned rubber. Why had he waited to eat dinner at Palfrey's? If the bad guys were heading to Tracy's, he could be too late.

He parked behind the complex, then walked along the driveway that led to the eight villas.

Although the motion activated driveway lights lit up, he'd also grabbed the heavy-duty torch he kept under the passenger seat. If necessary, it would make a good cosh for anyone lurking behind the Boxwood hedge. At the front door he called, "Anyone here?" and heard Shooter bark, the joyful bark that said *I'm glad you're home.* Since a menacing growl was not in his repertoire that meant nothing as far as clues went. He knocked.

A shaky voice said, "Who's there. We have a Rottweiler!"

Fiona, thought Bailey. "JB here. Are you OK? Let me in."

A dark eye appeared in the peephole and then the sound of the security chain sliding undone. Fiona stood there with a one-kilogram weight in her hand. Tracy stood against the wall holding the other one, Shooter obedient but dancing with anticipation at her side.

"Better than nothing," commented Bailey about the weights. Shooter pawed his leg until he acknowledged him by roughing his head. "How about a cup of tea?"

Tracy re-bolted and chained the front door before they trooped into the kitchen. The clock on the wall said 10:30 p.m. It felt later.

"Here's what we're going to do. You girls…" Tracy's glare interrupted him, "You young women are going to go and spend the night—maybe two at Tracy's father's place."

"He'll find some excuse to say no," argued Tracy.

"I will call him myself and insist!" An idea that had percolated on the drive came to the boil. "Most people find it in their best interest to agree to a police request." He took a sip of his tea to gather his thoughts. "Fiona – give me your phone, and Tracy…you too."

"It's not safe to catch an Uber without having a mobile," Tracy objected. "The driver might be a weirdo."

"Your father will come to collect you."

Tracy shook her head. "In your dreams."

"You'll be safe with him. And from now on you have to stop using my place as a flophouse. Give me the house key. When I told you where I kept it for emergencies, I didn´t give you permission to clone it!"

"What about when I pick up Shooter to go for a run?"

"We'll cross that bridge when we come to it. Pack some things and I'll make the call."

As expected, Tracy's father invented several self-serving reasons why he couldn't host two young women so late at night; but when Bailey carefully explained that he would be hindering police business—an offence that could see him in court not to mention featuring unfavourably in the *West Australian* newspaper, he capitulated. It took fifteen short minutes before he pulled up in his Prius.

Bailey first waved Shooter into the back. He didn´t want the dog around when he put his plan into place. "My leather seats," her father complained. Then, "they don't allow pets in my apartment block!"

"You have my number," plus a hard look from Bailey made him give it up. After the girls piled in, Tracy opened the passenger door again to say, "Would you undo the cat-flap? We had to lock her out in the garden because Shooter thought she was a toy."

Bailey nodded. Teenage girls were exhausting.

The car took off after some annoyed revving. Prius owners must miss leaving a cloud of exhaust fumes behind them when they're pissed off. Some parents didn't deserve to have such great children. Signing a maintenance cheque didn't make you a decent father. Bailey would give anything to have his own daughter back.

Before calling Palfrey, he first slid the SIM card back into Tracy's phone. Its location could now be traced.

"You know mate," he said without bothering to identify himself when his partner answered, "we've been too invested in finding these bastards. Why don't we let them come to us!"

"Maybe because indications are that they're big, strong ex Slovakian army blokes! I´m not sure the two of us are a match for one of them. Me especially."

"Wuss," said Bailey, going on to outline his idea.

"On my way," said Palfrey.

Bailey waited until Palfrey arrived before putting out a text. He was pretty sure the reason the perps had left Liam with his mobile phone was because they had loaded malware on it. Any text Liam received or sent would also go to them.

Hi Liam. Hope you're feeling much better. Me and Fiona are at home wishing you were with us. Mum's away for the night. Lost opportunities! LOL

"They'd use more abbreviations," objected Palfrey.

"Which ones? You're the grandfather."

"No idea."

Bailey googled *abbreviations and acronyms in text messages.*

"Acronyms?" asked Palfrey.

"Shut up."

They settled on—Hi L, *HRU? home 2NITE with Fiona. NGL Missing U. LOL BFF.*

"What if they're as hopeless as we are? We'll wait all night for them but they won't show," grouched Palfrey. "Plus, I think you should put *the mother isn't here* to make them complacent."

"I think they're already pretty sure of themselves. Anyway, I couldn't find the right shortcut! Texts shouldn't be too long. I guess perps can google just as well as we can. I left some real words in to make it easier."

"NGL?"

"Not gonna lie – I'm not a fan either." They laughed.

It was a while since they'd been on a stakeout. The majority of detective work was done in business hours interviewing witnesses or following up lines of thought. Bailey shut all the blinds and turned on a few lamps before showing Palfrey the laptop that Tracy had put on top of the bedroom wardrobe. It would begin infrared videoing when it detected motion. "What will they think of next?" marvelled Palfrey.

"Don't get too impressed. Perps use it to video the women they assault after giving them a date rape drug or whatever. That way when they watch it, they can experience the feeling of power over and over again. It wasn't invented for the good guys."

"Why does Tracy have it then?"

"It's her mother's laptop. God knows what she gets up to with her dates."

"Now I understand why people vote to turn the clock back to the 1950s."

"I thought you were one of those."

"That's why I understand them."

Time dragged on.

They put a romcom on the TV and turned up the sound. Atmosphere. "Oh joy," said Palfrey. "I've seen the Princess Bride at least twice."

"What time would Fiona and Tracy go to bed?"

"I dunno. Without parents around. About one?"

"OK."

They slunk down in the sofa and ate a couple of ginger nut biscuits they'd found in the cupboard. "What d'you reckon then? They'd come around 4 or 5am?"

"Three or four I'd say. Neighbours might get up for work around five."

They were both right. At 4:10 the front door knob turned with a slight squeak. Bailey nudged Palfrey awake. He nodded. They'd left the kitchen window a handspan ajar with a wooden rod behind it to stop anyone opening it too easily. It would however, be easy enough to snake an arm through and withdraw the rod. They'd put some pillows under the duvets in Tracy's bedroom to simulate the sleeping girls. Bailey in an inspired move, had downloaded the sound of waves and had it playing on Fiona's phone under one of the twin beds.

The sound of the outside thunder sharply intensified; a warning that the window had slid open. Two men dressed in black slipped out of the kitchen and down the hall. They were barely discernible and moved with the quiet stealth of predatory animals. Bailey, in turn, slipped behind them into the kitchen and quietly shut the window, pushing in the lock. All doors and windows were now locked and could only be opened with a key. If the men did manage to overpower the two policemen, they'd have to break out. He pinged the local police who'd agreed to include the address in their rounds and send a car by every so often. The complex was only minutes away from Scarborough´s centre, where hoons gathered nightly to do donuts in the carpark.

Bailey beckoned Palfrey to follow close behind him. Stopping at the bedroom door, they saw the two men a metre away having a whispered conversation. Bailey activated the police sirens and blue lights on his and Palfrey's cars. Colleague Fenton Farrell had long ago set up a mobile app to expedite this. As the alarms blared Bailey turned on the bedroom light.

"Police!" he said economically hoping both surprise and the noise of the sirens would stun them. Palfrey, standing with shoulders squared, scowled at his most menacing.

They turned. Not looking too worried. Army training. It was hardly a barrage. Bailey hoped the laptop was capturing the moment and their faces. Clearview AI—billed as the world's largest facial image network—had a software program most police forces in Australia used for facial recognition. It had 20 billion plus facial images stored from public sources, media and mug shots. Bailey put his hand in his pocket to turn off the sirens before speaking. The cacophony stopped. "You're under arrest for breaking and entering." Behind him, Palfrey shook his head to clear his ears.

The taller of the two well-built men smiled. Despite the cold weather, he wore a black singlet that displayed impressive tanned biceps and the tattoo Jazz had sketched to identify her attacker. His perfect white teeth were that of a male model. He wasn't the public's idea of a rapist—but then again, who was?

"What did we break?" His accent was so slight as to be almost undetectable. The shorter man looked older, but was equally as formidable. His muscles had muscles. He took a step back and flipped one of the doonas open to reveal the makeshift dummy. Tracy's cat had made a comfortable nest between the two pillows. Moving to his partner's he nudged him and lifted his chin to indicate the empty twin beds. "No problem. We'll be out on bail first thing this morning."

Bailey, impressed and somewhat discomfited by the men's cool acceptance of the situation, said, "Good. Glad we've got that sorted. Come forward. One at a time. Hands out in front of you."

The first man complied, taking a few lazy steps forward, but as Bailey looked down to snap on plastic ties in lieu of handcuffs, the second man ran forward and shoved both his accomplice and Bailey into Palfrey, momentarily leaving a space in the doorway to slip by them. Bailey heard the distinctive snick of a flick knife. "Look out," he yelled to Palfrey as he felt burning across his chest.

Palfrey had fallen to the floor and copped a hefty smack to the ribs as the man ran over him. He rolled over and grabbed the second man's leg as he leapfrogged past but the man shook him off. Palfrey made another desperate grab and caught his trainer, which flew into the air and bounced off a wall. The men ran down the passage into the kitchen where the sound of breaking glass indicated their escape route.

"Well, that went well," wheezed Palfrey, before noticing that Bailey had both hands clasped to his chest, blood seeping through the fingers. "Bloody hell!" He got onto his hands and knees then pawed up the wall before taking out his mobile and pressing the emergency number. "Ambulance. Man down." He shouted into the phone, reciting the address.

He put his left hand on top of Baileys hands and pressed hard to help stem the flow of blood. "Two POIs all in black. They may separate. Check any cars in the vicinity. I'll leave you on speaker." He turned and helped Bailey slide to the floor, then looking around and not finding anything useable handy, ripped off his cotton sweater and pressed it hard against the wound. Bailey's face was white and he kept repeating, "What a fuckup!" His words getting slower and slower.

"It's just a scratch," said Palfrey, who hoped he was right. "You've lost a bit of blood. That's all. Just don't move about until the ambulance gets here."

"Move about?" said Bailey, losing the thread of his profane litany. "Are you insane?"

The muffled voice of the emergency room responder could be heard on Palfrey's phone asking for details. "You'll have to break in through the front door or come in the kitchen window," barked Palfrey. "I can't leave my partner." He hadn't met Tracy's mother but he was pretty certain that what with her, his wife and their new boss, he and Bailey were in deep shit.

Chapter 24

Marcia Odell closed the door to her office then stalked past the waiting detectives to sit with a thump behind her desk. This was new. Their old boss always kept the door open, even when he was reaming them out. Especially when he was reaming them out.

"Stitched up and healthy, ready to go back to work?" she asked Bailey. Nothing in her tone indicated sympathy. Having a woman boss was harder than he and Palfrey had anticipated. If they couldn't predict how the women in their personal lives would react to a given situation – how the hell would they ever understand their new boss?

"Yes ma'am, Ms Odell. Twenty stitches. Not much more than a scratch. They only kept me overnight to pump some antibiotics into me." He didn't mention the night sweats.

She frowned at him, and gave no indication as to how she'd like to be addressed in the future. Great. It was like a lucky dip – who knew what you'd get for an infraction. Bailey decided on distraction. "What do we know about the perps?"

"Persons of Interest," she corrected him "We don't want to be contaminated by the language in melodramatic American television shows, do we?"

"No –um, I don't use perps outside of the squad, Ma'am." He felt like a naughty schoolboy.

Palfrey hid a smirk. He was leaving the running to Bailey and so far enjoying his discomfort.

Odell spoke, measuring her words. "As you know, we apprehended only one of the POIs. Serge Horvat. No major form—one or two D&Ds." Drunk and Disorderly convictions were summary, or simple offences, which only attracted imprisonment of up to three years, and more usually a fine. "Horvat has no form for violence and no B&Es. We′ll run his DNA through the unsolved system, but despite his assault on you, the lab isn′t calling it a priority."

"I thought the safety of police personnel was a priority, Ma′am. Or so the police commissioner said on the news the other day when he was explaining that the continuing loss of police personnel to the lucrative, and safer, mining industry, would just open the doors for new recruits with modern skills."

Ignoring him, she turned to Palfrey.

"Boss?" he said.

"I′ve read your report, but I′d like you to tell me again, using less police-speak."

Bailey interrupted, "—and the other man who attacked me? Did we get an ID?"

"Not from Horvat."

Which explained nothing.

"What about the face recognition software?" Bailey wasn′t ready to let it go.

"All in good time." Odell had an unlined face for her age. No smile lines. To be fair, no frown lines either.

Palfrey shuffled his feet, trying to decide if he could take one of the chairs in front of her desk, but she simply looked up at him and said, "Go on."

"It´s complicated, since you haven´t been here from the beginning."

"And what was the beginning."

"Perhaps JB, err DS Bailey, should tell you that part."

"No. I´m asking you. Con Tin You." She said it as if it were three words.

"A teenager, Tracy, came across an unaccompanied toddler when she was out on her early morning run. Bailey´s dog was following the child. Tracy thought the two were together and called the number on the dog´s registration tag and DS Bailey came to see what all the fuss was about." He scratched his nose and took an exploratory cough. "It later transpired that the child´s mother had been murdered and it became our case."

Odell circled her hand.

"Because she, the young girl, took a close interest in what happened to the infant, she and her mother got to know DS Bailey. Also, because we are long term partners in the squad, Tracy became known to my family."

"Sounds unorthodox," Odell raised her eyebrows. Her body language was so contained it was impossible to read.

"These things happen when you´re practically neighbours. I guess Perth is more parochial than

Melbourne" Palfrey said, picking up steam. "On Sunday, Tracy bumped into Bailey while in our home precinct of Scarborough and showed him a disturbing text she′d received from her boyfriend, Liam′s phone." Palfrey decided to leave out Evan′s participation. "Apparently Liam was out of contact with his parents—with whom he lives—and she, Tracy, was worried about both him and the implied threat to her in the text."

Odell impatiently waved him on again as he experimented with another bout of coughing.

"Confusingly, at the same time, conjointly—as these things tend to occur—JB happened upon a POI we′d been trying to identify from a partial photo on an ATM. He was thought to be a witness, or a suspect, in the murder of Hannah de Graf, the toddler′s mother."

Bailey could sense Palfrey contemplate asking whether Odell was with him so far, but then deciding it would not only impugn her intelligence, it would impugn his own. Even he was having trouble following the thread. Good enough so far. Best not to make it too coherent. For someone who habitually used shorthand speech he was exceeding expectations

"Liam was found in a drugged state stashed in an empty warehouse. Unconscious. Strangely not from one of the usual drugs of choice, but rather from a depressive drug more often used for heart patients with clogged arteries. Liam had gone to the Axial Night Club—the last thing he remembered before waking up in hospital. He has no idea what happened in the interim."

Odell sighed at his stilted delivery but nodded for him to go on.

"Because the text to Tracy had said *'We know where you live* DS Bailey was concerned for her safety. Not to mention that she and my grand-daughter, with whom she had formed a friendship, were going to be together at her home, alone, that night."

Bailey had never heard his partner say 'with whom' and covered a smile with his hand.

"DS Bailey and I convinced them to stay elsewhere for safety, then decided to wait at Tracy's address to see if anything untoward would happen. We advised the local force of that possibility."

Palfrey was beginning to sweat. Perspiration ran down one side of his cheek. He turned it away from Odell and wiped it across a raised shoulder.

"Where were the parents?"

Bailey chipped in. "They're divorced. Tracy lives with her mother, who was staying the night with her boyfriend."

Palfrey gave him a look. He had it in hand. Was he telling it or what! "We were just preparing to return home," he paused for a moment, "thinking the threat was a mere bagatelle, when the two intruders broke in. And the rest is history. Or at least, you have it in a concise, but detailed, form in my report. Having my partner attacked and left for dead shook me up a bit. I´d rather not go over it again. I´m still rather shaken. I hope it doesn´t have any long-term consequences." Palfrey was gently waving the workers compensation PTSS flag as a final distraction. Police administrators hated that, although they pretended the force´s mental health was a major concern.

Good one, Palfrey. Well done, I hope, Bailey thought.

"A bagatelle? If your partner uses such fanciful words when questioning witnesses, DS Bailey, I´m surprised at your solve rate." Without waiting for a response, she turned to Palfrey. "You seem to have left quite a bit out DC Palfrey."

Bailey interrupted to give Palfrey time to think. "Scrabble Ma'am. Since he's started playing the game with his grandchildren his vocabulary has changed. Some might say, improved. He does keep things simpler when interviewing suspects."

Palfrey cleared his throat but remained silent. He wasn´t going to fall for that one: filling in, where possibly no further information was required.

"The witness in Scarborough. What happened to him?" Odell asked.

Bailey decided to take it from here. "Through the Tor system, a member of the public has potentially identified him as the person who likely killed the boy´s mother. The informant said that he had confessed to the murder and threatened her."

Bailey hadn´t wasted his prescribed recovery time when the hospital released him. He had contacted

Brianna´s former madam. Known to him from a previous case, he´d asked her to convince Bree that both Bailey and the Tor system were to be trusted. "The information appears to be genuine, however we are following procedures to obtain a guilty conviction. It may take a little time. So far we have no DNA to put him at the scene of the crime."

Odell slowly nodded her head. A conviction early in her new position would do her no harm at all. She breathed in and out. "OK—let´s see where this goes," she said. "This young woman, Tracy, will confirm your version of what happened?" She looked at Bailey.

"Yes Ma´am, her ambition is to join the police force. She´d be very keen to talk to a successful high-ranking female detective. "

Odell rolled her eyes. "As you get to know me, DS Bailey, you will find I am immune to flattery." She indicated the door. "Well. Get on with it. I´ll let you know when I want to talk more on the subject."

Chapter 25

The doldrums had crept into the room. Searching for every speck of incriminating evidence against Fred Butcher was taking its toll on the murder squad. The fluorescent overhead lights left everyone feeling as dull as the autumn day. Evan had pushed his chair back from his computer and was staring at the wall with an equally blank look on his face. Tony and Pamela, recently reconciled from their early competitive partnership, had pushed their desks together to sit face to face to share ideas, earning them the nickname Topela. The large expanse of the joint desk was now littered with half empty cups of canteen coffee. Their faces reflected the same yellowy shade of tepid tan.

"News," said Bailey, swinging through the door to a general brightening of the atmosphere. Palfrey, who had been standing at the window frowning out at the rain, turned and put his hands in his pockets, the stance indicating his negativity.

"I just had a call from the honorary Consul to the Netherlands, Greta Meer. Apparently, at her instigation, Tom Watts and Ines de Graaf had a meeting with a family law solicitor and agreed that an application for a consent order be lodged with the court." Seeing Palfrey´s raised eyebrows, he clarified, "That means both the grandparents and the father have agreed to financial and custody arrangements for

Matey. The solicitor has filed an urgent request for the court to deal with the matter quickly due to Mrs de Graaf's wish to return to the Netherlands."

"So, who gets him?" asked Palfrey.

"He's not a parcel, Palfrey," Pamela scolded.

Bailey cleared his throat. "Well. It's complicated. Mrs de Graaf and her husband will have custody until Matey is of school age. They have waived any request for child support from Tom and have instead agreed that, until then, Tom will have Matey for three weeks holiday each year. They will either pay for Matey and an accompanying adult to come to Australia at a time when Tom is not working or, if he prefers, they will pay for Tom to travel to Amsterdam, and provide him and Matey with an independent place to stay."

"Jesus – for a father who's shown zero interest in his child up until now, he's got a cushy berth hasn't he?" Evan frowned. "Fathers who shirk responsibility for their children are the scum of the earth."

Bailey knew he was thinking about his own father and upbringing, with a single mother in poor health who struggled to make ends meet.

"Tracy's not going to be happy," Palfrey shrugged.

"Yeah, neither is Norma," Bailey turned from Palfrey to explain to the squad, "Norma is the foster mother who's been looking after Matey.

"And this is helpful to the investigation, how?" asked Evan.

"The success of a case is in the details. Any details that we miss, no matter how small, can lead to the derailment of a successful conviction."

"What else?" asked Tony, who was bitterly familiar with the family court, having gone through a contentious divorce and custody case when he came out as gay. He said the scars would never fade.

Bailey perched a hip on the edge of the Topola desk. The new configuration left just about six square inches of unused space. "In the consent order, the definition of school age was broadened from five to seven, so when Matey is seven, having gone to a bilingual kindergarten in Amsterdam, he will return to Australia and into Tom's custody until he is twelve. During that time Tom will be fully responsible for his keep but the grandparents will pay for a personal tutor to keep up his Dutch. The de Graaf's will also have visitation rights for three weeks a year. When Matey turns twelve, he will get to choose who he prefers to live with."

"Good luck with that," said Tony, whose children had chosen not to live with him. As the squad knew, they barely gave him the time of day unless there was money involved.

"That's a horrible choice for such a young child." Pamela straightened her collar and looked disapproving.

"Well that's how it is. Everyone will be happy except Norma and Tracy..."

"—and possibly Matey," chipped in Palfrey. "Mrs de Graaf is quite the Gorgon. Good thing you get on with Ms Meer, JB," he added slyly—the only one who knew of the budding relationship between them.

Bailey knew how to keep a poker face. He mostly did it well.

"Happy families then," said Evan, turning back to his computer. "I don't see an edge for us here. Back to the coalface. When I joined the force, I thought the days would be a bit more exciting than this."

"You've forgotten the mysterious relationship between Mrs de Graaf and Stinky Bill that we have yet to figure out," said Pamela. "What about the missing diamond pendant."

"I've got a headache," said Tony. "I need more coffee."

The afternoon ground on until the unexpected arrival of boss, Marcia Odell, together with Fenton Farrell, the IT specialist and ex-husband of Bailey's former wife. His department worked out of a lower floor which meant they didn't meet often. This suited them both.

Odell introduced Farrel to the room and looked around for the squad's newest member. "Where's Bob Hunter?"

Up until that moment, he was such a quiet presence that no one had missed him. Bailey shrugged, "Updating the profile on Fred Butcher, I expect."

"I like to know where my people are working and how they are helping the enquiry," Odell said with a tightening of her lips. "There´s no room for a maverick. Individuals who are not part of the team cause trouble."

Palfrey, not normally an advocate for Hunter, spoke up. "He often has to go to the library for research."

Pamela chipped in. "—and he is a valued member of the team. He helped enormously when we brought Butcher in for the interview.

Odell didn´t look her way. "Which library?" she asked Palfrey.

He shrugged. "City of Perth. State Library. Whichever. Ask him."

Odell turned to Bailey, who spoke before she asked the obvious question. "I have every confidence in my squad to operate collectively or independently and individually when necessary. Hunter´s skills as a psychology graduate are unique. He reports back when he has something of interest to add. We all value his input." He didn´t say that he had Hunter´s mobile if needed, because actually, he realised that he didn´t. He´d better rectify that.

Farrell, who had been standing a step behind Odell, was entertaining them all with a good supply of eye rolling and eyebrow raising. It made Evan laugh, a laugh that turned into a snort and a bout of hiccups.

Odell turned to Farrel and luckily only caught

him wide-eyed, as if in surprise. "Farrell," she said economically.

He stepped forward. "This is about another case altogether, although one involving certain members of the squad." He eyed Bailey and then Palfrey. "When JB was rather dramatically slashed by two home intruders, one dropped his mobile phone as he climbed out of the kitchen window…"

Odell interrupted, "—luckily it belonged to the suspect that we were not able to apprehend and identify. When questioned, the other POI, Serge Horvat, refused to speak a word. A lawyer then arrived and applied for bail. The…" she paused as if to expurgate an annoying thought and rephrase, "—magistrate released Horvat with a surety of $50,000." She nodded to Farrell to continue.

Farrell waited a good while before speaking, giving her a sideways glance that didn′t bode well for their future interaction. Bailey had to give it to him. Farrell was tougher than some. Or maybe he just didn′t care as much about promotion. He′d reached the pinnacle of his career in the IT department and his skills would always be sought after in the private sector.

"The mobile phone was password protected," Farrell said as he looked around the room knowing that half of their mobiles wouldn′t be. "Only thirty six percent of phones are protected with a 4 digit PIN, but of course now that we have Cellebrite software we can overcome this."

Everyone nodded, although most had no clue about the Israeli, multi-billion-dollar digital intelligence company, Cellebrite. They left most of the IT sleuthing to Evan, and if he was stumped, he passed it on to Farrell's division.

"Anyway, we now have a name—albeit probably a false one—and an interesting call history of what, where and when, the POI is about. Plus, some incriminating photos of his illegal activities."

Albeit? thought Bailey. Who uses the word albeit unless they were being deposed in court, which Farrell rarely was. "What type of activities? B&E. GBH. Drugs. Sexual assault?"

"All of the above."

Meanwhile Palfrey was breathing heavily. He put one hand out to lean on the window sill and the other on his chest.

"You OK?" asked Bailey.

"Feel a little unwell. Prawns for lunch. A big mistake."

Bailey knew his partner had actually eaten a cheese sandwich because they´d both had a quick bite together in the canteen.

"Let´s get you sitting down." He led Palfrey to Hunter´s desk in the corner. "Water!" he said to Pamela who jumped up and rummaged through the litter on her desk as if to find a hidden bottle. She then headed for the door, roughly brushing past Odell in her haste.

Palfrey was meanwhile whispering urgently to Bailey, "You´ve got to have a look at the photos on the phone to see if Jazz is on there."

"I will Palfrey. Don´t worry."

Odell looked put out at the distraction. "Well," she said, "This is a good result. I would have thought you´d be more interested, Detective Bailey."

"Of course, Boss. I am, and with your permission I´ll be talking with Fenton later in the day when I´m sure my partner is OK. But as you know, we were instructed not to interfere. It´s not our case since we were personally involved—plus nobody died. I think I´d best first take Palfrey to the ER to have him checked out."

"Don´t worry about me. I´ll be fine, JB," Palfrey said unconvincingly, again clasping his chest.

Bailey tried not to smile. Palfrey was pulling an act that was so successful in interrogations. He seemed harmless, even clueless, but he wasn´t.

Fenton looked at them both with suspicion. He knew something was up. "I´ll wait to fill you in then, JB," he said with an enquiring look at Odell. She nodded. Then without a word, turned on her heel and left the room.

When Bailey dropped Palfrey at home, eschewing the hassle of a bogus ER visit with phantom chest pains, Palfrey leaned on the open car door to ask, "You don´t think Odell will check the workers comp claims and see I didn´t go to the ER, do you?"

"Doubt it. Anyway we'll cross that bridge if and when we come to it. Don't worry about stuff that hasn't happened yet. Things are bad enough as it is."

Bailey's trip back to Perth was the usual traffic nightmare. Luckily the carpark at HQ was half empty. Bailey parked in his favoured corner spot and headed up the three flights of stairs to Farrell's office. Despite his protestations that he was fine after the attack, it had taken its toll on his fitness. The pain from the stitches had made him reluctant to work out in the gym. People who proclaimed that pain was all in the head and should be ignored obviously didn't have any.

"You're up to something, JB," Fenton said when he handed over a memory stick of photos and videos from the still unknown perpetrator's lost mobile. "You know I shouldn't really give you a copy."

"I'm going to run some of the photos past Liam, the young guy who was drugged, and see if he can shed any light. You can have the credit if we put a name and locale to the face."

"You and Palfrey normally bat away cases that don't belong to you."

"Fourteen stitches and a permanent scar on my chest tend to interest me."

Farrell nodded. "Fair enough. As long as there's no other, tortuous reason."

"Me? Complicated? You know better than that."

“Simple is not how Janet describes you.”

“What do ex-wives know about us, really?”

They smiled. Having been married to the same woman did give them a kind of perverse bond. Bailey wanted to ask Farrell if Janet had taken revenge after their divorce and slept her way around all his friends, but sense prevailed. Small victories weren´t worth it. Let it go. Best work towards a conviction. That was another bond they shared. That and the photo Bailey held in reserve. The photo of Janet with the black eye that Farrell had given her on their honeymoon. It got him a fair bit of cooperation.

“You´d better edit which photos you show Liam.

“Don´t worry. Will do.”

Fiona drew the Mini to a stop in Bailey´s driveway. Tracey and Palfrey piled out and the trio walked towards the front door. Tracy was thoroughly enjoying Fiona´s use of Liam´s wheels. It was actually more convenient than dating him. There were no awkward moments at the end of the night. When she turned sixteen, she´d get a licence and when she´d saved enough money she´d buy her own car. She´d start putting money away for a deposit now. Maybe look for a part time job at McDonalds. Not a job that would take up the mental space she´d need for her studies. Money was power. It was better not to be dependent on anyone else. Her plan to join the police force should provide a secure future. She couldn´t understand the school friends who were only focussed on marrying some type of professional with a large income so they could stay home with the kids. She had her mother′s example to demonstrate that didn′t work.

Shooter came barrelling through the screen door, greeting their presence with prolonged barking not to mention delighted prancing.

Tracy pointed to the ground and growled, "No!" to stop him jumping on her newly laundered jeans.

"Palfrey, I told you to come on your own," Bailey said.

"Try leaving them behind."

"At least you didn′t bring Jazz."

"She′s been in bed all day with the covers pulled over her head having yet another relapse. Best leave her to Diane."

"Good because the photos and videos are brutal."

"We′re here now, and we need to see them." Fiona looked unusually determined. Tracy nodded in agreement.

They traipsed into the kitchen, where Bailey had set up his laptop. "This will cost us our jobs if you tell anyone," he warned the girls, "I won′t show you the worst of it, just the faces Fenton enhanced."

They nodded. "Why would the men film it?" Tracy asked.

"The sex assault squad say perps often film themselves for future gratification. Not to mention there's a market to watch it on the dark web."

"You mean people will pay to watch it? Jazz being raped?" Tracy asked with incredulity.

Fiona made a choking noise and pushed her chair back. The sound of vomiting from the nearby bathroom followed. Tracy pressed her lips firmly together. If she wanted to join the police, she'd have to toughen up. "We're talking about her baby sister," she excused.

Palfrey looked away; no explanation needed. "What next?"

"I was wondering about using Nick Spagos—the nurse who looked after Liam—to get us closer. Maybe Fiona could accept his invitation to meet up at the bar he mentioned. The place where the ex-Slovakian army guys go to brag about the past. See if she could get a lead on the guy."

"And how would she accomplish that? She can't suddenly produce a cropped headshot and ask who it is. That's pretty far-fetched, not to mention dangerous. I'd rather not have two traumatised grandchildren, thank you very much." Palfrey rubbed a hand over his face.

"Well, we can't go there and ask. Everyone would clam up tighter than a duck's arse. But we could park outside and maybe follow him, if he's there."

"If, and it's a big if. Clutching at straws here."

The two detectives stared at each other.

Tracy leaned forward, amazed that she was going to be the source of restraint. "Why not do nothing? Just let the other detectives do what they're paid to do. They'll get the second guy in the end."

"Or they'll lose interest when another solvable case comes along and it will end up with all the cold cases."

"I want to do it," said Fiona. She was leaning on the doorframe wiping her mouth. "Anything to catch the bastard."

Bailey poured her a glass of water, "Farrell's going to send the photos to the Sexual Assault Squad. Tracy's right. It's not worth us getting involved. Plus, the B&E and assault charge is already being handled. They'll fast track an attack on one of their own."

"Don't even try to talk me out of it!" Fiona interrupted. "It's worth a try. If I had my way the guy would be castrated."

They all looked at her.

"What? I'm just saying what you're all thinking. I'm not the little innocent you seem to think I am." She stood up. "Come on, Tracy. Let's go. I'll call Nick and see when I can set up a date. The sooner the better. I want this to be over. Maybe then Jazz will finally get out of bed."

Chapter 26

Two days later Bailey turned to Palfrey and asked again, "So you´re sure this App to track Fiona will work?" He didn´t trust technology as much as he trusted the well-tested principle that if things could go wrong, they would go wrong. The LED lights in the kitchen made the conversation with his partner feel like an interrogation. Bailey wondered if the savings in energy were worth the lack of ambience.

"Jesus, JB—you´re turning into an old woman. Diane put the *Famisafe* App on both Jazz and Fiona´s mobiles after what we now call *the incident*. Unfortunately, it´s now on mine as well, so I can´t hide at your place drinking beer anymore."

"Save me a fortune," said Bailey.

"She´s been tracking the girls for a couple of weeks, and it´s been working just fine. Lots of parents download it to make sure their kids are where they should be. At football practice or whatever."

Bailey took a deep breath, but before he could say a word, Palfrey chipped in, "—and no, neither Jazz nor Fiona play footie, just in case you´re wondering."

"Ha ha. But what I´m really wondering—and worrying about, is that if Fiona goes off with this Spagos character or is grabbed by the perp, can we still track her?"

"If she has her phone."

"What if he throws her phone out the window and it´s run over by a truck?"

"That´s why we´re going to stake out the bar. She´s taking Liam´s Mini. He´s still under doctors' orders not to drive. She told Spagos she preferred to have her own wheels on a first date."

"OK. Good, I guess," but even though the idea was originally his, he´d changed his mind and he didn´t like it. They were way out on a limb and using an 18-year-old girl as bait.

Palfrey read his mind. "It was her strongly stated choice, JB. She was going to do it with or without us. At least we can reduce the risk. I´m aware that we can´t erase it."

Bailey wondered when it was that his partner stepped up, stopped listening to caution, and started making the hard decisions. "Diane OK with that?"

"About as OK as I am, which is not very; but we hope finding and bagging this guy will help Jazz. She´s scared shitless he´ll track her down. Until he´s behind bars she´ll never recover. Even then…it´s going to take a long time." Responding to a ping on his phone, he looked at it and added, "Fiona´s leaving in twenty minutes. The bar´s called *Strange Company.* It´s in Nairn St, Fremantle so let´s get going. All the one-way streets there might be a problem"

"Well that´s fucked things up already." Bailey threw his arms up. "What if we need to split up. You know I can´t bring the Camaro. It´s hopeless for covert work." They had decided to use Palfrey´s beat up four wheel drive. Over the years he had deliberately left all the usual scrapes and dings in the bodywork but mechanically, as he constantly told Bailey, it was a thing of beauty.

"*Strange Company* indeed. Been telling you for years you should drive a normal car."

"Too late now. We'll have to park out the front and hope for the best."

"Bloody hell. Parking on a Friday night in Fremantle's a bitch."

"The usual plan then. Rock up and improvise."

As it turned out, a delivery van was just leaving a parking space with a good view of the bar/restaurant. Palfrey nipped in behind it, earning him a loud blast from a Subaru, which had stopped to bag the space in reverse. Palfrey gave the driver the finger, and after a pause the car accelerated away. It drove around the block and pulled up dangerously close to Palfrey's door with a screech of tyres. Opening the window, Palfrey flashed his badge and yelled. "Piss off. Police business!" The car roared off again.

"Great," Bailey sighed. "He's probably one of the ex-Slovakian army blokes that Spagos drinks with, and we've blown our cover already."

"What's got into you. JB? I'm supposed to be the negative one."

Bailey just shook his head. Speechless.

Liam's distinctive lime green Mini passed by not long afterwards and turned into the driveway leading to the bar´s carpark. Palfrey tapped his fingers on the steering wheel. "I´d feel better if one of us could go inside."

"I´d feel better with a couple of large whiskies."

"Ditto. Fiona said they´re going to have a bite to eat and get to know each other. She´ll only have a spritzer since she´s driving. If our perp turns up, she´s going to excuse herself, go to the Ladies and let us know."

"You´ve told me this at least ten times."

An hour dragged by without a text. Three more cars turned into the bar´s car park. Palfrey got out to relieve himself against the car´s rear tyres. "Prostate," he said when he heaved his bulk back in.

"—and you´ve told me that at least a couple of hundred times!" complained Bailey.

"We´re starting to sound like *The Odd Couple*."

"What do you mean, starting?"

Another hour went by.

"The girl´s got a cast iron bladder. Couldn´t she at least update us?"

"No news means the guy´s not there."

"I know that, Palfrey. How long until your retirement?"

"Yeah. You´re aggravating me too."

Bailey knew the sniping didn´t mean a thing. It was a way to deal with the tension. Either the night would be a bust, or not. At least they now knew the name of the bar where the guy might drink. It was a start. They could pass the name on to Fenton as payment for allowing Bailey access to the perp´s phone. Fenton could advise the sexual assault squad. They had men undercover who´d blend in.

A noisy crowd spilled onto the pavement and turned left towards Pakenham Street. No one stood out as unusually bulked up or walked with the exaggerated swagger that pointed to a man being ex-army. In fact, they all looked like Joe Public on a Friday night with Jill Public by their side. Loud and annoying but unthreatening.

"Why this bar?" asked Palfrey.

"The name? Or one of the major players lives nearby? Why go to a particular bar?"

"Free drinks. Own the place. Proximity. Inertia?"

"Let´s hope for proximity."

Twenty minutes later, with the glut of Friday night cars coming and going, Palfrey´s mobile pinged with a text. "*He´s here and he´s leaving on foot out the front with two other guys. I´m on my way too. Nick´s going to walk me to the car.*"

Bailey got out and stepped into the shadows, his choice of black-on-black clothing deliberate. Three men swung out of the bar and turned towards the one-way traffic. Palfrey would have to make a U-turn. "Drive into the bar´s car park and then come back," Bailey hissed. "I´ll follow on this side of the road."

"He knows you, JB."

"That's why I wore a cap. And he knows you as well!"

"You should've stopped shaving and worn glasses. Betta hope he hasn't got his Stanley knife with him." And with that Palfrey pulled out into the street.

Bailey could hear the quiet voices of the men, who'd stopped to light cigarettes. They walked off close together, shoulder to shoulder. Occasionally, one would laugh and bump the shoulder of the guy next to him. They didn't say much and were speaking Slovak anyway so he was none the wiser. Their body language made it obvious they knew each other well. The camaraderie they displayed usually came from the military or a well-integrated sports team.

Visibility was limited in the badly lit street, making it easier to tail them, but it also made it difficult to know which guy was THE guy. He thought it was probably the one in the middle, with the two wingmen looking out for him. The one nearest the road turned once and looked towards Bailey, but Bailey kept on walking, adding a little stagger to his step. He hoped to look well and truly stonkered. Palfrey's four wheel drive drove slowly past, as if looking for a park. Luckily there weren't any. Friday nights sometimes worked in your favour. The men turned into a cul-de-sac and Palfrey drove slowly on.

Bailey crossed the road, unzipped and, following Palfrey's example, pissed against a tree—a crime that could bring $600 fine or 3 months' imprisonment, especially since he was not on lawful police business. He wished he´d thought to bring a pack of cigarettes as cover. The men stopped at a modern, attached villa, chatted for a bit and then the middle guy went inside. The other two wheeled around and looked across the road at Bailey, who was zipping up. They saw no threat and turned back in the direction of the bar. The lights went on in the villa, and Bailey, still in character, stumbled away to find Palfrey.

The Toyota took another turn around the block with Bailey on board. The two Slovakians weren´t in sight and Bailey presumed they´d gone back into the bar.

"Did you get the address?" Palfrey asked. "How about I go to the bar and have a drink? Get the lie of the land."

"We agreed not to do that." Bailey looked at his partner, dressed in his usual khakis and blue button-down shirt. However, instead of his usual police issue shoes, he was wearing loafers with no socks. Good call. It did help with the general public look.

"If Spagos thought the bar was OK for Fiona, I´m thinking it would be OK for me. The crowd that came out earlier looked pretty regular. Meanwhile, we shouldn´t get too close to the villa. The guy´s trained to be super alert. You stay in the car and wait and I´ll go in and see what´s what."

"If Spagos is still there and remembers you from when we visited Liam in hospital..."

"Shit." They looked at each other. With his bulk, Palfrey might be hard to forget.

Palfrey took out his phone. "I´ll call Fiona. Tell her to put it on speaker phone so some copper doesn´t pull her up for using her phone while she´s driving."

"Sometimes you think too much."

"One of us has to."

The phone rang out. Palfrey checked the App. "She´s not on her way home. Seems to be near the old Captain Stirling Hotel. Wait—she´s turning into a side street."

"Now what?"

While they pondered that, Palfrey´s phone rang.

"I was driving," said Fiona.

"You OK?"

"Jesus. Nag nag nag. I´m meeting up with Nick again to listen to some jazz at a club."

"Did you see Nick actually leave the bar?"

"I´m following him! Or I was until you called and I had to stop."

"OK, that´s fine. Just checking. Did you get to talk to any of his mates?"

"Kidding—right? The creeps came over and had a few words to say, but Nick soon got rid of them."

"Glad you´re safe. Have a good time."

"You can stop stalking me now. Turn the damn App off. Nick´s a super nice guy."

Palfrey put the phone back in his pocket with a sigh.

"You don′t know how to turn off an App do you?" Bailey grinned.

"Wouldn′t do it even if I did know how. Looks like we′re on."

Half an hour later, Palfrey slipped back to the SUV. "I propped myself at the bar and checked out a rowdy group of men in a corner. They were speaking in a foreign language with a few familiar four-letter words sprinkled in. I ordered a whisky and chatted to the barman for a bit, saying I was waiting for a Tinder date. Said it was my first time in the bar and I liked the place. Cheeky bastard looked me up and down and predicted my date would be a no show."

Bailey supressed a grin.

"At least I could use the Tinder pretext to text you and say our guy wasn′t there." He shifted in his seat and undid his collar. "I had another drink and wandered over to an empty table. Took my phone out and pretended to talk to my date, but actually took a few photos. They won′t have very good resolution, because I couldn′t use the flash, but the place was reasonably well lit, so we should be able to use face recognition software."

"Get any info from the barman on the men?"

"Said they came in a couple of times a week and didn′t cause any trouble."

"Anything else?"

"He didn't volunteer anything and since I couldn't show too much interest, I just said they were noisy sons of bitches and I couldn't understand why my date hadn't chosen to meet somewhere more intimate."

This time Bailey laughed out loud. The force would never use Palfrey undercover. His partner wasn't the sort of guy to blend in but Bailey suspected that, short as it was, Palfrey had relished the charade.

"You'll have to drive home, JB. After 2 double whiskies I'll be over the limit."

"Lucky bastard! We'll go past the perp's street and see if the light's still on. Count how many villas his is from the corner, and see what we can find out about the property."

"And then what?"

"We step back. Give it to Fenton. He can come up with whatever story makes him look good, as long as it keeps us out of the picture. Then we get to keep our jobs and our retirement."

"Inventive is he? Fenton?"

"He listed some pretty plausible reasons for me not to kick his arse after he gave Janet the black eye."

"Don't give me that! You love holding something over him."

"I do, Palfrey. I do."

"And don't tell me you haven't ever felt like giving Janet a shiner yourself."

Palfrey as always, wanted the last word. Bailey thought about saying *never,* but Palfrey would know that was a lie. Initially, he´d forgiven Janet´s infidelities with the excuse that she was blocking the pain of their daughter´s death. Later when she screwed his best friend from high school days, he realised the affairs were aimed at him. To punish him for unexplained crimes. for not keeping their daughter safe. Although with a drunk driver at 3 p.m. when school was out, how she had expected him to do that was anyone´s guess. They divorced not long after.

He turned on the ignition. The Sexual Assault Squad would do their job. He and Palfrey had found Jazz´s rapist and would hand over his whereabouts. The photos on the perp´s lost phone would almost certainly convict him. Or—since it was always hard to be certain how a court case would resolve—there was a probable 70:30 percent chance of a conviction ahead; leaving Jazz to get on with her life. She might be emotionally scarred and suffer from trust issues but at least she was alive. A better result than for the victims who made up the Homicide Squad´s daily workload.

Chapter 27

Bailey ignored Shooter´s mournful howl from the back yard. He´d taken him on a quick constitutional around the block after breakfast and whereas that might not make up for the daily run the dog took with Tracy, it would have to do until after work, later that day. Tracy had given back her house key and future dog-walking was to be by appointment only. He couldn´t have teenage girls using his home as a convenient clubhouse, thus buggering up his dormant love life. Greta had yet to reply to his message on her answering service.

He slammed the Camaro´s door and backed out of his driveway, then gunned the car down the road. He enjoyed the throaty roar and hoped his normally understanding neighbours wouldn´t mind the noise. Most were already up and off to work at that time, except the Johnsons across the road, who were retired. Judging by Mrs Johnson´s frequent offerings of vegetarian casseroles, they wouldn´t mind either.

Palfrey met him at his front door and ushered him back to the colourful sunroom where Diane, Jazz and Fiona sat together on the bamboo sofa. Bailey and Palfrey took the single chairs facing them. It being a family conference, Tracy was not invited. She was back living with her mother, weeks away from her sixteenth birthday and *my freedom* as she continually referred to it. Bailey wondered if her freedom would turn out to be all she hoped. Jazz was still in a fragile state with Diane tiptoeing around her. Bailey wasn´t completely onboard. Sooner or later, Jazz had to make a pact with reality and decide to get on with her life. If not, she would forever feel like quarry.

Palfrey had asked Bailey to run the family through the latest news. Apparently, a grandfather, despite his years of experience in the police force, was not to be trusted with explanations of the law or of any real-world happenings. Bailey had rehearsed the sequence during the 15-minute drive.

He began, "So, yesterday Vladimir Valcic— who was formally identified by material on his mobile phone— and Serge Horvat, his accomplice, were refused bail and remain in custody. And it´s thanks to Fiona´s help that we found Valcic´s whereabouts."

"Does that mean they will be kept in jail until the court case?" Jazz´s voice was high-pitched with anxiety.

"Ordinarily it would not, but fortunately the magistrate refused them bail because they conjointly face a number of other serious charges."

"Rape isn´t a serious enough charge to hold somebody!"

"Normally innocence until proven guilty is the norm, but let me continue," Bailey sighed and looked at Palfrey, who was sitting back sipping a coffee, face inscrutable. This was Bailey´s show and Palfrey was determined not to interrupt or add anything extraneous unless asked.

"The pair of them shared a rental property in Fremantle, which is where the police arrested Valcic and re-arrested Horvat, who had given a false address when bailed. They were initially charged with sexual assault and penetration without consent. One of the victims, who had been videoed on Valcic's mobile phone, had reported the rape when she underwent tests at St John of God's hospital. She is determined to give evidence at a future trial. If, as is usual, it is a jury trial there may be an 18-24 month wait."

"I'm not giving evidence. No way." Jazz raged. "I don't want one more person to know what happened to me. There are already far too many." And she glared at Bailey, who sighed again.

Diane patted Jazz's hand. "JB is here only to help you, dear. Because your grandpa is his partner. They've risked their careers to find the men involved. Plus, JB got a bloody great scar like a zipper down his front. Try to show a bit more gratitude and understanding."

Jazz's mutinous pout went unchanged.

Bailey had rarely heard Diane swear. Bloody was pretty extreme for her. He nodded his thanks. Teenage victims were often intractable. They had no experience of life's vicissitudes and tended to avoid wondering what part their decisions may have contributed to the problem. If Jazz, being underage, hadn't gone to the nightclub... He knew better than to blame the victim, but sometimes he did wonder about society′s current cluelessness when it came to personal safety.

He went on, "under warrant, the police searched the home in Fremantle and found marketable quantities of drugs, plus firearms and cash. Valcic and Horvat have been charged with numerous offences and investigations are ongoing to discover who else may be involved with the drug dealing. The police contested bail and the magistrate refused the men′s lawyer when he applied for it." Bailey decided not to say their sought-after defence counsel was extremely experienced, expensive and was batting about seven out of ten wins against the prosecution.

Jazz flinched and said, "Are you sure they won′t get out? Horvat managed to get released even after he attacked you!"

"The magistrate gave her reasons for not providing bail as:" Bailey ticked them off on his fingers, "the risk of flight, since they hold Croatian passports. Risk of further offences, because they had saleable quantities of drugs in their residence. The risk of intimidation of witnesses, since they are known to be highly trained ex-Croation military. Not to mention the number of sexual assaults detailed on the mobile phone—although their lawyer argued against the legitimacy of the phone′s contents being used at trial."

Seeing Diane′s relief at this, he added, "but we believe the mobile′s contents clearly will be allowed. At this point, it′s unlikely Jazz will be required to give evidence." Rape or domestic violence victims could not be compelled to give evidence, but they could still be held in contempt of court and fined for each day they refused to testify. All the same, he very much doubted a fourteen-year-old would be forced to testify against her will and saw no reason to suggest otherwise.

The three women clasped hands and gave a small cheer. Diane leant forward, "Does this mean there will be separate trials, and the sexual assault trial with the willing witness will be held first?"

"Probably. The investigation into the drug and firearm offences is in its early stages and with a specialist department. The upshot is that the two of them have a lot to answer for ahead of them and a minimal chance of being released in the meantime."

"Coffee?" Palfrey asked Bailey, judging it was now safe to speak.

"How about we take it to go? Work to do," and with that the men got up to head for Police headquarters, relieved to once more be pursuing Fred Butcher, Hannah de Graaf's suspected murderer.

The grey day outside had once again seeped through the windows into the mood of the homicide squad. Evan blew his nose loud and long then wiped his streaming eyes. "Late summer to autumn is the worst time for allergies."

Pamela looked up from her desk to ask, "Need some antihistamines? "

"Got some."

"Apart from that, do you have any good news?"

"Zilch."

Bailey looked over the room and realised the entire squad was shattered from too many unrewarding phone calls with no progress to show for it. Nor had surveillance achieved anything worthwhile. "Tell you what, let´s bring in Stinky Bill and interview him. You never know."

"The guy will never give it up. He´s as cunning as a shithouse rat." Palfrey was twirling around on his office chair making Formula 1 noises. For a man nearing retirement, he could be pretty childish. Bailey guessed that was what made him good with kids.

"Which is one of the reasons why, Palfrey, I´m going to ask Pamela and Tony to have a go at him. New faces. Less predictable. I want Hunter to sit in too, to interpret body language and to give us his take about what questions made Bill uncomfortable."

Tony laughed. "You think giving us this interview is some kind of reward for good work? Making the three of us sit in a room reeking of dead fish."

"I thought you wanted a rest from cold calls to people who don´t want to talk to you. People who either think you´re trying to scam them or sell something. Or do you want to have a face-to-face interview with a person of interest who could even be an accessory to murder? This is called the homicide squad for a reason you know. And yes, this was supposed to show you I value your input, and thought you´d done a good job interviewing Butcher, but I guess I suck at dispensing brownie points."

"OK. OK. I see where you´re coming from."

Palfrey did another twirl. "Rather you than me," he grinned at Tony.

"Don´t get too comfortable, Palfrey. You and me. We´ll go pick him up then hand him over to the Topela team. We´ll use your car. Mine´s boxed in."

The room erupted in laughter. Imprisoned in a car with Stinky Bill for half an hour. It´d be hard to get the smell out of the seat covers."

"We´ll take a squad car," said Palfrey, unphased.

Tony and Pamela mapped out a reasonably flexible order for the questions. Both had attended a recent refresher course on PEACE tactics for use during interviews and would attempt to follow the acronym. This was broken down into: Planning, Engagement. Account clarification, Closure and Evaluation. Pamela´s interview style was more personal than formal, an approach that tended to elicit more random information for them to confirm. Formal interviews made the interviewee stick to one answer and repeat it ad infinitum, if they spoke at all. Pamela would lead and Tony would jump in if required. They ran their thoughts past Hunter, who as usual nodded and said little.

"Anything you´d do differently?" asked Tony.

“Not that I can think of right now. Let´s just see how it goes.” Hunter replied.

Bailey, who preferred a more scripted approach, cautioned, “if you see a promising line of questioning, Bob, make some sort of sign. Rub a forefinger across your lip or uncross your legs—or cross them. If necessary, meet Tony or Pamela outside to give them your input. Three against one would signal to the defence a distinct sign of intimidation. It´s not that I think you wouldn´t do a good job during an interview, it´s just that Tony and Pamela are six months into a partnership so it makes sense for them to work together. Right?”

“Sure. Right.”

As usual, Bailey wasn´t at all certain what Hunter was thinking or whether he was on-side or not. He just had to hope for the best. Hunter was an asset to the squad, but an integrated part of the team he was not. Not yet anyway.

Once back at headquarters, Bailey and Palfrey had left Stinky Bill to cool his heels in one of the three interview rooms. He hadn´t asked for a solicitor to be present and since he was not yet under caution, they hadn´t offered him one. “Just want to run some things past you to see if you can help,” was Palfrey´s relaxed explanation when they broached Bill in his office. He´d been surrounded by watches and mobile phones, checking their functionality and adding prices. “Best we record the interview to teach the young guns how to conduct themselves."

Now Bailey and Palfrey stood behind the mirrored one-way glass and watched Bill approach it to smooth his moustache and then give them a wink. It wasn´t his first rodeo. He knew they were there observing him.

Pamela and Tony walked in with Hunter trailing behind.

"What´s this? A tag team?" Bill was already setting the parameters for an appeal in case he inadvertently gave them something to work with.

"DC Hunter´s new. Still learning." Pamela sat down and indicated the chair opposite her, behind the scuffed table. Bill stood for a moment, regarding Hunter who as usual gave nothing away. Just sat by the door, crossed his legs and leaned back.

"Was that a tell?" Palfrey asked Bailey.

"Don´t know. Forgot to ask what his signal would be."

"Well I hope he told Pamela and Tony."

Tony in the meantime was fiddling with the recording equipment and advising who was present, the day, date and time.

"Mr Johnson," Pamela began.

"Bill. Call me Bill, everyone else does."

"Thank you. Bill, we´re here to ask you about an encounter you had with a man by an ATM on May 17 in Scarborough." She nodded at Tony who cued the photo of Bill and Fred Butcher on his laptop and turned it towards him.

"No clue." Said Bill. "Don´t remember it."

"This man?" Tony showed him both the fuzzy photo captured by the bank´s security system and a still of the video Tracy had taken.

Bill slowly shook his head, leaned forward to examine the screen, then said, "No. Seems a bit familiar but I can´t put a name to him. Lots of people go through our doors selling stuff. Buying stuff. It´s impossible to remember them all."

Pamela took a sip of water. Her eyes were beginning to water from Bill´s noxious smell. "Hard Pawn is your own business, is that right Mr Johnson? Bill?"

Bill drummed his fingers on the table. "A proprietary limited company owns it."

"But you are the Managing Director and major shareholder. In fact, aside from a couple of other companies that are also shareholders, you pretty-well run things don´t you?"

Bill waggled his head and turned his mouth down. "I do my best. But I´m not superhuman. I can´t be there 24/7. I have sales managers, assistant sales managers, junior sales managers. I only employ managers. Gives them something to brag about at home."

Pamela laughed. "Sounds like your employees are lucky to have such an understanding boss." Bill preened a little. Hunter drew a finger across his upper lip. “Tell us about your day, Bill. What would an average one involve?”

Hunter′s tell was obviously a sign for Pamela to draw the question out. This she did in excruciating detail. Showing such a fascination that Bill had to ask if she were thinking of opening a pawn shop herself.

“Maybe in a second life. If I′m ever thrown off the force.”

“Can′t imagine that happening,” Bill said with a twisted grin.

Pamela eyed Tony to be ready for the next slide. “So, if I were to show you sales invoices, it could be anyone in your employ who was responsible for the sales,”

“No. Employees work on a base salary plus commission, so each employee signs the invoice. When take-home pay is involved, sales get quite competitive.”

“Do you personally sell the higher end products to ensure paying commission doesn′t get out of hand? It′s hard to make a profit these days, what with all the extras a boss has to pay, like superannuation, holiday pay, even long service leave.”

Bill chortled. “I doubt I′ve ever had to pay long service leave. Employees come and go all the time. Hundreds of ′em. Dealing with the public gets old pretty quickly. Especially if customers think the item they′re pawning is worth more than we′re willing to pay. They can get pretty aggressive. We have to employ security guards around the clock.”

"If you do happen to sell or buy an item yourself, do you sign the invoice?"

"Of course. Standard practice. Otherwise, someone else would try to get the credit—
and the commission."

Tony turned the laptop around again, showing the perfectly focussed photo of the Hard Pawn invoice they´d discovered when searching Butcher´s house. One Samsung OLEG 55inch flat screen TV Sold to Fred Butcher. Payment *deferred until further notice.* Signed by Bill Johnson. "This television is on a list of stolen property, Mr Butcher."

Behind the one-way mirror, Bailey gave Palfrey a high five. "Gotcha! Well done Pamela."

"News. To me," said Bill. "Sounds like an insurance dodge. The owner says his property´s stolen and also gives it to Butcher to sell. Gets paid out twice. Perhaps we should call my solicitor This seems to have gone beyond a friendly chat."

Chapter 28

With the eventual arrival of Bill´s lawyer, Graham Davis, and after a lengthy private consultation, the two agreed to resume the interview with Pamela and Tony. Davis objected to Hunter´s presence, believing that it was not in his client´s interest to train new police officers.

Davis would also not allow Bill to speak, nor answer any further questions. This was the usual ploy used by lawyers so that clients´ words could not be used against them in future court cases. "Mr Johnson freely agrees that he is acquainted with Fred Butcher, and that from time to time, Butcher acts as an intermediary, bringing goods to sell or pawn.

"As far as Mr Johnson is aware, Butcher works for a removal company, and in this job, customers advise him when they no longer wish to keep various personal items due to downsizing. Butcher then agrees to transport the goods to Hard Pawn to negotiate a price for them for a pre-approved commission—usually between 10 to 20% depending on the difficulty of transport. From time to time, Butcher prefers to take goods in lieu of cash for his commission.

"The second-hand television referred to on this invoice was one of these occasions." Davis looked at the two policeman, bright eyed. "Mr Johnson was confused when saying he didn´t know the person in the photo because the man in question was wearing reflective sunglasses. Had you shown him the invoice at the same time, of course it would have jogged his memory. Butcher is a casual acquaintance, not usually seen outside of office hours. "

Pamela rolled her neck around to free up a twinge. She had added a dark jacket to her normally tight shirt, professional to a tee. "And yet. Mr Johnson and Mr Butcher were seen together on the 5th April, which you will agree was only weeks ago."

"Mr Johnson bumped into him in the street. Butcher extended his hand for a handshake and said *it's good to see you.* Or something equally as forgettable. Nothing more than that."

"Does Mr Johnson keep a record of the transactions with Butcher?"

"He has a notebook in which he records the running total of whether he owes Butcher, or Butcher owes him."

"And does this notebook record every transaction?"

Davis looked at Bill who shook his head. "Only the running debit or credit balance."

"I also want to ask Mr Johnson about his relationship with a Mrs de Graff."

"I'm sorry. That's not in my brief."

Temporarily stumped, Pamela said, "In that case we may need to interview your client again under caution, unless you care to confer again."

The lawyer nodded. "Always happy to oblige DC Page but perhaps we can do this another day. I am due in court. DS Caravelli, please make a note of Mr Johnson's co-operation during this interview."

And with that Stinky Bill and his lawyer were free to go.

In the post-interview meeting, all agreed that things had not gone as well as they had first hoped, but nor were they surprised. "They don't call him Teflon Bill for nothing."

"Stinky, Teflon Bill?" queried Evan. "Seems a bit verbose."

"Forget the adjectives then." said Bailey.

"What now?" asked Tony.

"I guess we could interview Mrs de Graf about her connection with Bill."

"Want to do that through the honorary consul, Greta Meer?" asked Pamela.

"I'll leave that to you, Pamela." Bailey had no wish to be the one to call Greta on official business. Best keep well out of it and again trust Topela to do their job. He didn't want to give the impression that lack of progress was in any way Tony and Pamela's fault or that he had less confidence in them.

"How about letting Hunter have a go at her?" said Palfrey, surprising everyone. "Mrs de Graff is tricky and from what I heard, Pamela didn't exactly get off to a good start with her."

"OK with you, Pamela?" asked Bailey.

"Fine. Whatever. But sometimes a little aggravation can work in our favour"

"Maybe not this time," said Bailey, supposing he´d aggravated Greta enough.

Hunter as usual said nothing but did bare his ultra white teeth in a wide smile, which was a lot more than they usually got out of him. "You call Ms Meer, Bob." confirmed Bailey.

Palfrey smirked. Bailey read it as meaning *Bailey and his useless attempts at romantic trysts* and had to admit his partner had got it in one. Bailey didn´t have the knack for long-term relationships and should never have got involved in this one.

Hunter came back within minutes. "Not gonna happen, JB. Apparently today is the day Ms Meer´s going to accompany Mrs de Graff and Matey to the airport."

Bailey realised the squad had long since reverted to calling Bram by his nickname.

"Without letting us know? That´s rather sudden isn´t it?"

"Now that the custody arrangements are in place, Ms Meer said there was no reason to delay. The longer the child stayed with his foster parents, the more traumatic the separation."

"What time´s the flight?"

"10:20 tonight. Flying first class with Emirates. They have to be there three hours before take-off."

"Why weren´t we told about this?"

"I asked. It didn´t go down well. Ms Meer said that custody arrangements have nothing to do with the homicide squad."

"Wow! Severe," said Palfrey. "Doesn´t sound like we´ve made a friend there."

"I offered our best wishes. What else could I say?" Hunter looked more than usually thoughtful. "Strange, though. After all JB, you and your dog pretty well saved the kid´s life."

"Unfortunately, I didn´t hit it off with Hannah´s mother. She has a poor impression of the WA police force in general and me and Pamela in particular." Bailey replied.

"Well, you were getting along pretty well with Ms Meer," Palfrey interjected.

"Things change. Murder investigations put people off. We´re contaminated by association. That´s nothing new."

"Who´s waxing philosophical now? I thought that was Hunter´s job."

Hunter frowned at him. "I´m not a philosopher, Palfrey. I´m a qualified psychologist with a master´s degree AND I am a homicide detective." For Hunter., that was a long speech.

"Point taken." Palfrey bowed in submission.

Bailey stood up. "I´m not at all happy about this. Evan, see if you can get a warrant to stop Mrs de Graff and Matey from leaving. Her meeting with Bill stinks almost as much as he does. Once she´s back in Amsterdam, there´s a part of our investigation we can never get back. We need to know what that was all about."

Hunter nodded. “Something is off, for sure, I think…”

Pamela interrupted, “You won´t be popular with the boss, JB. Don´t you think you should run this past Odell? She´s new and wants to make her mark and not get involved in controversy.”

Pamela had obviously learned about the politics of running the squad during her affair with their previous boss. She may be right, but all the same Bailey wasn´t going to prejudice the outcome of the case due to internal politics.

“Not if Odell´s going to say no for public relation reasons. We´ll go ahead and then tell her later and let the flack fall on me.”

“What reasons do I give in the warrant?” Evan asked. “It´s pretty late in the day. I´ll have to make it quick.”

“Reasonable and probable grounds of collusion in a crime. Reasonable suspicion.”

“That´s pretty weak.”

“I do have the power to arrest her without a warrant.”

“—and see you career go down the toilet,” said Pamela. “It´s one thing to prevent her from leaving *at this time*. Quite another to arrest her.”

“Well, do the best you can, Evan. Shop it around if necessary. If that fails, we could still interview her before she flies out.”

“Less than ideal without the ability to record.” said Palfrey.

"Hunter, call the airport and ask them to make a room available for us. We can record on a mobile device or laptop."

Bailey and Hunter left for the airport at six, figuring to be half an hour ahead of Mrs de Graff and whoever accompanied her and Matey. Odell wasn't in her office as they passed by on their way to the lift. Small mercies. "Oh dear. Ms Odell seems to have left for home," Bailey said for the record.

Hunter grimaced, knowing Bailey was commenting out loud for his benefit and that he'd be required to repeat it. He was along on the theory that, as the latest recruit to the squad, the Commissioner wouldn't expect him to have pushed back. He would therefore not incur any repercussions should things go badly. That aside, Hunter's ability to read body language would be helpful. Bailey was pretty good at knowing when a subject lied but Hunter seemed to intuit why or what they were hiding.

They were met by the airport's head of PR. She asked whether the passenger would, or could, check in before being ushered to the room selected for the interview.

"Maybe issue the boarding pass, but set aside the luggage. How late can you get it on the plane if we see no reason to detain her?"

"An hour?"

"That's probably all the time we need," said Bailey, fingers crossed behind his back. Not normally superstitious, this was a high-risk gamble. Airport security would usher Mrs de Graff to the room after check-in. Perhaps that might just make her realise how seriously the police considered her departure from Australia without notifying them,

"All set?" he asked Hunter, who was setting up both a mobile and tablet to record.

"No worries."

They arranged several uncomfortable green and gold patterned chairs around a bleached oak desk and tried to appear unworried. "This is a better solution to the warrant," said Bailey, wanting to convince them both.

Hunter nodded. Evan hadn´t managed to persuade any of his usual contacts that the matter required judicial interference so they had no warrant. "It is what it is," Hunter said, unhelpfully in Bailey´s opinion.

The door opened and Mrs de Graff entered the room with a flood of complaints. Greta followed with Matey perched on a hip. The two security men quickly departed, shutting the door without a word. Hunter placed his chair against the door where Bailey could see him.

"This is outrageous." Greta began.

"What is outrageous, Ms Meer, is that we were not informed that Hannah´s mother had opted to leave Australia without informing us. The police department is trying to solve a crime and would like the co-operation of the victim´s closest relative. We had no idea she was contemplating departure at this time."

Greta shook her head. "Unbelievable. I strongly protest. A grandmother just wants to start leading a normal life with her grandson…"

"Please take a seat and let Mrs de Graff respond to our questions without any further comment or interruptions from you."

Greta let Matey down to the floor and sat. Matey ran towards Bailey saying, "Dog?" his feet seeming clumsy in his new shoes. Just as Greta reached out to grab him, he tripped and flew forward, hitting the side of his forehead on the corner of the desk. His scream had the pitch of a fire engine. Bailey got to him first.

"It´s alright little fella. What a big bump you´re going to be showing your grandpa." He rubbed the boy´s head softly. "There. There."

Matey quietened down in his arms and said, "Big shoes! Off!"

"Sure. The big shoes can come off."

"Zee shoes stay on!" insisted Mrs de Graaf firmly. "Zay are zee correct size for a growing boy. "We are not staying here. You have no right to keep us."

"Do we not, indeed?" Bailey said. Hunter was rubbing his hand across his lip rather anxiously. Walking back behind the desk, Bailey sat with Matey on his lap. He wanted to comfort him, but also knew the woman across from him couldn´t leave without her grandchild. Matey seemed happy, and whispered hopefully. “Norma here?” Bailey raised his head towards Greta in enquiry. She pursed her lips and shook her head.

Matey looked at her and then turned to whisper, “Norma mama.”

“Give me the child,” demanded Mrs de Graff.

“When you´ve answered our questions to our satisfaction.”

“I know nussing, except you have not found my daughter´s murderer”

“What is your relationship with Bill Johnson.”

“Who?”

“The man who owns the pawn shop, Hard Pawn. The man I found talking to you in your hotel room.”

“Oh Please. A business acquaintance gave me his name. A possible place to sell our low-quality diamond jewellery. It didn´t work out. Wiz my daughter dead, how could I possibly sell anyzing in zis town? Ze longest, most boring city in the world wiz nossing to recommend it. I spit on it.” She gave a token spit into her lace handkerchief. “Ptttp.”

Bailey didn´t take the denigration directed at his hometown to heart. Persons of interest often tried to distract interrogators by attempting to change the topic.

“I recall there was talk of Hannah having a diamond pendant identical to the one you showed me?”

"I never said zat." Mrs de Graff drew the pendant out of its resting place between her ample breasts. "I wasn't sure if Hannah had brought the pendant wiz her. I just wanted to know if Mr Johnson had seen anyzing like it. When he said he had not, I asked if he had any customers for zis type of high-end sale. He did not. Not only was he a smelly man, his business was not what I had been led to believe." She sniffed and screwed up her mouth as if Stinky Bill was in the room.

"Better get some ice!" said Hunter suddenly. "The bump on Bram's head is growing before my eyes. Ms Meer could you go and ask security if they could bring some ice for it."

Matey stirred in Bailey's lap and bent to undo the Velcro bindings of his shoes.

"No!" shrieked Mrs de Graff. "He must learn to do as he is told. Zis child has been thoroughly spoiled here in Australia. He must learn to listen to Oma and to obey."

Bailey helped Matey discard one shoe. He turned it over. It had kangaroos on the sole. The shoe seemed heavier than necessary. He turned it back and pulled out the insole. There was a second larger insole about 1.5centemetres thick glued to the sides to make the shoe fit Matey's foot. He took the small Swiss army knife off his belt and sliced into the edge and turned the shoe upside down. Lustrous round pearls poured onto the table. He took off the second shoe, disassembled it and pierced the larger insole and was treated to a shower of diamonds.

He thought of Hannah´s boyfriend Tom Watts. Matey´s father. How he worked for one of the largest cultured south sea pearl producers in the world. Pearls. Diamonds. And a shady Pawn empire. The stench of collusion couldn´t be denied.

"I know nossing!" shouted Mrs de Graff

Bailey blessed the fact that Australian laws were different to those portrayed on American crime series. Miranda warnings were not entrenched in the law and if a person refused to answer detective´s questions, a jury was entitled to draw adverse conclusions.

"Mrs de Graff I am arresting you for obstruction of justice. Do you understand? And do you wish to ask for an attorney?"

EPILOGUE

Sunday picnics by the Swan River at the Point Walter Reserve were one of Perth´s well established family favourites. Bailey got there early so as to bag the best spot for the dozen or more people who were expected. A young man stormed up to say his family always had that particular spot, but soon shied away when Bailey flashed his badge. "Sorry mate, it´s on a first come basis. You´re welcome to attend the wake," Bailey said, only half joking. He frowned at Shooter who had sidled up to the man´s board shorts and was licking his knee.

"Ged out of it," said the man without heat.

Yes, they were celebrating the end of the case. As far as he knew, the entire homicide squad team were coming with their significant other—if they had one. He and Palfrey were also using the picnic to draw a line under their pursuit of Jazz´s rapists—however the rest of the squad would simply see this as Palfrey bringing his extended family. He and Diane were bringing Jazz. Fiona had invited Nick Spagos, who had to first finish his shift so they would arrive later. Palfrey´s elusive son, father of the girls, said he may be there later too, in time for the sausages.

Norma was bringing Matey. Her husband Bill was on some sort of secret civil-service, taxation mission overseas. Mining. Bailey supposed Australian mining companies had many associated companies overseas and a lot of opportunities to fiddle the books. Tracy, the heroine of the hour, would be driving Liam, using L-plates on his Mini now that she was sixteen.

Greta had begged off. Friends from the Netherlands was her excuse. Not to mention as the honorary consul, she felt her position to be not a little ambiguous. Her countrywoman was charged with smuggling diamonds into Australia and for receiving stolen pearls. Bailey wasn´t surprised by Greta´s absence. That romance was dead. It looked like he was destined to be a loner.

The new boss, Marcia Odell, had declined as well. She wasn´t one to party with the underlings. Maybe she´d loosen up as she got to know them better. Or maybe her management style meant keeping a disciplined distance between management and staff. As long as she was a straight talker and honest with them, Bailey didn´t care. She seemed pleased enough with the outcome so far, although they had yet to have their day in court.

Tom Watts had been charged with the theft of pearls and would likely be convicted and serve time. He was no longer employed in the pearling industry. The family court, advised by the child protection services, would consider his suitability as a parent once he´d been released.

Butcher was being held without bail while his lawyers debated the charge of murder versus unlawful homicide. The argument being that the ice-fuelled frenzy of the attack showed a lack of mental capacity, was unintentional and unplanned. The outcome being a difference between twenty years in prison or life.

Stinky Bill, as usual, was Teflon coated. He′d received no diamonds and denied any knowledge of the plan. Butcher hadn′t given him up during interrogation. Probably because Bill was surreptitiously paying for his defence. They′d get Bill next time. There was always a next time.

Bailey tossed a ball into the river for Shooter to fetch and watched a pelican swoop down and make a skid landing further out on the smooth water. Shooter immediately forgot about the ball and changed direction. "NO Shooter. NO!" he shouted. In a nearby pine tree, a Kookaburra laughed. The ironic joys of a Sunday picnic. He hoped the Department of Agriculture hadn′t chosen that Sunday to spray for the borers decimating local pine plantations. Government departments weren′t famous for common sense.

He heard a "Hoy!" and to his surprise discovered that Bob Hunter was the first to arrive together with his friend from Broome, Claire Foy. A friendly girl and budding chef, she gave him a hug. "Good to be out in the sunshine, JB, and not in the kitchen," she said. "You do know there are bull sharks in the river and not long ago one attacked a young girl who was swimming!"

"Shooter!" yelled Bailey, knowing it was fruitless. The dog would come when he was good and ready.

Hunter merely lifted his chin in greeting and set up the portable barbeque. “Light it in half an hour, you reckon? Most people like the sausages well done.”

“Sounds about right. Tony and Maurice are bringing a camp stove plus a giant pot of meatballs with home-made pasta.”

“Can´t take Italy out of the wop,” grinned Hunter and winked a sly wink. Bailey was pretty sure if anyone called him a pejorative indigenous name, they´d get a solid cuff around the ears.

Claire opened an exquisite wicker basket and displayed a neat array of sandwiches and pretty iced cupcakes. “I have my reputation to think of,” she said. “Or rather, the one I´m building. You never know, I might have my own café one day.”

The squad arrived in dribs and drabs, spreading blankets, unfolding outdoor tables and chairs. Some brought tablecloths. Everyone brought an esky full of wine, low alcohol beer and soft drinks. Bailey had made it clear that he didn´t want the entire team pulled over for drink driving on the way home.

Pamela arrived, puffing under the weight of a box of prawns on ice. Her sister and brother-in law were dawdling along behind her. “I didn´t think you´d mind me bringing my sis along, considering the bounty.”

“Well, as long as there´s no mutiny to go with it, she´s more than welcome of course.” Sometimes Bailey forgot Pamela´s history. After her father killed their mother in a murder/suicide, the sisters were brought up by an aunt. They were mega close. The brother-in-law not so much. He was engrossed in his iPhone. Why hadn´t he carried the seafood? OK. Pamela was a rufty-tufty homicide detective, but all the same…

Pamela looked around. Beamed. "This is great. We should do it more often."

Tony and Maurice sauntered up and enclosed her in a group hug. Bailey smiled, glad he´d thought to forge the Topela partnership. It had worked out well in the end. For a change he wasn´t second guessing himself. The case was behind them for the moment and it was going to be a terrific day.

Evan had invited his bosomy high-school-aged girlfriend. "We´re secretly engaged," he confided. The girlfriend didn´t say a word, just gazed adoringly at Evan. Bailey never remembered her name. Unusual for him with his prodigious memory. Maybe the breasts were too much of a distraction. They were epic. Just as well thoughts were private.

And then there was…

"Your fucking dog…" yelled Tracy, arriving just as Shooter proudly spat out the slimy tennis ball and shook river water over the assembled crowd.

"Dog!," Matey hooted, slipping away from Norma and toddling over to slam dunk a pat on Shooter´s head. "Big black dog,"

The gang were all here.

Printed in Great Britain
by Amazon